She saw something out of the corner of her eye. Or at least, she almost saw it, a fleeting movement in the trees to her left, too quick to pin down. Faye kept going, hoping she was imagining things. Instead, to focus her thoughts, she concentrated on where she put her feet among the hidden, snowy tree roots, wishing now that she hadn't worn heels. But then she saw it again – a fluid shape, sliding swiftly between the tree trunks. A cold slice of fear shivered down her spine.

It was a wolf, its yellow eyes flickering in the dark of the forest.

www.rbooks.co.uk

Mortal Kiss

ALICE MOSS

BANTAM BOOKS

MORTAL KISS
A BANTAM BOOK
978 0 857 51056 3

Published in Great Britain by Bantam
an imprint of Random House Children's Books
A Random House Group Company

First published 2010 on www.stardoll.com
Bantam edition published 2011

1 3 5 7 9 10 8 6 4 2

The Random House Group Limited supports the Forest Stewardship
Council (FSC), the leading international forest certification organization.
All our titles that are printed on Greenpeace-approved FSC-certified paper
carry the FSC logo. Our paper procurement policy can be found at
www.**rbooks**.co.uk/environment.

Mixed Sources
Product group from well-managed
forests and other controlled sources
www.fsc.org Cert no. TT-COC-2139
FSC © 1996 Forest Stewardship Council

Set in Palatino 10/13pt
by Falcon Oast Graphic Art

Random House Children's Books
61–63 Uxbridge Road, London W5 5SA

www.**kids**at**random**hou**se**.co.uk
www.**rbooks**.co.uk

Addresses for companies within The Random House Group Limited
can be found at: www.**randomhouse**.co.uk/offices.htm

THE RANDOM HOUSE GROUP Limited Reg. No. 954009

A CIP catalogue record for this book is available from the British Library.

Printed and bound in Great Britain by CPI Bookmarque, Croydon, CR0 4TD

Chapter One

Back to School

Faye McCarron tucked a windblown strand of brown hair back beneath her stripy wool hat before crouching down to snap another picture. She didn't know how long the snow would last, but there was no sense in missing an opportunity.

'Do you really want to be late for the first day of school?' Liz Wilson asked, impatiently. 'You know how cranky you get when you're late . . .'

Faye glanced at Liz, sticking her tongue out before turning to snap another image of the flowers outside Winter Mill High's gate.

'The bell's about to ring,' Liz warned.

Faye straightened up with a sigh. She was taller than her best friend by a few centimetres, something Liz was always complaining about, though Faye couldn't see that it made much difference. 'Liz, come on. Look – these roses are covered in snow – and it's only the first week of September!'

'I know, right?' Liz agreed, shaking her curly brown hair out of her perfectly made up dark eyes. 'It's weird. I mean, maybe one freak snowfall would be OK – but anyone would think it was Christmas. The whole town looks like a greetings card.'

'Exactly,' said Faye, taking another picture. 'Which is why these photos will make a great story in *The Miller*.'

Liz snorted. 'Sure, because it's not as if the school paper

won't have tons of dorks sending them pictures of their *really cool* snowmen.'

Faye looked at her friend, knowing she was teasing. 'Are you calling me a dork?'

There was a brief silence. 'So . . .' asked Liz, smoothly changing the subject, 'any news from your dad this morning?'

Faye shook her head. 'No.'

'And he hasn't emailed? Or called?'

'No.'

Liz was quiet for another moment before she said brightly, 'Oh well, he's probably just busy, or something. Where's the latest dig?'

Faye took her last picture and straightened up, fitting the lens cap to her digital SLR. It had been a Christmas present from her dad the previous year, the most expensive thing he'd ever given her. The plan was that when she was older, Faye would join him on one of his archaeology trips as an intern photographer. She couldn't wait – it was something Faye had wanted to do for ages. To actually visit all the incredible places her dad had told her about, with him there too, would just be awesome. Until then, though, Faye wished he could find a way to stay in touch more often when he was away. Sometimes weeks went by without a word, and Faye always worried, though she tried to hide it.

'He's in Tanzania.'

Liz frowned. 'In Australia?'

'No . . . Liz, that's Tasmania.'

'Oh.'

'Tanzania's in Africa.'

'There you go! The mail probably isn't too good there, right? Or phones. Or the Internet . . .'

Despite herself Faye grinned, pulling her friend into a brief hug. 'Thanks, Lizzie.'

2

'For what?'

'Trying to make me feel better.'

Liz hugged her back. 'That's what friends are for.'

The sudden noise of a loud car behind them made them both jump. They turned to see a sleek black Cadillac slide to a halt a few metres away, wheels carving deep tracks in the snow.

'Oh my god!' squeaked Liz in excitement, 'I bet that's him!'

'Who?'

'The Morrow kid! Lucas!'

The two girls watched as the passenger door opened and a boy of about sixteen stepped out. He was tall and broad-shouldered, with very pale blond hair that flopped across his brow above piercing blue eyes. He slung a rucksack over his shoulder, reaching to push his hair back as he glanced up at the school.

'Oh my god,' Liz stage-whispered. 'He's gorgeous. Take a picture!'

'What?'

'For the paper – you can do a story. About ... about his arrival, and the whole Morrow mystery.'

' "The Morrow mystery"? What are you talking about?'

'The whole town's chatting about it. Come on, Faye, you must have heard about the Morrows arriving?'

Faye had. Everyone was excited about the fact that Mercy Morrow, the fabulously wealthy heiress, had bought the old mansion in the woods.

'I know the whole town seems to be fascinated by them,' said Faye. 'But I don't see what's so mysterious.'

Liz sighed dramatically, as if she couldn't believe what she was hearing. 'Faye. Why on earth would Mercy Morrow, one of the richest women in America, take a house here in quiet old Winter Mill?' she asked, repeating what many people in the town were saying. 'She could go anywhere – Los Angeles, Monaco, Rome . . . but she came here' – she paused for dramatic effect – *'and nobody knows why.'*

'Maybe she wanted to be in a place where no one would talk about her?' Faye suggested wryly.

'Come on, Faye. Just take a picture.'

'OK, OK . . .' She unhooked her lens cap and raised the camera, but before she could snap a shot, the driver's door opened. A tall, pale man appeared, barking at them in an unpleasant, gravelly voice. His narrow face looked as if someone had taken a skull and covered it with skin-coloured paint, it was so gaunt. His eyes were sunken in their sockets, dark and cruel. Just looking at him creeped Faye out.

'No pictures,' he said, roughly.

'It's just for the school paper,' said Faye.

'I *said*, no pictures.'

'It's OK, Ballard,' Lucas Morrow said, pushing the car door shut. 'I got it. Go back to Mom.'

The man stared at Faye coldly before slowly getting into the car again. A moment later, the Cadillac pulled away.

'Wow. My first locals,' said the boy with a slight smile as he reached them.

'Hi,' said Faye, slightly thrown off-balance by her run-in with the man called Ballard. 'So you're Lucas Morrow? It's nice to meet you. I'm Faye, and this is Liz . . .'

Lucas looked them both up and down. 'So, you're like . . . What? The top girl reporters of the small-town *National Enquirer*?'

Faye narrowed her eyes. '*The National Enquirer*?'

Lucas smirked. 'Yeah. It's a trash mag.'

'I *know* what it is.'

Faye watched, annoyed, as Lucas turned on his most

4

charming smile. It showed his perfectly white, even teeth. 'It's . . . funny. Sometimes.'

Faye refused to be charmed, still upset by his trash mag jibe. 'Sure it is.'

There was a brief, awkward, pause. 'Sorry,' Lucas muttered. 'That was supposed to be a joke. Guess I'm more nervous than I thought. It's my first day . . .'

Faye shook her head. 'It's fine'

Lucas looked up at her, a mischievous look in his eye. 'No? Are you sure? Because you don't look fine. You look *angry*. Your eyes are flashing.'

'Oh, don't worry about that,' Liz piped up, before Faye could answer. 'They always do it. All her family have crazy green eyes.'

Lucas's eyebrows shot up. 'Crazy green eyes?'

'Oh, no,' said Liz, realizing what she'd said, 'I didn't mean . . . not *crazy*, crazy – they're just, you know, really green.'

Lucas laughed. 'Well, that's good. "Crazy Faye" isn't much of a nickname.'

Faye found her voice. 'I don't have a nickname. And please ignore my best friend – she's . . . challenged.'

Liz gasped in outrage. 'Hey!'

Lucas laughed again. 'If you two are representative of the whole school, I think my stay here might be more interesting than I thought.'

Faye smiled sweetly. 'Does that mean you'll let me take a picture for the school paper?'

Lucas shrugged, 'Maybe. How about we strike a deal? You let me give you a nickname – and I'll let you take a picture.'

Faye shook her head. 'Oh, I don't think so.'

Lucas sighed regretfully. 'Too late. I've already thought of the perfect nickname. Flash. I think it suits you.'

5

'Flash?' Faye repeated, horrified.

'Sure. For your green eyes, and your addiction to snapping pictures. Perfect, isn't it?'

'Actually, that's pretty good,' said Liz, with a nod.

Lucas smiled at her. 'Thank you. It's a talent of mine. One of many.'

Faye dug an elbow into Liz's ribs. 'You will *not* call me "Flash"! No one's going to call me Flash!'

'Aw, come on, Flash, don't be a killjoy,' teased Lucas.

'I'm not—' Faye began, but Lucas had already started to walk away.

Faye and Liz watched as he headed for Winter Mill High's main doors.

'Hey!' Faye shouted, suddenly. 'I didn't take your picture!'

The boy looked over his shoulder with a grin, but didn't stop. Faye raised her camera, snapping off two quick shots before he disappeared through the main doors.

'Oh . . . My . . . God!' Liz breathed. 'Isn't he just the most gorgeous boy you've ever seen?'

Faye shook her head, unsure whether to be angry or amused. Flash – he'd called her *Flash*! What a terrible nickname. 'Come on,' she said to Liz, running for the doors as the bell rang. 'We're late!'

'Hey, wait up!' Liz called after her. 'So, are you going to write about the Morrow Mystery, or not?'

Chapter Two

New Arrivals

By the time school was let out, Faye had just about had enough of Liz's constant talk of the 'utterly awesome' Lucas Morrow. Liz had spent the whole day talking about nothing else, and it was beginning to drive Faye nuts. It didn't help that Liz was now calling her 'Flash' at every opportunity. It wasn't often she didn't want to be with Liz, but right now Faye wished she was going home alone.

Every day after school, the two girls headed back to Faye's house to study. Liz spent so much time there that Aunt Pam sometimes suggested she just move right in. Faye's mom had died when she was little, and ever since then Faye and her dad had lived with Aunt Pam, her dad's sister. Her aunt owned the only bookshop in Winter Mill, and knew everything there was to know about the town and its history. In actual fact, Aunt Pam knew a lot about all kinds of history and cultures. She'd spent most of her twenties and thirties travelling all over the world, and had even lived in eastern Europe and India for a few years before coming back to Winter Mill to start her own business. Faye loved her like a mother.

'Aunt Pam! We're home,' Faye called loudly as she and Liz pushed open the store's wooden door. The cluttered shop floor was quiet, but Pamela McCarron appeared from the back room as Faye and Liz stamped their snowy feet on the mat. Her wavy red hair was bound in a printed African scarf, and despite the snow outside, she wore her usual T-shirt and long skirt.

'There's no need to shout,' Aunt Pam said calmly. 'You've lived here long enough to know I can't be more than a few metres away, now, haven't you?'

Faye crossed the floor to give her aunt a kiss on the cheek. 'Sorry. Anything from Dad?'

Aunt Pam squeezed her arm with a shake of her head. 'Not yet, but try not to worry.'

Faye nodded, but her stomach twisted. Her dad had been out of contact for longer than usual.

'I know it's hard, but you know what he's like. He'll pop up in a day or two,' Aunt Pam told her, warmly. 'Now, there are some ginger cookies up in the kitchen for you. Let me know what books you girls need for your homework and I'll look them out.'

Liz threw her arms around Pam. 'What about something on how to make the boy of your dreams fall in love with you?'

'What's this, now?'

'Ignore her,' sighed Faye. 'She just hasn't stopped going on about the new boy since she saw him this morning.'

'Oh?' asked Aunt Pam. 'What new boy?'

'Lucas Morrow. He's amazing. Just *amazing*, Aunt Pam,' Liz gushed. 'He's gorgeous and clever and funny . . .'

'And annoying.' Faye added.

Liz rolled her eyes. 'Faye doesn't like him.'

'It's not that I don't like him. I don't know him. And what's more, I don't think I *want* to know him.'

'Faye,' Aunt Pam chided. 'Don't be like that. He's new in town. You should be a bit more welcoming.'

'He calls me Flash!' Faye squeaked. 'It's so embarrassing – Liz is already doing it. If the two of them don't stop, it's going to catch on and the whole school will be calling me Flash, too! I wish I'd never met him!'

Faye saw Aunt Pam trying to keep a straight face. 'Flash? You know, that's actually—'

'Oh, don't you start,' groused Faye.

'If that's the worse that he can come up with, I think you should probably give him the benefit of the doubt,' laughed her aunt.

'Did I mention that he's totally gorgeous, Aunt Pam?' Liz added. 'He has this amazing hair that just—'

'Argh!' Faye put her hands over her ears. 'Please, no more about the wonderful new boy. Can we just have thirty minutes without a single mention of him? Please?'

'Oh, all right,' sighed Liz. 'Come on, I want one of those cookies—' She stopped short as the sudden sound of loud engines shattered the peace of the quiet street outside.

'What on earth is that?' Faye asked, going to the front door. She opened it as Liz and her aunt joined her, all of them staring out into the snowy street.

Six huge black bikes were roaring slowly down the road, churning up the snow as they went. They were in formation, a large V-shape that took up so much room that no other cars could pass. The riders were all dressed in thick black leather and wore dark glasses that hid their eyes. The leader of the pack had a grey beard and long, straggly grey hair that blew out behind him as he cruised past.

All along the street, the people of Winter Mill were coming out of their homes, startled by the thunder of the motorbikes.

'Wow,' Faye said, raising her voice so Pam and Liz could hear her. 'What a noise!'

'Who are they?' Liz asked, shouting too. 'I don't recognize any of them.'

9

Aunt Pam watched the bikes carefully. 'They've been in the area for a couple of days,' she said. 'But this is the first time they've all come down into town together. I think they're introducing themselves. Somehow I don't think they're going to be very welcome here.'

The riders drew level with the bookstore. Faye was fascinated – she'd never seen real bikers before. She scrabbled for her camera, eager to take a picture: the bikers would make a great article for *The Miller*. Looking through the viewfinder, Faye realized one of the bikers was staring right at her. He was younger than the rest of the gang, and she thought he probably wasn't much older than she was. His dark hair was cropped close beneath his helmet, and she couldn't see his eyes properly because of his shades. But something about him made Faye pause, looking over her camera, as he passed.

'I think he's the one who came in here a couple of days ago,' Aunt Pam said into Faye's ear. 'He didn't look quite so fearsome then!'

Faye looked at her aunt. 'You didn't tell me about that!'

Aunt Pam shrugged. 'It didn't cross my mind.'

'Look,' Faye heard Liz say. 'There's my dad, in his squad car.'

Following in the bikers' wake was Sergeant Wilson, the big police officer that headed up Winter Mill's local law enforcement. Rather than driving past the bookstore, though, he pulled to a stop outside it and opened the door, pressing his hat firmly on to his head as he got out.

'Mitch,' greeted Pam. 'Looks like we have some new people in town.'

Sergeant Wilson nodded with a frown. 'I'm not too happy about it either, I can tell you.'

'Maybe this is a sign that they're moving on?'

He shook his head. 'Not a chance. They're still camped up in the woods. Mind if I come in, Pam?'

'Of course. Nothing serious, I hope?'

Sergeant Wilson looked grave. 'It might be. I need to talk to the girls.'

Chapter Three

Bad Dogs

Liz watched as her dad shook the snow from his boots. It was closing up time, so Aunt Pam locked the door behind him and removed the store's cash register drawer. Then they all crowded upstairs into the McCarrons' small kitchen. Outside, the snow was beginning to fall again, huge soft flakes piling against the window.

Liz's dad sat at the large kitchen table, still frowning. Liz was worried, and tried to think of something that she might have done wrong. Her dad was pretty strict, but she couldn't imagine what it was. Unless – maybe somehow he'd got hold of her grade sheet early? But it was only the first day of term! That couldn't be it, could it? That would so not be fair …

Liz forced herself not to panic. She sat down opposite Faye and helped herself to a ginger cookie as Aunt Pam poured tea from a china pot.

'So what is it, Dad?' she asked. 'You look worried. What's wrong?'

The police officer sighed, rubbing a hand through his hair distractedly. 'We found a body up in the woods, about half a mile out of town. A man. I don't recognize him, so I don't think he's local. We're trying to find out who he is right now.'

'No!' said Liz, shocked. 'That's terrible. What happened to him?'

'We don't know yet. And I can't tell you too much while the investigation is underway, obviously. But let's just say . . . we're not ruling anything out at this stage.'

Liz stared at Faye, who was obviously thinking the same thing she was. 'You don't mean . . . you don't think he was murdered, do you, Dad? *Here?* In Winter Mill?'

Her father took a mouthful of tea, and Liz saw him cast a strange look at Faye over the rim of the cup. She wondered what it meant, but a second later it was gone and her dad shrugged. 'Like I said, we're not ruling anything out.'

'But – but Winter Mill is such a peaceful place,' Faye gasped, her eyes wide. 'I don't think I've ever heard of anything like a murder happening here! Have you, Aunt Pam?'

Aunt Pam shook her head. 'Not in the time that I've been here, and I think I'd have to go back a long way to find the last one.'

'Well, we don't know for sure that it is murder yet,' Sergeant Wilson reminded them. 'We haven't established a cause of death so far. I'll have to wait for the pathologist's verdict before I start a manhunt. And to be honest . . .' He shook his head. 'Just getting around is going to be difficult in this weather. All the roads in and out of town are treacherous.'

Liz was alarmed. 'Do you think the town will get cut off if it carries on snowing like this? Are we – do we have enough food and stuff if that happens?'

'I don't think that's likely to happen, Liz,' said Faye. 'The town has plans for that kind of thing.'

Liz's dad covered her hand with his own, patting it gently. 'Faye's right. Don't worry. We're laying down grit to make sure that doesn't happen. We just have to make sure we don't run out – and hope that this cold snap doesn't last.'

'But what if it does?' Liz asked, worried. 'It hasn't given up

14

for the last five days! What if it just carries on snowing like this?'

'It can't, can it?' Faye asked. 'This can't be the start of winter. It's only September!'

'You know, I was doing some research today,' said Aunt Pam, 'and I can't find any mention in the town records of snow falling this early in the year. Not as far back as sixteen-eighty. It's amazing – I think this snowfall may be unique in the history of Winter Mill, maybe even in the entire history of New England.'

'I'm not so worried about the snow,' said Sergeant Wilson. 'My big concern right now is the bikers.'

'Do you think they have something to do with the body you found?' Faye asked.

'There's no direct link – not yet, anyway,' he told her. 'It's just a feeling. They're trouble, and I don't believe in coincidences. They turn up and a couple of days later I'm investigating the first unexplained death Winter Mill has had in decades.' Sergeant Wilson shook his head. 'I don't like it.'

Aunt Pam poured the sergeant another cup. 'Try not to judge on appearances, Mitch. I had one of them in here the day before yesterday. He was only young.'

Mitch frowned. 'What did he want?'

'He flicked through some books, but I think he mainly wanted to get out of the cold. Finn, his name was. I told him he was welcome, but that if he really wanted to get warm he'd need to help me fix the heating, as it had been playing up in the cold snap.' Aunt Pam settled at the table. 'He did a good job. He seemed harmless to me, Mitch, if a bit quiet. Are you sure the Black Dogs are involved?'

'*The Black Dogs?*' Liz repeated, confused.

Her dad looked up from his tea. 'That's the name of their

gang, Liz. They're the sort of folks who like to make a good first impression,' he added wryly.

'But what does any of this have to do with us, Sergeant Wilson?' Faye asked. 'You said you needed to talk to Liz and me.'

'I just don't want you girls up there in the woods.' Sergeant Wilson sighed. 'It's not just you two – I plan on getting the word out to all the Winter Mill kids. I know it's tempting, what with the early snow. It's lying thick, and it's perfect for skiing, tobogganing, snowboarding . . . I don't want to be a killjoy, but until the bikers are gone, and until I know what happened to this man . . .'

Faye nodded. 'We'll be careful,' she promised.

'You don't need to worry,' Liz agreed, taking another cookie. 'We're not going to mess with them.'

Her dad's phone rang, and he glanced apologetically at Aunt Pam before answering it.

'I have to go,' he said, as soon as he rang off, finishing his tea and standing up. 'The pathologist just finished the post mortem.'

Chapter Four

Unnatural Causes

Liz decided to hitch a ride with her dad instead of staying to finish her homework with Faye. She didn't really feel like trekking home through the snow, and Liz was still put out by Faye's apparent dislike of Lucas. On the one hand, of course, it was a good thing – at least they didn't both want to date him, which meant Liz could have Lucas Morrow all to herself. On the other hand, she wanted her best friend to at least be friendly to the person that Liz had already decided was her future boyfriend. Not that Liz had had many steady boyfriends before – most boys in Winter Mill were too scared of her dad to ask her out!

She trod through the snow towards her father's big four-by-four, watching his hunched shoulders. Sergeant Wilson was known in the town as being strict but fair – and the same went for his parenting style. In fact, sometimes he was way too strict, as far as she was concerned. He had set ideas about things and she knew when not to cross the line. But right now there was something she really, really wanted . . . and it looked as if he was going to be very busy, possibly for a long time. So if Liz didn't ask for it now, who knew when she'd get another chance?

Her dad revved the engine as she pulled the door shut, waiting until Liz had fastened her seatbelt before pulling out. It was rush-hour and Winter Mill's shops were beginning to shut, and the snowy roads were as busy as the small town ever got.

'Are you really worried about those bikers, Dad?' Liz asked, feeling the truck's snow chains bite into the clogged road.

'Well, they haven't given me a reason not to be, so far,' her father muttered, glancing in the rear-view mirror as he negotiated a junction. 'And in my experience, it's always better to be safe rather than sorry.'

'I will be, I promise.'

Her dad patted her knee. 'I know you will, sweetheart.'

They drove in silence for another couple of moments before Liz spoke again. 'Dad . . .'

'Yes?'

'I've been thinking . . . now that we're back at school, and this year is going to be a really tough year . . . And I want to do really well, you know I do . . .'

'Yes, Lizzie?'

'Well, I wondered,' Liz bit her lip before continuing, in a rush. 'I wondered if you and Mom could increase my allowance?'

Her dad sighed, 'Liz . . .'

'Dad, *please*. It's been a year since the last one. And now that I'm older, I really, really need a new wardrobe. You should have seen the looks I got at school today, turning up in the same coat I had last year. Besides,' Liz added innocently, 'if this really is winter setting in so early, I definitely need new clothes, don't I? You know, nice warm ones . . . ?'

Liz knew she'd get what she wanted when she saw him trying to stifle a smile. Before he had a chance to say anything, Liz threw her arms around her dad and kissed him on the cheek.

'Liz! I'm driving!'

'Sorry,' she said, as they pulled up outside her family's pretty clapboard house. 'Thanks, Dad! Ohmigod! This is going to be so great. There's this new boutique in the mall, and I can't wait to go there!'

'Hey! I haven't said yes yet!'

Liz stopped talking immediately and sat very still, looking at him with large eyes.

'OK, OK,' said the big policeman, conceding defeat with another sigh. 'You can have a raise. But,' he warned, as Liz went to hug him again, 'I want straight As from you this year, you understand?'

'Sure Dad. Piece of cake,' grinned Liz, already planning her next shopping trip. She reached for the car door, pulling out her cellphone – she had to call Faye immediately! 'Thanks, Dad. I love you.'

'And I meant what I said about the woods. If I catch you or Faye up there . . .'

Liz's feet hit the cold snow as she slid out of the car. 'I know. Don't worry.'

'And absolutely no short skirts! I love you. Kiss your mother for me – tell her I'll call her when I can.'

Liz was already dialling.

Sergeant Wilson watched his daughter in the rear-view mirror as he pulled away, smiling to himself as she talked excitedly on her phone. She'd been dropping hints about getting a bigger allowance for weeks, but he'd ignored them as long as he could. Who knew what she'd spend it on – to his mind, Liz seemed to own every item of clothing she'd ever need already. But, as her mother kept telling him, that was teenage girls for you. It was just that they hadn't seemed to have the same problem with Poppy, Liz's older sister . . .

19

His mind turned back to more troubling matters as he drove on to the town's small morgue and parked in his usual spot. Winter Mill shared a pathologist with three other local towns.

'Pat,' he nodded, as an older man opened the door, dressed in scrubs. 'Sorry to call you out on a night like this.'

'Had to be done, Mitch,' said Pat Thompson, ushering him back through to the autopsy room. 'Although I'm not sure what good I'm going to be able to do you.'

The body had already been stitched back up, and lay, grey and still, on a metal trolley in the centre of the room. It was cold, the dim lights casting odd shapes against the sterile white walls. Sergeant Wilson gave an involuntary shudder. He didn't want to be there any longer than necessary.

'Have you got a cause of death?'

Pat reached for his notes, shaking his head. 'No. The only injury I can find on the body is a slight cut on one arm. It's shallow, and smooth – a knife cut, probably, but it would not have been fatal. Other than that, the body seems unharmed.'

'Natural causes, then?'

'I can't confirm that, either. All his vital organs were sound. There are no signs of hypothermia. It's as if one moment he was walking around, right as rain, and the next he just . . . died. The only thing that might fit what I'm seeing is a massive anaphylactic reaction, but to what I couldn't say.'

Mitch frowned. 'And what about identification?'

'I ran the prints, but didn't get a hit.'

'How about through dental records?'

'Again, I've got nothing,' said the coroner, handing the sergeant his notes so he could see for himself. 'Nothing, that is, except for more mystery.'

'Oh?'

'Take a look. You'll see what I mean.'

Mitch scanned the summary before looking back at Pat with raised eyebrows. 'What the— World War Two dentistry? Seriously?'

'Absolutely. This man has fillings applied in a way discontinued after nineteen forty-seven.'

'But he doesn't look . . .'

'Above thirty. I know.'

'What about his clothing?'

'What about it? He was in rags, Mitch, you know that. No labels on what was there, either.'

Mitch's stomach turned with anxiety. Something wasn't right here, and it made his skin crawl. 'Can I see the locket you found near him again?'

'Sure.' Pat pointed towards a metal bowl. 'It's in there.'

Sergeant Wilson picked it up, running the fine antique chain between his fingers before opening the small case. He couldn't stop the shiver that ran down his spine. He'd hoped his memory had deceived him, that when he looked at the photograph inside again he'd see something different.

But to him, the dark-haired girl inside looked for all the world like Faye McCarron.

Chapter Five

RSVP

The snow was still falling as Faye pulled the door of McCarron's Bookstore closed behind her. She had her camera with her, as always, but Faye had taken a shot the day before that was so good she doubted she'd be able to get anything similar again. It was of one of her neighbours, trying to dig his car out of a deep snowdrift, while behind him, a dark, dramatic sky threatened to send even more unseasonal weather down on top of him. Aunt Pam had told her to send it to one of the national papers, convinced that it would get used – stories of Winter Mill's unusual weather was beginning to cause interest in the outside world, too. Faye had done as her aunt had suggested and emailed it to *The New York Times* editor, but she doubted she'd hear anything back. Still, it was worth a try.

As Faye pushed on towards Winter Mill High, she thought about her conversation with Liz the previous evening. Her friend had called less than fifteen minutes after leaving with Sergeant Wilson, desperate to tell her the great news about her allowance increase. And it was great news – Faye's dad had given her a raise before he'd gone away on his latest dig, and now the two girls could have the *perfect* shopping trip at the new store in town. Their chat hadn't really covered more than the latest clothes they'd both love to buy, but it had reminded Faye of how important a friend Liz was. They spent so much time together that sometimes Faye forgot how much she missed Liz when she wasn't around. The last thing Faye wanted was something like a boy to come between them, and so she resolved to make more of an effort to be nice to Lucas Morrow, however annoying he was.

'I'll just have to pretend to like him, for Liz's sake,' she muttered aloud to herself as she reached the school gates. 'And who knows? Maybe he'll grow on me.'

'Hey, McCarron – wait up.'

Faye turned to see Candi Thorsson a few steps behind her. As usual, the blonde girl was dressed exactly as if she'd just stepped out of a magazine. Faye stopped and watched her enviously. Candi always looked fantastic. Right now she was wearing beautiful tan leather boots and an amazing coat. It was a delicate shade of mink with a large collar that draped round Candi's shoulders and perfectly set off the girl's ice-blue eyes. It was an extravagant outfit, even for Candi, and Faye knew that something must be up.

'Hi, Candi,' Faye greeted her. 'You look great.'

Candi beamed a huge smile. 'Thanks! Isn't this coat gorge? It's honest-to-goodness real Chanel! My dad sent it up from New York for me to say sorry for missing my birthday.'

'He's not coming up this weekend? I'm sorry.'

Candi shrugged carelessly. 'If he did, he'd only moan about my grades. I'd rather have the coat! So, listen, are you free on Saturday night?'

'Sure.'

'Then come to my party. Seriously, it's going to be awesome. I've borrowed the Mathesons' cabin up on the hill. Everyone's going to be there. So, will you come?'

Candi's parties were legendary. She always hired her own staff to mix the best virgin cocktails you'd ever had in your life and there was usually some amazing band as well.

Faye smiled. 'I'd love to! Thanks.'

'Wild!' Candi hugged her briefly before floating away on a cloud of perfume, heading for another knot of students. 'See you there!'

Before Faye could make it to the front gates, she heard another shout behind her. This time it was Liz, wearing a smile as big as the Golden Gate Bridge, which told Faye her friend had already heard about the party.

'Wow!' exclaimed Liz, as she reached Faye. 'Isn't it awesome? An allowance raise *and* a party to shop for. And did Candi tell you that Lucas Morrow is going to be there? I should die right now. Life just can't get better than this!'

'Don't you think you'd better go to the party first?' laughed Faye. This was another reason she loved Liz – her characteristic excitement. No matter what was going on, you could always count on Liz to be in the middle of it – usually making the most noise!

'Very true, very true. Now, come on. This is important. We have to draw up a shopping schedule!'

Faye laughed again. 'Why don't we just go straight to the mall tonight, right after school?'

'Good plan. Hey – where are you going?' Liz asked, as Faye went in a different direction.

'You go ahead, I'll be there before roll call. I just want to go into the school newspaper office and see Ms Finch.'

The Miller had been a Winter Mill High institution for years. Some of the student contributors to the school newspaper had gone on to have stellar careers – one of the girls who had graduated just a few years before worked at *National Geographic* magazine, which sounded to Faye like the most perfect job in the world. The paper mainly covered school activities and soft, local interest stories like the recent cold snap. But Faye had her sights set on covering a real story for once.

'Hi, Ms Finch.' Barbie Finch, the school's deputy principal, was seated behind the large desk that dominated the room that formed *The Miller*'s headquarters. She was a prim-looking woman in her fifties who always dressed in sharply tailored suits. She looked up as Faye approached.

'Good morning, Faye,' Ms Finch glanced at the clock on the wall. 'Aren't you going to be late?'

'I just wanted to ask you about a piece I'd like to work on. For the paper?'

'Oh yes?'

'Did you hear about the body that Sergeant Wilson found up in the woods?'

The teacher took her glasses from her nose and raised an eyebrow. 'A body?'

'Yes . . . they even think it might be murder. And the sergeant is worried that it's linked to the arrival of the Black Dogs.'

'The what now?'

'The Black Dogs – the bikers that have been camping outside town?'

'Faye, I'm not sure that any of this is appropriate for a school newspaper.'

'But it's perfect! It could be a real investigative piece. We can do background sidebars on the bikers – why they're called the Black Dogs, for example, and where they come from. And we can publish more articles as the case goes on. And if it is murder, and there's a trial—'

Ms Finch held up a hand. 'Faye, stop. Just stop. I admire your enthusiasm, but really, this is not a subject for the school magazine.'

'But Ms Finch—'

'How exactly would you research the bikers? Does your aunt have a book on the subject?'

'Not on the Black Dogs, no . . .'

'How, then?'

'Well, I was thinking that I could interview one of them.'

'Faye McCarron, you will do no such thing.'

'But—'

'No arguments, Faye. The Black Dogs are off-limits.'

'OK, well, then I'll concentrate on the body. I can interview Sergeant Wilson.'

'Faye—' sighed Ms Finch. 'Please drop this idea. We don't want the school mixed up in anything untoward.' Seeing Faye's downcast expression, she offered a warm smile. 'I do have an assignment I was going to suggest for you, though. And it's a good one.'

'Oh?' said Faye, unable to imagine anything as interesting as the story she'd just proposed.

'I want you to get an interview with Mercy Morrow. A human-interest article about why she came to Winter Mill. I think it'll be fascinating, especially as she and Lucas are the talk of the town at the moment. They're quite the mystery. Can you do that?'

Faye shrugged, uninspired. 'Sure.'

'It won't be easy. But I think it'll be worth it. And better than getting mixed up with those bikers. OK?'

Faye mustered a smile, quashing a sigh as she swung her book bag back over her shoulder. 'OK, Ms Finch. I won't let you down.'

But as she left, Faye couldn't help thinking about Lucas's creepy driver, Ballard, and shivered. If that was the sort of person Mercy Morrow employed, what would she be like?

Chapter Six

Mall Dogs Go to Heaven

Faye couldn't help but be a little excited as she and Liz headed for Winter Mill's shopping mall. She hadn't been shopping in ages, and it was time she spiced up her wardrobe.

'OK,' said Liz, as she pulled her car into the parking lot with Faye in the passenger seat. 'Here's my plan. Candi's party is definitely going to be in contention for Party of the Season, right?'

'Probably,' agreed Faye.

'So it calls for a serious outfit overhaul,' Liz declared. 'I'm thinking that I'm going to blow almost all of my shiny new allowance at MK – I can't wait!'

MK was the newest boutique to open in Winter Mill's little mall, and the girls had been dying to shop there. It stocked the latest lines from all the top designers, which meant that at Christmas it would be bursting with the most incredible gowns. But the owner had also dedicated a section to the town's younger population, promising to fill it with the latest new designs from labels like Pretty in Pink, Wunderkind, Bisou, Rachel Roy and anything else the owner liked the look of. It was, quite simply, Faye and Liz's idea of heaven.

'Whoa,' muttered Liz, breaking into Faye's happy shopping reverie as she parked the car. 'Look over there.'

Across the parking lot, near the mall entrance, were six large black and silver bikes. There was no sign of their owners.

'I guess they're inside,' murmured Faye, staring. The bikes were oddly hypnotic – they looked powerful, like huge crouching creatures, ready to pounce at the slightest provocation. In spite of Ms Finch's order, Faye still wanted to find out more about the gang. Sergeant Wilson had said they were camping up in the woods, and Faye wondered if they had homes that they usually lived in, or if they were always on the move. That boy she had seen didn't seem much older than her. What would that be like, to live on the road? She sighed, frustrated. She knew there was a really good article there, if only she was allowed to work on it!

Beside her, Liz shivered. 'Come on, Faye. You know what my dad said.'

'Yeah,' echoed Faye, attention still on the bikes as they headed for the mall doors. 'Yeah, I know.'

MK was even more fabulous that the girls had expected. Everywhere they looked were clothes they would kill to own.

'Oh. My. God!' Liz said as soon as they walked in. 'That just might be the cutest knit dress I've ever seen.'

'It's cute,' agreed Faye, running her fingers over the soft texture. 'But I'm not sure it's really right for a party in the snow!'

Liz stuck out her tongue and wandered on. 'So what style do you think I should go for?' she asked, over her shoulder. 'Young and fun? Or deep and sophisticated?'

'This is to impress Lucas Morrow?'

'Of course,' Liz looked at Faye, narrowing her eyes slightly. 'You're not going to go on about how annoying he is again, are you?'

Faye held up her hands. 'I promise. If you like him, Liz, then so do I.'

'OK. That's good. As long as you don't .. you know . . . like him, like him . . .'

Faye sighed, shaking her head with a smile. She pushed Liz gently on the arm. 'Just go and shop! I need new clothes too, you know!'

Liz grinned. 'I'm going, I'm going . . .'

Faye headed off, pushing between the racks of clothes. She pulled pieces out and held them against her, realizing that she really didn't know what she was looking for.

'Can I help you?' Faye looked up to see a shop assistant smiling at her.

'I don't know,' admitted Faye. 'I've got this party to go to . . . I'd like something new, but I just don't know what.'

'I'm sure we can find something,' said the assistant. 'Maybe you're looking for something a little different to what you usually wear?'

The assistant ushered her to another rack, by the window. 'We've just had these in from a new young designer. No one else stocks them at the moment. I think they're just divine. The designer uses sheer fabrics and silks, lots of florals and adornments. Dramatic and stylish! Have a look. Try on whatever you want.'

'Thank you,' murmured Faye, already running her fingers along an exquisite top. It was sheer white, striped with angora knit and lace-trimmed. It was like nothing that Faye had ever seen before. She pulled it from the rack, matching it with some great skinny slashed blue jeans and a pair of dove-coloured heels, and hurried to the changing rooms.

'Faye, are you in there?' came Liz's voice, through the curtain. 'I want to see what you've got!'

'I'll be out in a second,' Faye called back. 'Have you found something?'

'You would not believe the things I've found,' said her friend, dramatically. 'This place is a-mazing!'

Faye laughed. She glanced at herself in the mirror, surprised by what she saw. The top was a perfect fit, and the loose turtle neck highlighted her features exquisitely. The white made her skin paler, and her green eyes even greener.

Turning, Faye pulled open the curtain and stepped out as Liz continued to chatter away, her back to her friend.

'Just look at this!' Liz said, pulling out a luxurious grey, tassel striped vest from another rack of clothes. 'This would look amazing with a short skirt and high heels. Like this, maybe—' she pulled out a pale blue skirt with bandage-like structures over the front. 'There are just so many possibilities!'

'Well, what do you think of this one?' Faye asked.

Liz turned around, looking her up and down. 'Wow,' she said.

'Do you like it?'

'Yeah – the top is fantastic! It's kind of—'

Something caught Faye's attention – a movement outside. She looked up, and found herself staring into a pair of deep brown eyes. They belonged to a boy who was standing, completely still, on the other side of the window. Everything about him was dark. His hair was black and clipped short. He wore a heavy black-leather jacket and scrappy black jeans with chunky black boots. And . . .

And he was staring right at her. Faye couldn't look away. Her heart began to beat harder, and as she watched, she saw the boy unclench his fists and raise them towards the glass, as if he were reaching for her.

Faye's heart beat faster and faster, until it was crashing against her ribcage. She felt as if she should look away, but somehow she just couldn't.

Beside her, Liz whispered loudly, 'He's one of those Black Dogs. It must be the one your aunt was talking about – Finn.'

Suddenly a shout echoed from outside MK and the boy turned his head. A man that Faye recognized as Mr Purser from the CD shop ran up to the boy, still shouting. Instinctively, Faye ran out of the door, eager to see what was happening. Liz followed close behind her, their footsteps clattering on the tiled mall floor.

'I know what you're doing!' Mr Purser said, angrily. 'All of you. You're looking for what you can steal. You're waiting until we aren't looking, and then you're taking whatever you can! Why don't you just get out of here?'

From nowhere, the other bikers appeared. They strode past Faye and Liz like a force of nature. It was the first time that Faye had seen them so close. She'd left her camera in her bag in the changing room, but she tried to get an impression of each of them into her mind. The leader was hugely tall and wore a leather jacket emblazoned with the gang's symbol – a dog or perhaps a wolf, howling at the moon. Two of the other, older, bikers looked as if they could be brothers. Both had grizzled, scarred faces and wore the same leather jacket, but cut off at the shoulder to show their massive, muscled arms, covered in tattoos. Only one of the group was shorter than Finn – he was shorter, even, than Faye and Liz, but made up for it with a fearsome scowl, framed by long plaits of thick grey hair that looked as if it had never once been cut. This one removed his dark glasses as he stalked towards Mr Purser. One by one, they surrounded Finn and the shop owner; not one of them said a word, but their anger fairly crackled in the air.

Security appeared almost as quickly, demanding to know what Finn had been planning.

'Wait!' Faye heard herself say. 'Wait, I don't think . . .'

'Faye,' Liz hissed, catching her arm. 'What are you doing?'

One of the guards came towards her. 'Miss? Do you have something to say about this incident?'

'I didn't see him steal anything,' Faye said, feeling the boy's eyes still on her, and wondering what on earth she was doing. 'I didn't – I don't think he was going to steal anything. He was just – he was just standing there.'

The security guard nodded before turning his back on her to talk to the bikers' leader, the big man with grey hair and fury in his eyes. 'All right. Here's what I'm going to do. We won't take this any further. This time. But I want you and your gang to leave. Right now.'

It looked for a moment as if the bikers were going to protest. Their leader stepped forwards until he was nose-to-nose with the security guard, who tried, unsuccessfully, to hide his fear. 'I . . . I don't want any trouble here,' he stuttered.

The biker smiled coldly. 'Then here's some advice. Don't let your people start any. Because next time, I won't be so inclined to be peaceable. Understand?'

The security guard nodded quickly. The leader stood still for another minute. Then he lifted his chin in the direction of the mall's exit. The bikers all began to walk away, slowly, passing Faye one by one, smelling of engine oil and gas. Finn hung back.

'Hey,' he muttered, as he reached her. 'Thanks.'

'Y-you're welcome,' Faye stuttered, confused again by the sudden racing of her heart.

'Maybe I'll see you around?'

'M-maybe.'

He looked her up and down before flashing her a brief smile. 'That looks good on you,' he added, before sliding on a pair of dark glasses. 'You should buy it.'

It was only when Finn had turned and strolled outside to join the others that Faye realized what he meant: she'd run out of MK in clothes she hadn't even paid for!

Chapter Seven

The Man in the Shadows

'Hey!' came an angry voice from behind her. 'What do you think you're doing?'

She turned to see the store owner marching towards her, pointing at her chest.

'I'm so sorry!' Faye exclaimed. 'I didn't mean to – I didn't think! I just had to speak to the security guards.'

'I don't appreciate customers who walk out without paying,' the owner said. 'Where I come from, we call that stealing.'

Faye was shocked. She'd never been accused of trying to steal anything before. 'Oh, but I wasn't – I wouldn't—'

'Faye wouldn't steal!' Liz said, leaping to her defence. 'She was just trying to help the bikers.'

'Give me one reason why I shouldn't call security back here again, right now,' the owner demanded. 'Were you two girls with those men? Were they creating a distraction so you could steal this?'

'No!' both girls said, together, horrified.

'Well, you're lucky you didn't keep walking, that's all I can say,' said the woman, her hands on her hips. 'As it is, you'd better not try to hang those things back up. If you were planning on buying them, you'd better pay for them, right now.'

Faye hesitated. She really couldn't afford the whole outfit . . .

'Faye,' Liz hissed. 'Just buy it!'

She forced a smile on her face. 'Of course I'm going to pay for it!'

'Good,' said the owner. 'And then both of you can leave. You're not welcome in this store – not now, and not in the future. Do you understand?'

'What on earth were you thinking?' Liz raged, as they left the store. 'After everything Barbie Finch said to you. After everything my dad said to you!'

Faye had rarely seen Liz so angry, and never with her. She followed her out of MK, trying to think of a way to make it up to her. But though she was worried about Liz's mood, most of her thoughts kept going back to Finn. Faye still didn't know why she'd done it. She didn't know him. Why did it matter to her what happened to him?

'I'm sorry,' Faye murmured. 'I just ... he wasn't doing anything.'

'And how do you know that? Those bikers might have been doing exactly what Mr Purser said they were!'

'But you saw for yourself,' Faye protested. 'He was just looking through the window, he wasn't doing anything bad ...'

Liz stopped marching and turned on her, eyes full of anger. 'Look. I know you wanted to do a piece on them. And maybe it isn't fair that you can't. But you know what I think isn't fair? Me getting kicked out of the best clothes store in town because you tried to steal an outfit on our first visit!'

'I didn't try to steal it! I just—'

'But that's what it looked like, isn't it?' Liz turned her back again, still heading for the exit. 'All I wanted to do was have something perfect to wear for the party. Doesn't that matter to you at all?'

'Hey,' Faye protested, hurt. 'Liz, I'm sorry about that. Of

course it matters to me! Tomorrow I'll call the store and apologize again. Even if I can't go back, there's no reason for them to stop you from shopping there.'

'They'd better not,' Liz snapped as they walked out of the mall's main doors and headed in the direction of the car.

The man watched the argument in the mall with interest. The bikers weren't really his priority at the moment, but he snapped a couple of quick photographs of the incident all the same. He even managed to get one of the dark-haired girl and Finn together.

He followed the two girls at a safe distance once they finally left the store. It took him a few minutes to notice that they were heading for the exit. He was surprised, as he'd been expecting their shopping trip to last far longer. Then he realized that the one called Liz was angry. She stalked ahead as Faye tried in vain to talk to her.

Outside, the Black Dogs were preparing to leave, pulling on their helmets and kicking their engines into gear. The girls had to walk right past the gathered bikes to reach their own ride.

He watched as Faye turned her head to look for Finn, slowing down, but the other girl caught the sleeve of her coat and dragged her away.

'Last chance, Faye,' he heard Liz say. 'You come, or I leave you here. I'm not losing the allowance I only just managed to get. Got it?'

He couldn't make out Faye's reply, but she followed her friend, sliding into the car when Liz unlocked it. Faye didn't look at the group of bikers again, holding a hand against her temple to shield her face. But he saw Finn watch her go.

Stowing his camera, the man hurried to the pick-up truck he'd borrowed. It wouldn't be his usual choice of transport, but in this situation, it at least blended in. The plan worked, too. Neither of the girls noticed him following them as Liz drove away, decidedly too fast for such a snowy evening.

Glancing in his rear-view mirror, he smiled. The young biker was staring after the two girls in the speeding car, clearly intrigued. He stood there so long, in fact, that it took a sharp, annoyed shout from the leader of the gang to get him moving again. In a fury of gas fumes, the Black Dogs rolled out of the Winter Hill Mall car lot. They followed his truck for a couple of turns before peeling off onto the road out of town.

Ahead of him, the man could still see the two girls in their little car. He pulled a cellphone from his pocket and hit speed-dial before listening to it ring in his Bluetooth earpiece. His employer would want to know of his success.

The ringing telephone was answered almost immediately. 'Yes?' The voice on the other end of the line was curt and clipped, same as it ever was.

'Finn has seen the girl.'

'They were in contact?'

'Oh yes. I don't think either of them will forget the encounter.'

'Excellent. Did you get photographs?'

'I did.'

'Good. Anything else of interest?'

He nodded to himself absently as he watched the red tail-lights of the car in front bite into the falling dark of a winter's night. 'I think there may be some tension between our little friends.'

'The bikers?'

'No, the two girls.'

'That could work in our favour.'

'My thoughts, exactly . . .'

'So? You are clear on what must be done?'

'Yes. This weekend is all arranged – this party really is perfect for our plans. The only problem we may have is if the enemy chooses to interfere before we are ready for them.'

'They won't,' drawled the voice, confidently. 'They know their limitations.'

'But if they do?'

'Then they'll go ahead and start a war they really can't win, won't they?'

Chapter Eight

Home Sweet Home

It was heading towards dusk as Lucas Morrow reached the front gate of his new home and started the long walk up the snowy pathway. He called it home, but it didn't feel like one. Lucas had moved a lot in his life, and he usually didn't have much say in where he ended up, but this place had really shocked him. His mother liked rich people and rich places, and that usually meant somewhere a bit busier than Winter Mill. *Winter Mill!* God, even the name sounded rustic. He wondered how long they'd stay. Surely his mother would soon get bored. Of course, that would mean he'd have to change schools again . . . but Lucas was used to that.

He walked up the front steps and unlocked the imposing front door. Inside, the mansion was as quiet as a tomb. But then, it was so big that you could land a jet plane on the top floor and no one in the rest of the house would even hear it, let alone notice several hundred new arrivals. His mother certainly wouldn't – she'd be too busy looking at herself in the mirror. With just Lucas, his mom and Ballard in residence at the mansion, the place was as good as empty.

Lucas walked into the middle of the large, marble-floored entrance hall. Stairs curved upwards before him, splitting into two as they reached the mansion's second level. It was cold.

'Hello?' he called, but he got no answer except the echo of his own voice, bouncing back at him.

With a sigh, Lucas walked towards the door to the living room looking for his mother. He figured he should probably speak to her at least once today before heading out to the Thorsson party – you know, as if they were a regular family. He'd almost said no when the girl asked him to go. He didn't feel like spending a whole evening being gawped at; it had been bad enough at school. But what else was he going to do? Hang around this place on his own? So in the end, he'd said yes. Who knew, maybe it would be fun. The locals couldn't be worse than the super-rich fake-tan junkies he usually found himself surrounded by, and maybe he'd meet someone interesting to talk to. That girl Faye – Flash – for example. She seemed smart. She was cute too.

'Hello?' he said again, pushing open another door. There were two lamps lit, casting a shallow glow over the living room, but there was still no sign of his mother.

Lucas looked around the room. He hadn't been in it before, yet another corner of the house he'd not bothered to explore. Now, though, he noticed the huge, ornate mirror that hung over the disused fireplace. All the furniture was arranged around it, as if it were a TV or a particularly beautiful painting.

'Ah,' he said. 'So that's where she's put you, is it? Thought I hadn't seen your ugly face for a while.'

Lucas moved until he stood in front of the mirror, studying its ancient, intricately carved wooden frame. This mirror featured in so many of his memories. No matter where they went, no matter how far they travelled, this thing always came with them. It must cost his mother a small fortune to transport it, and yet she did it, every time. He'd never asked why, though Lucas kind of assumed it was a valuable family heirloom. On the other hand, his mother never got tired of looking at her own reflection. Maybe she just liked the way this mirror made her look.

Lucas stared into the glass. He realized that although the mirror had been around for as long as he could remember, he had rarely looked at himself in it. It coloured everything in a bluish tint, as if each reflection contained within it was further away than it really should be. He regarded himself, and wondered if, as everyone was fond of telling him, his face really was similar to his mother's. He had her eyes, he knew that, but everything else – his nose, his mouth, his chin ... they held nothing of her.

He put his fingers to his face, wondering what his father looked like. Mercy never spoke about him, had never offered Lucas even a hint of who he might be. Maybe she didn't know – she certainly didn't want to talk about it. But the older he got, the more Lucas wondered. Was his father out there, somewhere? Did he even know he had a son? There were pictures of Lucas everywhere in the press – perhaps his father looked at them, and wondered too? Perhaps he recognized part of himself in his long-lost son, somehow?

The whole of Lucas's life, it had just been him and his mom. Well, the two of them plus whatever dumb bodyguards were following his mother around like trained animals. Ballard was just the latest. Lucas couldn't stand them. He'd never felt as if he'd really known his mother: not properly, not like other children seemed to know their parents. He had spent most of his life in the care of one idiot employee after another. And even if they hadn't been there, there was nothing to say that—

Something suddenly skittered at the edge of his vision. It was barely there, a movement deep within the mirror, something scuttling, insect-like, beneath its surface. Lucas stepped back, spooked, and knocked into the occasional table behind him, nearly sending a lamp crashing to the floor.

'Honestly, Lucas,' came his mother's bored voice. 'You really are as clumsy as an ox. At least try to be more careful, can't you?'

Lucas turned to see Mercy Morrow standing in the doorway, one slim and perfectly manicured hand grasping the antique handle. It was no wonder, he thought, that the rest of the world thought her so beautiful. She was beautiful. Her tall figure was a perfect hourglass shape. Her thick blonde hair was swept up as usual in a complicated arrangement of twists and curls that must have taken hours to complete, framing her delicate, pale oval face. Her almond-shaped eyes, bluer even than Lucas's own, shone in the lamp light, her lashes so long that they cast shadows on her high cheekbones. Her full lips were curved in a smile that Lucas wasn't sure was reflected in her eyes. She wore a tailored trouser suit of fine, natural-coloured linen over a simple white cotton shirt, with strings of baroque pearls at her throat. The light suit served to accentuate the pale serenity of her face, but she wore little make-up, which would probably shock the gossip journalists of the world. Mercy Morrow looked as perfect without cosmetics as she did with them. In her son's mind, she hadn't changed since he was a little kid – but then, Lucas supposed, parents always looked the same to their children.

'Hi, Mom. Good day?'

Mercy shrugged and walked over to him. 'I went down to the town's little spa and got a woman to give me a massage. It was . . . acceptable. Though she did chatter so.'

Lucas gave a derisive snort. 'Busy as usual then, huh?'

His mother narrowed her eyes. 'Don't be flippant, Lucas. It's boring. Rather like this commonplace little town.'

He sighed, exasperated. 'Honestly, Mom – why are we here? This place is like – it's like the ends of the earth! There's nothing to do, and you know you're going to get bored in two weeks. Can't we just go somewhere else? You know – somewhere alive?'

'I wanted us to unwind somewhere quiet,' Mercy said coldly. 'Somewhere . . . with a little history.'

'History? Sure, this place has history – if you count Abe Lincoln staying at the town inn for one night. I guess that was all he could stand, too.' Lucas threw up his hands. 'If you wanted to go somewhere quiet we could have gone to Barbados. You would have got an acceptable massage and I could have gone windsurfing. But instead we come out to the backwoods, where every local wants to peer in our windows and there's nothing to do but check your toes for frostbite every half hour.'

'Do not take that tone with me, Lucas,' Mercy hissed angrily. 'I don't recall you doing anything to earn your keep, and until you do, we go where I say, when I say. Is that clear?'

'It's not like I have a choice, is it?'

Mercy smiled before she turned her attention to the mirror behind him, checking her hair. 'I'm glad we understand each other.'

'Fine. I'm going out. And I really don't care if you mind or not.'

Mercy raised one long arm and flicked her fingers impatiently. 'Go, do. As long as you're not skulking around here, whining about your lot in life, I don't care.'

Lucas pushed past her, angry, slamming the door as he left

the room. Feeling someone watching him, he looked up to see Ballard standing on the other side of the entrance hall, an unpleasant smile on his face.

Chapter Nine

A Dog's Life

Finn stared into the fire they'd built to warm the camp, thinking about what had happened at the mall. It wasn't the incident with the shop owner and the security guards – he was used to attitudes like theirs, and had long ago learned that the best way to combat them was to rise above it. Actions spoke louder than words, as the old cliché went, and anyone who really cared to look would soon see that the bikers were not the thieving vagabonds they were so often accused of being. No, what had stayed with Finn was his encounter with the girl. Faye, her friend had called her. But it was another name that haunted Finn's dreams – another name that also matched that face. He'd glanced through that window, and it had been like seeing a ghost. He could still feel the shock that had spiked through his heart at the sight of her, even now.

Finn heard the crunch of footsteps behind him and turned to see his dad approaching through the fresh layer of snow. Joe Crowley had been leading the Black Dogs for too many years to count, and the group respected him more than anyone else. He was a big man with broad shoulders, and the leathers that he always wore made him look even bigger. Everyone said that Finn was getting more and more like his father every day, and the boy had no problem with that at all.

'Hey, Dad. Everything all right?'

Joe nodded as he came to stand beside his son, throwing an arm around Finn's shoulders. 'All quiet, at least for the moment. Just thought I'd see how you were doing.'

'I'm fine.'

'Listen – you should probably stay away from the town for a few days. I can send someone else down there for supplies.'

Finn sighed. 'I've no reason to hide. I did nothing wrong.'

'I know. But they'll be watching you now.'

Finn shook his head. 'I said I'd go back and check on that woman's heater. In the bookshop. I ought to keep my word.'

'I can get Archie to check on it.'

'I'd rather do it myself. Come on, Dad. You know I'll be careful.'

Joe was silent for a few moments. Finn glanced up to find his dad watching him carefully.

'I'll be fine,' he said. 'Come on, I can't just sit here until something happens. I'll go crazy with boredom.'

After another moment, Joe nodded. 'All right. But I want you to promise me one thing.'

'What's that?'

'Don't go looking for her while you're down there.'

Finn stared down at his feet, watching fresh snowflakes settle and then melt on the heavy steel toecaps of his boots. 'What do you mean?'

'You know what I mean. That girl. The one you saw in the mall.'

The boy nodded, still not looking at his father. 'Did you know? Did you know about her?'

At the edge of his vision, he saw Joe shrug. 'Why would I? I don't even know who she is.'

'She looks so much like—'

'Finn.' His father cut him off, his tone of voice holding an unmistakable order. 'You know it's not her. And if you saw her again, you'd probably realize that yourself, too. You only saw her for a few moments.'

It was enough, thought Finn. But to his dad he said, 'You're probably right. I know you are. But it's just . . . sometimes I feel as if I'm forgetting. Sometimes I think I can't quite remember what she looked like.'

Joe clasped a big hand over his son's shoulder and squeezed gently. 'That's just time, Finn. It's just the way we heal.'

The boy shook his head. He didn't want to forget, but his dad didn't seem to understand that. 'Is that what it was like with you? I mean, with you and Mom? Can you remember what she looked like?'

A flicker of emotion passed over Joe's face, and he glanced away, into the dark forest. 'No,' he admitted, at last. 'No, I don't think I'll ever forget what your mother looked like. I don't think I'd be able to. But I wish I could. It . . . would make things easier.'

Finn smiled grimly. 'Don't be so sure about that.'

Joe looked back at him, and for a moment Finn thought he was going to say something. But then he shook his head, apparently changing his mind. Joe moved away, heading back towards the ring of tents and bikes. 'Come and have some food. Doesn't that stew smell good?'

Finn smiled slightly. 'I'll be there in a minute.'

His eyes watched his dad walk away, but his mind was full of the girl called Faye.

Faye stood in front of her mirror and pulled a face. She wished Liz was there with her – they usually always got ready for parties together. For Candi's birthday Faye was trying out a really cool new colour of smoky grey eyeshadow. Instead of being a flat all-over colour, it had flecks of silver and petrol blue running through it, and Faye had decided to smudge it beneath her eyes as well as dusting it onto her eyelids. It would have been great to know what Liz thought of the look, especially since she'd only just managed to make the mall incident up to her best friend. But Liz's older sister, Poppy, was home from college for a rare family weekend. At first Liz was worried that her mom and dad would insist she ditch the party completely so they could spend time together. Instead, she'd been allowed to attend only so long as she spent all day at home before it.

Faye understood – if she'd had a family – a proper one, with a mom who was alive and a dad who didn't travel so much, and maybe a brother or sister – she'd want to spend time with them too.

She sighed. It wasn't that she didn't love her aunt Pam, and her dad's job was so cool – but without Liz and the rest of her friends at school, Faye sometimes felt that she'd be very, very alone.

The phone on her bedside table rang. Faye hadn't even got it to her ear before she heard Liz's trademark screech of despair.

'Faye!' Liz wailed. 'I don't know what to do!'

'Liz?' Faye frowned. 'What's happened? Are you all right?'

'No, I'm not all right! We're about to go to the most important party of our lives and . . . *I don't know what to wear!*'

Faye heaved a sigh of relief that there hadn't been a worse tragedy. 'I thought you went back to MK last night?' she asked. 'I thought the manager agreed—'

'I did go back! It was great!'

'So . . . What's wrong? Couldn't you find anything you liked?'

'Oh yeah . . . I found plenty – which is the problem,' sobbed her friend. 'I spent my whole allowance in one go, which was just *so* bad of me. I bought so many gorgeous things, you wouldn't believe it. But now I don't know which of them to wear! It's almost as bad as not having anything at all! You've got to help me!'

'Well . . . why don't you go for the first thing you chose at the store?' Faye suggested. 'If it was the first thing that caught your eye, it must have something awesome about it, right?'

'But then I can't wear these amazing shoes I found!'

'Um, OK . . .' said Faye, trying to think of a solution.

'Are you dressed?' asked Liz. 'I want to see – send me a picture from your cell! Oh – hold on . . .'

There was the sound of knocking in the background, followed by muffled conversation as Liz put her hand over the receiver to talk to someone. A moment later she came back on the line with a theatrical sigh.

'I've got to go,' she said. 'My dad wants to talk.' Liz emphasized the word 'talk' as if it left a terrible taste in her mouth. 'Send me that picture. And wish me luck. And I'll see you in two hours! This is going to be the best party ever!'

And with that, she hung up.

Chapter Ten

A Question of Style

Liz put down the phone and turned to her dad, who was look-ing around her bedroom as if he was worried there had been a break-in. Admittedly, it was even more of a mess than usual. Liz had been laying out different combinations of her new clothes, and had then decided to mix in a few pieces from her old ones. The general effect looked as if a bomb had gone off in her wardrobe.

'I'll clear it up,' Liz said, in what she hoped was a contrite voice. 'I promise, Dad.'

He nodded, stepping further into the room. Liz realized that he'd only just come off-shift. He hadn't even changed out of his uniform yet.

'Please don't tell me I can't go to this party,' she begged, suddenly scared that he was about to do just that. 'I know we haven't been able to spend the time together with Poppy that Mom wanted because you worked late, but we can do that tomorrow, can't we?'

Her dad glanced at her. 'Actually, I have to work tomorrow too. I've got a meeting with Mercy Morrow.'

Liz squealed. 'Oh my god! That's amazing! What for?'

'Well, it's a bit of a meet and greet – she wants to get to know some of the locals. I guess I'm an obvious choice. But I think she's also worried about photographers. They've been a bit of an issue at places she's lived in the past, apparently.'

Liz was almost jumping up and down with excitement. 'Can I come? Dad, please? Can I come?'

'Of course not! It's official police business!'

'But you said she wanted to get to know the locals,' Liz pouted. 'I'm a local, aren't I?'

'Liz,' sighed her father, 'be sensible.'

Liz was suddenly worried. 'Oh, no. You're not going to tell me I can't go out tonight because you have to work tomorrow, aren't you? Oh, that's so not fair—'

Mitch Wilson held up a hand. 'Don't worry, I'm not going to stop you going to the party.'

'Oh,' said Liz, with relief. 'Thanks, Dad, you're the best.'

'But I do want to have a serious talk with you before you go, OK?'

Liz managed to stop herself from rolling her eyes, but only just. 'Dad, we'll be fine. It's at the Mathesons' cabin – you've been there a million times.'

Her dad pushed a pile of tops out of the way and sat on the edge of his daughter's bed. 'Yes I have, which is how I know that it's one of the most isolated spots within the town limits. I'm not too happy about that, I can tell you.'

'But, Dad – I can run home from there in twenty minutes! How is that isolated?'

'It is, I believe, right in the woods I told you and Faye to stay out of, for a start. I know I told you that we now think the body up there was a vagrant who got caught out in the snow, but I'm still not comfortable with the bikers hanging around.'

'But the Mathesons'—'

'Won't be there. Instead, it'll be a big, unsupervised gathering of teenagers. Teenagers – including boys.'

Liz cringed. 'Dad, please don't . . .'

He interrupted her protest. 'Your mom tells me you've been talking a lot about the new boy this week. Lucas Morrow?'

She turned away, shuddering in embarrassment and pretending to be absorbed in picking non-existent stray threads from one of her new skirts. 'Yeah. So?'

'So will he be there tonight?'

Liz shrugged. 'Maybe.'

Mitch sighed. 'Lizzie, I just want you to be careful.'

'Dad! It's a party. All my friends will be there – it's not like it's just going to be me and Lucas.' *Though I wish it was*, Liz thought to herself.

'I know that, Liz, but I also know what can happen at parties like this. Things get out of hand, and before you know it—'

There was another knock at her bedroom door, and without waiting for an answer, Poppy stuck her head round the door.

'There you both are!' she exclaimed. 'Can I come in?' Poppy shot Liz a look that clearly said, *I'm here to rescue you from another one of Dad's lectures.*

Liz grinned. 'Of course you can!'

'Liz, I haven't finished—' began Mitch, but was cut off by a bear-hug from Poppy.

'Dad, I haven't even seen you yet! You don't have to go out again tonight, do you?'

'No, I don't, but—'

'Great, then we can have a proper catch-up. By the way, I think Mom wants you downstairs. Something about tasting the chilli? I think she's worried it's too hot.'

Poppy moved to stand next to her little sister and both girls looked at their father expectantly. He frowned, shaking his head as he looked between them. He knew he'd been beaten.

'Liz, just be careful, OK?' Mitch said, as he left. 'Keep your cellphone to hand at all times. One call and I'll be right there.'

Liz smiled. 'I know, Dad. Don't worry. I'll be fine.'

With a last nod, he left the room, closing the door behind him softly.

'Phew,' said Poppy, breathing out with relief. 'That could have been a long one.'

Liz hugged her sister. 'Thanks for the intervention, Popsicle. I swear he's got worse since you went off to college.'

'Poor Dad. He really doesn't like his little girls growing up.'

'Well, never mind about that right now,' said Liz, remembering the task at hand. 'I am in such a mess. I have to leave for the party of the year in' – she looked at her watch – 'an hour and forty-five, and I have no idea what to wear!'

Liz watched as Poppy surveyed the vast array of clothing strewn around the room. At nineteen, Poppy was her elder sister by three years, and the girls had always had a very different style of dress. Liz loved anything sparkly – little skirts with embellishments, tops strewn with gorgeous glitter, high heels that she wore whenever she could get out of the house without her dad seeing. Poppy, on the other hand, loved to work the boho look. She wore her long dark hair in a plait, or loosely pulled back from her face with a cute patterned band. She often wore gypsy tops, pairing them with long, country-style skirts or vintage jeans and boots.

'I've got a great idea,' said Poppy. 'Why don't you let me give you a makeover?'

'A makeover?'

'Sure. I can lend you some of my things – they'll mix really well with some of your new clothes.'

'I don't know,' Liz said, doubtfully. 'I mean, you always look great, but I'm not sure it's my style . . .'

'You don't have to wear it exactly the way I do,' said her

sister. 'You can make it your own. I think it could look really amazing.' Poppy picked up a corset-style top. 'This would layer so well with loads of stuff, and I've got a fantastic belt that would go with it. Come on, Liz – it'll be fun. I can do your make-up too.'

Liz grinned again. 'OK. Let's do it! But we'll have to be quick. And you have to promise that I'll look drop dead gorgeous. This could be the biggest night of my life!'

Poppy hugged her. 'I promise. That boy won't know what's hit him!'

Chapter Eleven

Making an Entrance

Faye was standing outside the door of the bookshop, patiently waiting for Liz to swing by and pick her up. Punctuality wasn't one of Liz's strong points even on a good day, and from the phone call they'd shared earlier, Faye had known her friend would be late tonight.

Faye shivered slightly in the evening chill. Above her, the sky was a deep blue as the last of the day's light bled away into evening. The stars were coming out, one by one. It was going to be another cold night. Faye stamped her feet, sending up tiny flurries of snow. The snowy weather still hadn't let up, and the town was beginning to get used to the idea of an extremely early winter. Even Aunt Pam had been stockpiling food in case the town actually did get cut off.

Liz's little car rattled skiddily round the corner, going too fast, as usual. Faye saw her friend raise one hand from the steering wheel in a wave before she pulled up, her face bright with excitement.

'Get in, get in, get in!' Liz babbled, as Faye opened the door. 'I'm so sorry I'm late!'

'It's fine,' Faye said, as she slid into the passenger seat, twisting to drop her camera case on the back seat. She turned to look at Liz properly for the first time as they pulled away. 'Wow, Liz – you look amazing! That's a really, really good look for you!'

'I know, right?' Liz said, excitedly. 'I really wasn't sure when Poppy first suggested it, but now I really like it. Aren't these earrings awesome? Look!' Liz waggled her head, sending the long drops tinkling before glancing at Faye. 'Love your make-up too. Very glam-goth!'

Faye glanced in the rear-view mirror and smiled. She was wearing the new top she'd bought at MK, but instead of the jeans, she'd chosen a short black tulip-style skirt, which looked great with her black high-heeled ankle boots. She'd accessorized the look with a chunky black-and-silver necklace and a row of silver bangles. Besides the smoky eyeshadow, Faye had also picked a deep red lipstick. Overall, it was a bolder look than Faye usually went for – but it felt great. 'Thanks,' she said. 'You're sure it's not too much?'

'Definitely not. Anyway, what have you been doing today? I'm sorry I've been tied up.'

'Don't be silly. It must be lovely to have Poppy home.'

'Well, Mom's happy,' Liz rolled her eyes. 'She thinks Poppy's a good influence on me. Keeps getting her to talk to me about things she thinks I need to hear. As if I don't get enough of that from Dad. Ooh!' Liz added. 'Speaking of Dad – guess what?'

'He's given you a curfew of eight-thirty p.m.?' Faye was only half-joking – once the girls had gone to a firework display alone, and Mitch Wilson had tried to demand that Liz be home before the sun had even set properly!

Liz shuddered. 'Don't even joke about it. He almost gave me a talk about the dangers of boys. Seriously, you should have seen me cringe! But no, this is actually quite cool – he's going to meet Mercy Morrow tomorrow!'

'Really?' Faye pricked her ears up, genuinely interested.

'Yeah, he's going to get to see inside their mansion and everything!'

'Maybe he can put in a good word for me,' said Faye, as the car left the town lights behind and headed into the woods. 'Ms Finch wants me to write a piece about her for *The Miller*. I've been researching her all day.'

'I said you should write about her! See? You should so listen to me more. Although I thought you didn't want to?'

'I didn't, but Ms Finch didn't give me much of a choice. And, actually – Mercy Morrow's kind of interesting.'

'I knew she would be!' Liz exclaimed. 'What did you find out?'

'Well, for one thing, she and Lucas sure move around a lot. They've lived everywhere – all over the States and Europe. They've even spent some time in Egypt and other parts of north Africa.'

'Ah, the lives of the rich and famous,' sighed Liz enviously.

'I don't know, I think it probably sucks, having to live in so many different places,' said Faye. 'Especially for Lucas. He must find it hard to make friends.'

Liz looked over at her again. 'Does that mean you're going to start being nice to him?'

Faye smiled. 'Well, I am hoping that I can chat to him at this party, maybe pick up some useful material for this piece.'

'It might be a good opportunity,' agreed Liz. 'Hey – listen to that!'

The sound of music and happy raised voices floated out of the trees as Liz turned the car up the track towards the Mathesons' cabin. The little road had been lit with fairy lights to lead the way, but the rest of the forest was dark. The music got louder and louder – and then, up ahead, a pool of light splashed into the darkness. The cabin was lit by floodlights and surrounded by cars. Guys from school swarmed every-where, congregating on the wide wooden steps, leaning against the cabin walls. Liz searched for a space to park as, through the windows of the cabin, strobe lighting coloured the cold air.

'You know what?' Liz said, as she killed the engine.

'What?'

'Talking might not be that easy after all!'

Faye laughed, her spirits lifted by the sight of so many of her friends all having a good time. She picked up her camera and grabbed the gift she'd picked up for Candi – a new charm for the bracelet that Faye had bought her friend for Christmas. This one was really cute – a miniature working pocket-watch in a silver filigree case that opened like a tiny locket. Sliding out of the car, Faye shut the door and followed Liz towards the cabin's entrance.

'Hey, Faye! Liz!' Jimmy Paulson called from the steps, waving as the two girls approached. 'There you are! You're late!'

'That would be *fashionably* late, Jimmy,' Liz told him breezily, as she headed up the stairs.

'Um . . . uh . . .' Jimmy's face fell, and he began to stutter. 'Of-of course, b-b-being late is far better than b-b-being on time . . .'

Faye gave Jimmy a quick hug. They worked on *The Miller* together, and she'd got to know him a lot better in the past year – so she knew he had a bit of a crush on Liz. Jimmy may have looked like a bit of a geek – Faye kept telling him his glasses were too big, and the knapsack he carried everywhere was a long-standing joke at Winter Mill High – but everyone loved Jimmy. Well, everyone except Liz, who just couldn't see him as anything other than a likeable loser, and had often told Faye as much.

'S-so,' said Jimmy, bravely trying to engage Liz in conversation again. 'Have you two heard about The B-Battle of the

B-Bands? It's c-coming to W-Winter Mill! It's g-going to be a-amazing!'

'What is it?' Faye asked, watching out of the corner of her eye as Liz scanned the crowd of kids, obviously searching for Lucas Morrow.

'I-it's great! I-it's this big competition that tours high schools—'

Jimmy stopped as a new sound was heard over the noise of the party. It was a finely tuned engine, making its way up the track to the cabin. The noise grew louder and louder, and as everyone turned to look, a flash of red could be seen moving through the trees. A car appeared, sleek and fast-looking.

'Oh my g-goodness,' exclaimed Jimmy, pushing his glasses up his nose. 'That's a Ferrari. A four-five-eight. You can't get them here in America yet – they have to be specially ordered from Italy . . .'

The car swung in a tight arc and backed smoothly into a space. Faye looked up at Liz. Her friend's eyes were as big as saucers. There was a ripple among the gathered partygoers as the door opened and Lucas Morrow stepped out. He wore slouch jeans and a crisp white shirt, open at the collar. He'd spiked his hair into an amazing style. Even Faye had to admit he looked incredibly gorgeous. Faye pulled out her camera, framing a shot of the scarlet car's smooth lines against the haphazard roughness of the snowy trees behind it.

She felt Liz grip her arm in silent excitement as Lucas walked through the crowd, nodding at people as he went. He glanced up to where the two girls were standing – and then headed straight for them! He jogged up the steps, stopping in front of Faye.

'Hey Flash,' he said, smiling his charming smile. 'How's the party?'

'It – er – it's great, I think. We only just got here ourselves,' said Faye, trying to involve Liz, who was digging her fingers into Faye's arm.

'Great,' Lucas said, blue eyes sparkling in the party lights. 'Then I guess you and I can find out together!'

Chapter Twelve

What Are Friends For?

Liz couldn't believe it. This evening was supposed to have been the most fun she'd had all year, but it had turned into a massive, humiliating disaster. She should have been getting to know Lucas, chatting to him, maybe even dancing with him by now. But instead, Liz had been made to watch as Lucas and Faye got closer and closer. Sure, at first Faye had tried to involve her . . . but as the evening had gone on, Faye had obviously decided that she wanted Lucas for herself.

Liz swallowed the lump in her throat, scrabbling in her purse for her mirror to wipe away the tears that suddenly threatened her make-up. Snapping open her compact, she checked her mascara, relieved to see that it hadn't run. *There's no point crying*, she told herself harshly. *You just have to do something about it*. Liz stared at her reflection in the little mirror so hard that she went dizzy. For a second, it felt as if she were falling. Then a knife of anger stabbed through her. She snapped the compact shut, looking around for her so-called best friend.

They were standing together, sipping drinks, chatting as if they'd known each other their whole lives! It wasn't fair. Lucas had totally ignored her since he got to the party. It was humiliating.

'Hey, Liz!' Candi Thorsson slipped up behind her, giving

her a quick hug. 'Thanks so much for coming! The necklace you bought me is gorgeous! Are you having fun?'

Liz forced a smile onto her face and hugged her friend back. 'Oh yeah – this is the most amazing party I've ever been to!'

Candi laughed. 'I think my mom and dad feel bad for not being around that much. What do you think of the band?'

'Er – yeah, they're great.' Liz turned to look at the five-piece rock outfit that had been playing since she arrived. To tell the truth she'd not really noticed them, too preoccupied with the Lucas and Faye situation.

'Are you OK?'

Liz looked up at Candi's question and smiled again. 'Sure. Why?'

Her friend smiled back and shrugged. 'Never mind. Hey, doesn't Lucas look great? He's like, my star guest – everyone wants to talk to him! How amazing would it be to be that popular?'

Liz actually laughed for real at that. 'Candi – you are that popular!'

'Yeah, but he's like *mega*-popular. It's a kind of popular that you and I can only dream of, Liz. I wouldn't have thought he was Faye's type, though.' Candi nodded towards where the pair was still chatting. 'They've been talking for ages.'

Liz felt the knife twist again, and turned away. 'I think she's writing a piece on him for *The Miller*,' she muttered.

'I don't get it,' said Faye. 'If you've got an amazing car like that, why does that man drive you to school every day?'

Lucas shrugged. 'It's Mom's car, not mine. I'm not supposed to have it.'

Faye raised her eyebrows. 'Will you get into trouble?'

Lucas shrugged. 'So, what's your favourite band?' he asked, ignoring her question.

'I'm the one that's supposed to be asking you the questions,' laughed Faye. 'And you haven't given me a proper answer to any of them yet!'

Lucas grinned. 'Well, maybe the ones you're asking just aren't any good,' he suggested.

'Hey!' Faye feigned outrage. She had to admit, an evening in Lucas's company had changed her mind about him. He could be sarcastic, but he was charming and funny, too. She made a mental note to tell Liz as much when her friend appeared from wherever she'd disappeared off to. 'I'll have you know I'm a brilliant school journalist. I've won prizes and everything.'

'Oh yes? Let me guess – for that amazing story you did on Farmer Giles's giant potato last year?'

Faye felt her mouth drop open. 'The farmer's name was Baxter, actually. And you've been researching me?'

Lucas shrugged. 'Well, you were so angry with me for that *National Enquirer* joke I made when we first met, I thought I'd better see who I was dealing with, Flash.' He glanced at her, serious for a second. 'We didn't really get off on the right foot, I guess.'

Faye shrugged. 'Maybe not.'

'I'd like to be friends now, though,' Lucas added, clinking his glass against hers. 'I could really do with some fun people to hang out with here.'

'Ah, then you really need to meet Liz properly,' said Faye, looking around for her best friend. 'She's the most fun person I know.'

'Is that the pretty girl you hang out with a lot?'

'Yeah – she's been my best friend since we were like, three. She's brilliant.' Faye smiled. 'You think she's pretty?'

Lucas shrugged. 'Sure. I mean, it's not an opinion, or anything. She just is. I like her outfit tonight. It's different to what she usually wears.'

Faye nodded, pleased that Lucas had noticed – Liz would love that! 'She looks gorgeous. Look, I'll go find her so you two can get to know each other. I don't know where she's disappeared to . . .'

Jimmy Paulson was going on about something to do with the International Space Station, and Liz had just about had enough. She kept staring at his little quiff and trying to work out if it was actually cute, as Faye seemed to think, or just stupid. But thinking about Faye then took her back to Faye and Lucas, which was just too awful to contemplate. She'd had to go stand somewhere that she at least couldn't see them being together, so it wouldn't hurt so much.

This was the worst party *ever*.

'Liz!'

Liz looked in the direction of the voice to see Faye pushing through the crowd. She'd like to turn her back and make it clear that her *former* best friend was the last person she wanted to talk to right now, but Liz already had her back to the wall.

'What?' she said brusquely, instead, pulling out her mirror again and making a show of reapplying her lipstick. Her reflection stared back, and Liz could see the hurt in her own eyes. Anger surged through her. She shoved the mirror back in her purse, stepping a little closer to Jimmy as if the two of them had been in an intense personal conversation.

'I've been looking all over for you! Where did you go?' Faye looked perfectly happy, as if she was having the time of her life. *Which she probably is*, Liz thought, furious, *since she's spent all evening with Lucas Morrow!*

'Oh, you've been looking all over, have you?'

'Yeah . . .' Obviously picking up on her sarcastic tone, Faye looked at her strangely. 'What's the matter?'

'So, when you were looking all over for me, Faye – was that just in the ten seconds this evening when you haven't been glued to Lucas Morrow's face?'

Faye looked shocked. 'What?'

'It's disgusting,' Liz stormed. 'You've been all over him. Everyone's talking about it!'

Jimmy tried to interject, timidly putting up his hand. 'Um, I'm not . . .'

'Oh, go away, Jimmy,' Liz snapped.

'Don't talk to Jimmy like that!' Faye protested. 'Stop being an idiot, Liz – come on, come talk to Lucas. He thinks—'

'Oh, so now I'm an idiot, am I?' Liz's rage was beginning to bubble over. 'Some best friend you turned out to be, Faye McCarron.'

'Liz, I don't understand what you're talking about. One minute we were both talking to Lucas, and the next minute you'd vanished. I only stayed there because I wanted to chat to him for the article. And it was a good talk, I think.'

'Sure,' spat Liz. 'It looked really good from where I was standing – good for you, that is. You knew I liked him, Faye. And now you're going after him yourself. How could you?'

'I'm not! We were just talking!'

Liz had had enough. She pushed away from the wall and shoved Faye out of the way, spilling some of her drink in the process. 'Well, don't think that you're getting a ride home from me, McCarron. You can walk, for all I care!'

Chapter Thirteen

Night Terrors

Faye couldn't believe what had just happened. How on earth could her best friend think that she would do such a thing, especially when Liz had made it so clear that she was totally head over heels for Lucas?

And then, as Faye thought about it, anger began to take over. *What sort of friend thought about another like that, period? And over a stupid boy! And even if Faye had wanted Lucas for herself – what right did Liz have to get upset about it? As if she'd somehow put a label on him saying TAKEN, or something? Unbelievable!*

Faye looked at her watch. It was ten-thirty p.m. – early, considering the party was due to carry on until midnight and Aunt Pam had told her she could stay right to the end. But she was no longer in the party mood, and anyway, she'd just lost her ride. She didn't feel like going around to all her friends, begging them to drive her. Faye would have to explain why she wasn't going back with Liz, which would just be embarrassing, and add fuel to whatever rumours were already going around the party. Anyway, Faye didn't really feel like spending any more time in the same room as Liz. Even if she hadn't been doing what her friend had accused her of, Faye had to admit that she'd had fun talking to Lucas – which just made her feel more confused and angry. Faye just wanted to go home, alone, right away.

Making up her mind to walk, Faye was about to search for Candi to say goodbye when she spotted Liz. She had her arms around Lucas's waist, and was pulling him towards the dance floor. Faye turned away, feeling something suspiciously like jealousy. She had to get out of there.

Heading for the door, Faye slipped out of the cabin unnoticed and made her way into the woods.

Though it was dark, the sky was so clear that the moon shone silver on the snow, lighting her way. Faye set off in the direction of Winter Mill, avoiding the track and instead cutting through the trees, heading for the road into town. She wasn't worried about getting lost – she'd spent so much time up here as a child, exploring with her father, that Faye knew the forest as well as she knew the town itself. The music and chatter followed her for a while, but soon it faded until all she could hear was the crunch of her boots on the undisturbed snow.

Faye had just topped a small ridge when a horrible noise shattered the quiet. It was a raw, animal howl – a noise unlike anything Faye had ever heard before. She froze, terror gripping her heart and thumping it against her ribcage.

She waited there, not daring to move, but after several minutes there had been no more awful sounds. Her heart calmed, and her fear gradually faded away.

It must have been an owl, she thought to herself. *Or maybe someone up at the party, making stupid noises. You weren't listening properly, that's all. There's nothing scary in these woods.*

Faye began to move again, more quickly. Her party clothes really weren't that warm, and standing still had chilled her to the bone. Faye rubbed her hands up and down her arms to warm herself. Maybe walking wasn't such a great idea after all . . .

Then she saw something out of the corner of her eye. Or at

least, she *almost* saw it, a fleeting movement among the trees to her left, too quick to pin down. Faye kept going, hoping she was imagining things. Instead, to focus her thoughts, she concentrated on where she put her feet among the hidden, snowy tree roots, wishing now that she hadn't worn heels. But then she saw it again – a fluid shape, sliding swiftly between the tree trunks. A cold slice of fear shivered down her spine.

It was a wolf, its yellow eyes flickering in the dark of the forest.

Her heart began to beat faster again. She changed direction, moving to her right, away from the predator. But then she saw another – they were either side of her, moving quietly through the trees.

Faye's heart jumped and stuttered. Two wolves? She'd heard of them in these woods – loners, coming over the border from Canada to hunt – but never of more than one at a time. What if there was a whole pack?

There came another howl, high-pitched and terrifying. And then, something else – another sound, further away but just as baleful – the creepy, mournful wail of a horn, that rose and then died away on the wind.

The howl went on and on. It came from somewhere behind her, and Faye found herself running, trying to open her bag to pull out her phone. She looked left and right and saw that the wolves were still following her, easily keeping up. They wound around tree trunks as they loped through the woods, faster and faster, closer and closer ... Faye managed to pull her cell out, but her cold fingers fumbled as she dialled and she lost her grip. The phone fell, disappearing into a snow drift. Sobbing, Faye didn't dare stop. Instead she ran on, gathering all her strength.

She heard snuffling close to her right as one of the wolves checked her scent. Then the horrible sound of the horn pierced the breeze again, dousing Faye in a fear so cold that she felt numb.

She slipped, went sprawling headlong in the snow. Faye thought she felt the creature's breath on her neck, and forced herself back to her feet, not even pausing to brush off the snow as she ran again. Her clothes were wet now, and she was freezing cold. She felt her teeth began to chatter, and her fingers ached. Her mind flashed, suddenly, to the body in the woods. Is this what had happened to him? Maybe he hadn't died from cold after all, maybe . . . Faye shook herself, clearing her head. Panicking wouldn't get her anywhere.

It can't be that much further to the road, she told herself, trying to keep calm enough to think clearly. *Just keep going. If you can make it to the road . . .*

Something snapped at her heels and she screamed, the sound echoing into the trees as she twisted to get away. Faye spurred herself forwards, feeling branches scratch at her face and pull at her hair.

Then the wolf was at her heels again, grazing its teeth against her calf. She stepped on a rotten tree branch, concealed beneath the flawless snow. It crumbled under her foot, and she stumbled, right under the beast's nose.

Chapter Fourteen

An Unexpected Encounter

Faye tried to right herself, but the stumble turned into a fall and suddenly she was rolling down the slope at full tilt. She opened her mouth to scream, but shut it again as dirty snow and dead leaves made her cough instead.

Faye scrabbled desperately with her hands, trying to catch onto the trees as they passed, but she couldn't. She thought she was going to fall for ever, but suddenly the ground levelled out. Her head struck something harder than the surrounding mulch – tarmac! She had rolled onto the road, which had been salted against the snow.

She could still hear the wolves howling as they chased down her scent. Faye scrambled to her feet, ignoring a sharp pain in her elbow.

A roar sounded behind her – but it wasn't an animal this time. Faye spun on her heel, throwing up her hands to shield her eyes from the fierce glare of the headlight that appeared round the bend in the road, cutting through the darkness like a knife. She tried to get out of the way, but, disoriented by the chase and her fall, didn't know which way to leap. She recognized the sound of the vehicle as a motorbike as it bore down on her.

Faye held her breath, but in the split second that she waited for the collision, the bike skidded around her. The girl watched as the rider fought to control his bike. Its back wheel kicked out against the blacktop as it hit a patch of stubborn snow and slid until it was almost horizontal against the road's icy surface. She could see the rider holding on, grimly, his leather-gloved fingers gripping the handlebars for dear life. He and the bike spun in a semicircle round her quaking figure. Faye stood, rooted to the spot, waiting for the rider to crash to the ground.

But he didn't. With a monumental effort, he pulled the bike upright, completing the semicircle he had cut on the treacherous ice and coming to a standstill with his front wheel just inches from her legs. The engine idled, suddenly quiet.

In the vast moment of silence that followed, Faye could hear her breathing, even louder than the beating of her terrified heart. She could feel herself shaking, her teeth chattering with cold and fright.

'What the—?' said the rider, struggling to catch his own breath. '*Faye?* It's Faye, isn't it? What the hell are you doing out here? I could have hit you! I could have killed—'

She had a second to wonder how on earth he knew her name before the rider's words were cut off by another wolfish howl from somewhere in the trees. He pulled off his helmet, and Faye found herself face to face with Finn, the biker boy from the mall. He stared up at the forest, his face dark with anger.

'Get on,' he ordered. 'Behind me. I'll take you home.'

Faye didn't hesitate. She straddled the bike's wide seat and wrapped her arms around his waist. As soon as he felt her weight behind him, Finn kicked the engine into gear and roared off down the road towards the lights of Winter Mill.

She'd never been on a bike before. It was exhilarating, to race with the wind through the night. Faye held on as tightly to the boy as she dared, her face against his warm, heavy jacket. It smelled of leather, an old smell, but not unpleasant. Her heart was still beating hard, but as she felt the muscles of his back move where she was pressed close to him, her fear melted into deep excitement.

'Where do you live?' she heard him shout as they approached the town.

'McCarron's Bookstore,' Faye called back, hoping that the wind hadn't snatched her words away before he had heard them.

The ride was less than ten minutes, though as the bike pulled up Faye wished it could have lasted an hour. The boy killed the engine and kicked down the stand, leaning the bike into it. Faye slid off, pushing her windswept hair back from her face, and found she had to catch her breath once again. 'Thank you,' she managed, as he removed his helmet and pushed himself off the bike.

He stood in front of her, eyes shadowed so that Faye couldn't tell what he was thinking. 'I guess that makes us even,' he said at last.

'Even?'

He smiled then, briefly. 'For what you did in the mall.'

'Oh. Right. You didn't owe me—'

'What were you doing out there in the woods?' he asked, cutting her off. 'Don't you ever go out there alone, you hear me?'

She was shaken by the urgent tone of his voice, talking about a landscape she'd known since she was a child. 'I was just walking home. I've done it a thousand times.'

'Well, don't. Not now. Not any more.'

'Why?' she asked, trying to make sense of everything that had happened. 'Those were wolves out there. They were chasing me – but there was something else, too. It sounded like . . . like a horn, or something. Do you know what that was?'

The boy looked away. 'I don't know. I just know it's not safe up there. Please ... Faye, please promise me you won't go up there again.'

Faye felt her heart lurch. 'How do you know my name?'

Finn shrugged. 'I heard your friend call you it. At the mall.'

'Thank you,' she whispered. 'I was afraid. Really afraid.'

Finn took a step towards her. Faye held her breath as he raised one hand and traced a finger along her cheekbone where a branch had scratched her. 'You don't have to be afraid,' he told her, softly. 'Not while I'm here. Never while I'm here.'

He was so close. Her eyes flicked to his lips, and she wanted, suddenly, to feel his arms around her. Her heart stuttered and she met Finn's gaze to find it so intense that she could hardly breathe. He dipped his head forwards and Faye thought he was about kiss her. But then he froze. Finn dropped his hand as if her skin had burned him and stepped back, turning abruptly to look up at the McCarron's sign.

'So the woman that runs the shop – that's your mom?'

'Uh – no,' said Faye, sent off-balance by the sudden change of atmosphere. She swallowed her disappointment, embarrassed that she'd misread his intention. 'No, my mom's dead. That's my aunt Pam.'

Finn nodded, glancing at his boots and then the bike key in his hand – anywhere, apparently, to avoid looking back at her. 'I like her. Anyway, I've got to go.'

'You were out there,' Faye blurted, suddenly desperate for him to stay. 'You were out in the woods tonight. Why?'

He stared at her for a second and shrugged. 'I like the moonlight.'

Then he jammed on his crash helmet and swung his leg over the bike, gunning the engine. A second later, he was gone, without even pausing to say goodbye.

Chapter Fifteen

Home Visit

Nerves bubbled in Liz's gut as she pulled up outside the Morrow mansion. Part of it was the idea of seeing Lucas at home, part of it was the idea of being in such an amazing house at all, and part of it was left over from the fight with Faye the night before. Sometime after their showdown, Liz had looked around the party and realized that Faye was no longer there. She must have left soon after she'd told her friend she wasn't going to get a ride home.

Liz looked in the mirror, adjusting her make-up and re-applying her coral-pink lipgloss, trying to ignore the shadow of guilt that haunted her. *It was her own fault*, Liz told herself. *You just don't do that to a friend . . .*

Friends don't leave each other to walk home alone in the dark, either, said another voice, one that Liz was determined to ignore. She climbed out of her old rust-bucket of a car and slammed the door shut, looking up at Lucas's home.

It was huge and imposing, just as her dad had said. He'd come back from his meeting with Mercy a couple of hours ago and Liz had been eager to learn as much as she could. He'd been in a strange mood, though – unwilling to talk. The only thing he'd said before he shut himself in his study was that Mercy's mansion was a lonely place. That was what had made Liz's mind up about paying this surprise visit. She imagined Lucas,

81

holed up in this big house with no company, and had told herself he'd welcome a visit; after Faye had left the party, they'd had quite a lot of fun, even if he had kept asking where she had gone.

Liz ran up the steps and rang the doorbell. A few moments later there was the sound of heavy footsteps, and the door opened to reveal the man who had driven Lucas to school on his first day. Liz tried not to shiver as she looked at him, but he really did look scary. He was big and broad-shouldered, with a bald, shiny head – not even a hint of hair. It was his face, though, that was really alarming. His eyes were deep-set and very dark, and seemed to be permanently angry. His nose was flattened as if it had been broken at some point, and his lower lip bore a long scar that ran down and cut into his chin.

The man looked her up and down. His expression was openly hostile. 'Help you?'

'It's Mr Ballard, isn't it? I, uh – I've come to see Lucas. Is he in?'

He stared at her for another moment before opening the door wider and gesturing for Liz to step inside.

Ballard led her up the massive stone staircase swiftly, turning left at the top, then right into another corridor, and then right again into yet another. Liz looked around her, intimidated by the sheer size of the house – it was like a maze! There were doors everywhere, all shut. They kept walking, and Liz became aware of the sound of music up ahead. It came from behind a door at the end of the last corridor they had turned into. Ballard walked up to it and knocked twice, hard.

There was a pause before the door was flung open and Lucas stood in the doorway, a scowl on his face. 'What?'

Ballard flicked his head towards Liz. 'Friend of yours to see you.'

82

Lucas looked past him and offered a faint smile. 'Oh, hey Liz. Come in . . .' He nodded curtly at Ballard, who stalked past her and away down the echoing corridor. 'I wasn't expecting any visitors . . .'

'Um . . . I just thought I'd pay a friendly visit,' Liz said, as Lucas shut the door behind her. 'That's OK, isn't it?'

Lucas wandered further into the room. 'Well, I don't mind – but Mom can be a bit funny about it. She doesn't really like uninvited guests.'

'Oh,' said Liz, beginning to feel uneasy. 'Sorry.'

Lucas shrugged dismissively. 'Do you want a drink? I've got juice, or Coke . . .'

'Coke would be great, thanks.' She glanced around the room, taking in the drinks refrigerator. Music was pouring from an expensive-looking sound system in the corner. A large, slouchy sofa stood beside it – Lucas had obviously been lying on it reading, because it was surrounded by music and car magazines. A large flat-screen TV hung on the wall opposite, but Liz was most impressed by the drum kit, keyboard, guitar and microphone, all set up as if a band had just left.

Then she realized something else. 'You don't have a bed!' she blurted, surprised.

Lucas walked to the sound system, glancing at her as he turned it down. 'This is just my den. My bedroom's next door.'

'Oh. Right. Of course . . . That makes sense . . .' Liz said, kicking herself. *Way to seem like a poor hick, Liz.*

'So . . .' Lucas said, handing her a Coke and waving for her to sit down. 'Was there a specific reason for you coming over?'

'No, not really. I just thought . . . you left the party pretty suddenly last night. I just thought I'd see if you were OK.'

Lucas raised an eyebrow, a cheeky sparkle in his eye. 'Really? Just that? You didn't think it might be a good excuse to have a look inside the Mysterious Morrow Mansion? Seriously. I think I spent most of my night last night ignoring hints. Everyone wants to come over to hang out.'

'No!' Liz protested, feeling herself flush – because if she was really honest with herself, that was exactly one of the reasons she'd come. 'I just . . . I just thought you might like some company, that's all. Stuck here in this big house with nothing to do.'

'Take a look around,' Lucas teased. 'I think I've got plenty to do, don't you?'

Liz swallowed, trying to stop herself blushing. She was desperate to act cool around him, but that plan seemed to be failing. 'So, which do you play then?' she asked. 'Or do you sing?'

'I play guitar mostly. I had lessons when I was younger. I write songs, too – or at least, I used to. Haven't for a while, now.'

'Did you hear what Jimmy said last night about the Battle of the Bands?'

'Jimmy. That's the little geeky one, right? With the crazy glasses.'

'Yes,' Liz laughed. 'He's a geek, all right. Really smart, though. He was telling me about this competition that tours around high schools looking for the best new talent. It's run by all these big music executives. Anyone can enter – you can sing or play, either solo or in a band. And the best gets a record contract. And it's coming here, next week. How cool is that?'

Lucas grinned. 'That depends.'

Liz frowned. 'Depends on what?'

'On whether there's any talent around here! Won't be much of a show if these guys turn up and there's nothing good going on.'

'Oh, a few of my friends are going to enter,' Liz said. 'Rachel

Hogan's got an amazing voice. And Trey Finkler plays electric guitar really well. And then there's Matt . . .'

'Don't tell me,' Lucas interrupted. 'He's a drummer, right? He must be. All drummers are called Matt.'

Liz laughed. 'Actually, he plays keyboards. But Winter Mill High has a couple of good drummers, too.'

Lucas sighed theatrically. 'Sounds like I'm going to have competition.'

'Really? So you're going to enter?'

He shrugged. 'Sure, why not? All I need is the perfect song. And I kind of got inspired by someone last night.'

Liz's heart beat a little faster, and suddenly found herself playing nervously with her Coke can. 'Oh?'

Lucas nodded. 'Yeah. Cheesy, I know, but meeting a girl you like is always good inspiration. Especially when she's so . . . different.'

She risked a look at his face, Was he talking about her? *Oh, please*, she begged silently, *please let him mean me. We danced, after all. We had fun. He must mean—*

'Does she always carry that camera around with her?' Lucas asked, suddenly. 'I don't think I've ever seen her without it.'

Liz's vision blurred slightly, and she swallowed hard. Faye. He was talking about Faye.

'Uh – Faye, you mean? Yeah, she's always got it with her. She wants to be a photographer. She's really good.'

Lucas nodded. 'So . . . is she seeing anyone? You know – has she got a boyfriend? Someone she's going steady with?'

Liz stood up, placing her half-empty drink on the floor and keeping her back to Lucas so he couldn't see her face. 'No . . . no, she doesn't. I mean, she did, for a while, last year – there was this guy called Ryan . . . but they were never serious.

He moved away, and they haven't kept in touch.'

'That's really great!' Lucas said, standing up, 'So . . . do you think you could put in a good word for me? I know you and she are really close.'

'Me?' Liz asked, faintly.

'Yeah,' Lucas barrelled on, apparently oblivious to her discomfort. 'I'm not sure that she likes me. I thought I'd made up for that stupid gag when we first met, but then last night she just left, without saying goodbye. I couldn't find her anywhere.'

'Um . . .' Liz didn't know what to say. She just wanted to get out of there.

'She was right about you, you know,' he said.

'Right about me?'

'Yeah. She said you were brilliant fun and a really good friend. Thanks for making me feel welcome, Liz – at school, and at the party last night. I thought being here in Winter Mill was going to be a drag, but maybe I was wrong.'

'So . . . so you really like Faye, huh?' Liz asked, forcing herself to smile and look him in the eye.

Lucas nodded, looking slightly embarrassed. 'Yeah. That first time that I met you both? When she was mad at me for calling her Flash? I kept thinking about her all day.' He shrugged. 'Girls don't usually get me that way. It just felt . . . As if I'd seen her before somewhere, but I can't have, can I?'

Liz managed to get through the rest of the conversation without showing how she really felt, but only just.

Chapter Sixteen

Belongings

Lucas watched from his window as Liz's little car pulled away from the front door and rattled off down the driveway. She'd gone a bit quiet after he'd asked her about Faye. Maybe he'd sounded like an idiot, with all that stuff about being inspired, but he just couldn't get Faye out of his head. Talking to her at the party had filled him with a kind of hope. Maybe he and his mom should stay in Winter Mill for a while – a long while. Lucas could have proper friends. And a girlfriend. It'd be like having normal life, where he was just one of the crowd, with a home that he lived in for more than just a few weeks and there were no photographers nosing around to see what his mom was up to. That would be great.

The car disappeared round a snowy bend and Lucas let the blind fall back into place. He was excited by what Liz had told him about the Battle of the Bands competition, too. All he needed to do was come up with a killer song. Who knew, maybe this was his chance? His chance to prove that he was more than just a kid permanently in his mother's shadow. And if Lucas did win – well, it would mean he wouldn't need her any more. He could get away, build his own life, his own home.

Determined to start right away, Lucas went to his guitar. It had been so long since he'd even played that he realized he didn't know where his guitar picks were. He searched his desk and drawers, but couldn't find them. With a sigh, he figured that they were probably still in a box somewhere with the rest of the stuff that Mercy and Ballard hadn't unpacked yet. Lucas was usually careful to make sure he had all of his own stuff, but he must have missed a box. He'd just have to go looking for it.

Leaving the den and heading along the corridor, Lucas pushed his way into one of the other unused bedrooms. There were stacks of boxes all over the floor, and even on the old four-poster bed. The house was so big that he wasn't even sure he'd been in this room before. He'd left the heavy lifting to Ballard – if his mother was going to insist on having him around, Lucas wasn't going to make life easy for him. The guy creeped him out.

Lucas noticed that his mother had put another of her mirrors on the old, dusty mantelpiece. *Really, mother, what is the point?* he asked her, silently. *Do you actually need to have a mirror in every room? No one's ever even going to stay in this one!*

He turned away and surveyed the mess of boxes. Not sure where to start his search, Lucas went to the nearest and opened it. Inside was an assortment of glass ornaments, but no sign of anything belonging to him. He moved on, opening box after box, but failing to find what he was looking for.

'Come on,' he muttered to himself. 'They've got to be here somewhere . . .'

Lucas knelt and pulled open yet another box, sighing when he saw it was stuffed with what looked like a leather jacket. He was about to shut the box again and move on, but something made him pause. He ran his fingers over the soft black leather, and then took the jacket from the box. Holding it up, Lucas saw that the back was emblazoned with a large embroidered silhouette of a wolf, set against a blood-red moon. Beneath were the words 'Black Dogs'. It looked like a biker jacket, but he had no idea what that would be doing in their house. Mercy had never owned a bike, and in any case, this was a man's jacket. It was old, too – the elbows were scuffed from one too many brushes with the asphalt, and the collar had curled with age.

Without thinking, Lucas pulled on the jacket. It fitted perfectly. It was comfortable, too, as if it had been someone's favourite piece of clothing, and worn often. He wondered who the owner was, and where he was now. Was he still riding the motorbike he rode when he wore this? It – and the rider – must be pretty ancient by now if he was!

Standing, Lucas walked to the mirror and looked at himself in it. The jacket made him look older, somehow. He ran one hand through his unruly hair, sticking the other in one of the deep pockets. His fingers brushed against something – a piece of stiff paper, crushed at the very bottom. Pulling it out, Lucas saw that it was a photograph, badly crumpled.

Walking to the bed, Lucas sat and tried to flatten the photograph out. It was obviously really old – it had that strange pale-brown colour to it, and it had faded at the edges. He stroked his fingers over its damaged surface, seeing that it was a picture of a young woman. Her hair was dark, pulled back from her face with a simple Alice band. She was dressed in old-fashioned clothes, like something out of a period movie about the pioneer days. Her eyes were dark too, and sad, but her face was beautiful. In fact, her face—

A cold tingle ran down Lucas's spine. Her face looked exactly like Faye's. He blinked, wondering if he was imagining the likeness, but no – this photograph was so like Flash it was uncanny. This girl had the same high cheekbones, the same cute lips. Her hair was neater, but Lucas could see that it had the same tendency to look wild and untamed. He stared at

89

the picture as if it could give up its secrets, and the more he stared at it, the more confused Lucas became.

The door opened sharply, hard enough to bang against the wall and make him jump up from the bed. Ballard stood in the doorway, scowling, his face black with anger.

'What are you doing in here?' The man took in what Lucas was wearing and made a curt gesture with his hand. 'Take that off.'

Lucas bristled. 'Why should I?'

Ballard stepped towards him, menacingly. 'Because I told you to. Don't stick your nose in where it doesn't belong, you little brat.'

'Tell me what to do again – talk to me like that again,' seethed Lucas, 'and I swear I'll have my mother fire you.'

Ballard threw back his head and laughed, a cruel, dry sound. 'I'd like to see you try, *Master* Lucas, I really would. Now, get out of here before I lose my temper.'

Lucas stood his ground. 'Who does this jacket belong to? And who is this girl?'

Ballard strode even closer, grabbing the picture from Lucas's hand before he had a chance to step backwards. Glancing at it once, Ballard crushed it in his fist and shoved it into his pocket. 'What do you want me to tell you? It's an old photograph. It was probably left here by the previous owners.'

'Yeah, right,' Lucas said, 'because of course they would have left it inside a jacket pocket in a sealed box that *we brought with us.*'

Ballard growled in anger. 'Out, now. Or shall I tell your mother how you've been rooting through her private things? I'm sure she'll love that, won't she?'

Lucas shrugged, still wearing the jacket as he walked to the door. 'I was looking for a box of mine. If you'd done your job and unpacked everything already, I wouldn't have had to, would I?'

Ballard ignored him, and following him out of the room shut the door behind both of them. 'The next time you want something, ask me for it,' he told Lucas, before striding away.

Lucas stared after him. Before Ballard had thrust the photo in his pocket, there had been a flash of recognition on the man's face.

Lucas was sure of it.

Chapter Seventeen

Making up is Hard to Do

Liz drove straight to the mall after her seeing Lucas, planning to go to Griffin's, the diner that was the regular hang-out for Winter Mill High teens. She thought Candi would probably be there, as well as Rachel and a few others. But, as she walked through the mall, trying to cheer herself up with some window shopping, Liz just kept thinking about Faye. She'd said some horrible things the previous night, and now she wished she could take them all back. It looked like it had been love at first sight for Lucas; he hadn't ever looked at Liz that way, not even once. So what was the point of losing her best friend over him?

Nothing is the same without Faye, Liz thought to herself, as she stared at a jeweller's window display. *And what did Aunt Pam say? Never let a boy come between you.*

Liz wracked her brain, trying to think of a good way to apologize properly to her friend. And, as she looked at a really cute range of silver Best Friend Forever charms, Liz formulated a plan.

Pulling out her cellphone, she sent Faye a text asking her to come to the mall as she had a present for her. Liz waited nervously for a reply – maybe Faye was so mad that she'd just ignore the text, or, even worse, text back and say that she never wanted to speak to Liz again.

93

Liz paced up and down. She couldn't lose Faye's friendship over a stupid boy, she couldn't . . .

'Liz? Are you OK?' She turned to see Jimmy Paulson standing a few paces away. He looked concerned. 'You seem worried,' he added.

Liz shook her head with a faint smile. 'Thanks, Jimmy, but I'm OK.' Then she realized that she probably owed him an apology too. She sighed. Last night really hadn't been her finest hour. 'Look – I'm really sorry about yesterday. At the party, I mean.'

Jimmy stared at his feet, pushing his glasses up his nose, the way he always did when he was nervous, which was most of the time. 'Oh – you don't have anything to say sorry for, Liz.'

'Yes, I do,' she insisted. 'I was feeling bad, and I took it out on you, when you were just being nice. So I'm sorry.' She sighed. 'I think I'll be doing a lot of apologizing today.'

Jimmy smiled, 'Well, thanks. But I had a good time. It was nice . . . just talking to you.' He cleared his throat, embarrassed. 'So – you're sure you're OK?'

Liz nodded, smiling back. 'Yeah. I'm OK. Thanks for checking, though. So what are you doing here, anyway? We don't often see you at the mall.'

'Oh,' he shrugged. 'Mom doesn't seem to be feeling well today, so I thought I'd get her something to cheer her up. Some flowers, maybe. Any suggestions?'

'Aw, Jimmy, that's really sweet,' Liz said, a little surprised. There weren't many of her male friends who would be so thoughtful. 'I'm sure she'd love flowers.'

Jimmy smiled awkwardly. 'Well, I'll leave you to it. See you at school, I guess.'

He gave her a little wave and walked away, just as Liz's

phone vibrated in her pocket. Liz opened the message nervously, but then smiled.

I'LL BE THERE AS SOON AS I CAN, it said.

Faye walked into Winter Mill Mall, not quite sure what she would find, but happy that Liz wanted to talk. Faye hadn't really slept the night before, there had been so much going round in her mind. The fight with Liz, her horrible fright in the forest – not to mention the amazing bike ride home with Finn. If she were going to tell anyone about what had happened, it would be her best friend – but after the previous night, Faye hadn't been sure they'd ever speak again. This, at least, was a step in the right direction.

She saw Liz standing right where she said she'd be, beside the Millie's Cookies concession. She had what looked like a box of cookies in one hand, and a small white bag in the other.

'Hi,' Faye said quietly, when she got nearer.

'Hi,' her friend answered, with an uncertain smile. There was a pause, during which neither of them knew quite what to say. Then, 'Thanks for coming. Look . . . I'm really, really sorry about last night,' Liz offered.

Faye shook her head, feeling a flood of emotion fill her. 'No, Liz – I'm sorry. I should have realized—'

'Faye, you have nothing to apologize for. I was just being an idiot, like you said. You can't help it if he likes you. I don't know why I got so angry.'

'He doesn't like me, Liz, we were just chatting, that's all. I'm sure—'

Liz sighed, shaking her head. 'I'm telling you, he does. And it's fine. Really.'

'It's not fine!' Faye exclaimed. 'And anyway, I don't like him. At least – not like that. He's just a friend, Liz, that's all.' In her head, the memory of being pressed against Finn's back as they raced into town sent a flush rising to her face. OK, so she knew Lucas was cute, but next to Finn . . .

'Well, whatever,' Liz's words broke into Faye's thoughts. 'I just don't want to lose you over him. I'm just – sorry.' Liz held out the cookies and the little bag. 'And these are to prove it!'

Faye laughed, 'I thought we swore we'd never eat cookies again?'

Liz shrugged. 'Desperate times, desperate measures, as Aunt Pam would say.' She shook the little white bag. 'Open it, go on.'

Faye took it. Inside was a little jewellery box that held the cutest silver bracelet she had ever seen. It had a small BFF charm hanging from it.

'Oh Liz – it's lovely. You didn't have to do that. And how did you afford it? I thought you'd spent your allowance?'

'Poppy lent me some money yesterday. It was supposed to be for emergencies because she knew I was broke, but I wanted to buy you this,' Liz said softly. 'Because you deserve it. And because if I don't have you, I don't have anyone.'

Faye felt tears in her eyes, and pulled Liz into a fierce hug. 'Funny,' she said, 'I was thinking the same thing about you this morning.'

Liz pulled away with a shaky sigh. 'So – friends?'

'Definitely friends,' agreed Faye, slipping on the bracelet and holding it up to the light.

Liz smiled, a flash of her usual sunny self breaking through. 'In that case . . . I've got another surprise for you!'

Faye followed Liz through the mall, expecting them to end up in Griffin's. Instead, her friend led her to the door of MK. Liz headed straight in, but Faye held back.

'Liz, I can't go in here!'

'Sure you can. Come on, they've got some great new stuff! I

can't spend any more money, but that doesn't mean I can't plan what I'm going to buy with my next allowance, does it?'

'No, Liz, the owner lifted the ban on you, but she didn't do the same for me! They'll call security if I try to go in there!'

Liz turned, her hands on her hips. 'Well, that was yesterday. This is today.'

'And why should today be any different?' Faye asked.

Liz walked towards her, linking her arm and pulling her into the shop. 'Because today I got Barbie Finch to call the owner and give you a glowing reference, that's why. And now we're both fine to shop here whenever we want.'

Faye blinked, touched. 'Really? You did that for me?'

Liz grinned. 'Really. So come on – let's separate and find the perfect outfit. Meet you at the changing rooms in twenty minutes!'

Maybe it was a side effect of making up with Liz, or maybe it was because she kept trying to imagine what Finn would think about each item she picked up, but this time Faye found it far easier to find something she wanted to try on. She picked out a cute green top with an appliquéd flower on it, a light sequined scarf in a matching colour and a distressed pair of dark blue jeans. She went to wait for Liz at the changing rooms as instructed, trying not to let her mind wander back to the previous night.

'Look what I've found,' Liz exclaimed when she'd finally decided what to try on. She was holding up the same green top that Faye had slung over her arm.

Faye laughed as she realized they'd both picked out identical outfits – right down to the same little neck scarf!

'Well, we can't both wear it,' giggled Liz. 'What would Candi say?'

'Let's both try it on, and see who looks best,' Faye suggested.

They each ducked into a cubicle and began to pull on their new outfits. Faye loved the jeans, the careful stylized fading on them was great.

'How's it going so far?' Liz called from the next cubicle.

'I love the jeans!'

'Oh, no – me too!'

Faye had just pulled on the top when she saw a reflection in the mirror. There was a woman of about forty, with anxious, tired eyes, standing just behind her. Thinking that the woman had mistaken the cubicle as empty, Faye turned round.

'Oh, I'm sorry, I'll be done in just a—'

Faye stopped dead. There was no one there. She pulled back the curtain and looked around the shop, but the woman was nowhere to be seen. Shaken, she returned her gaze to the mirror. The woman was still there, staring at Faye with mournful, empty eyes. Faye shivered as the temperature suddenly dropped. Tiny patterns of ice began to creep up the edges of the mirror. She grabbed her camera to take a picture, but by the time she'd got the lens cap off and put it to her eye, the mirror was empty, reflecting nothing but her own worried face.

'Faye?' asked Liz, appearing from the other cubicle, wearing the outfit. 'Did you say something?'

Chapter Eighteen

Forest Speedway

Finn took his coffee extra strong that morning. He hadn't really slept, far too wired from his encounter with Faye to settle. Instead he'd stayed out on his bike until the early hours, only returning when the sun was beginning to stain the forest floor with light. Even then he hadn't felt like sleeping. Instead, he'd sat by the campfire with his penknife and a piece of wood, and as the rest of the bikers slowly began to stir around him, Finn began to whittle it into shape. But carving didn't calm his thoughts, as it usually would. He just couldn't tear his mind away from Faye.

He couldn't shake the image of her from his mind, and he couldn't erase the feel of her arms around him during that fast, fleeting ride. She looked so much like Eve, with that same fragile beauty that he'd fallen head over heels for all those many years ago. And Finn was torn. Torn between running away as fast as he could, and never leaving her side again. It had to be a sign, didn't it? That she was here at all, and especially now?

Finn put down his knife and took another mouthful of coffee, letting the bitterness wash around his mouth. That moment they'd shared, outside her aunt's shop – he'd sworn he'd keep her safe, but could he? Could he save her from the evil that was sweeping these woods?

'Finn?' His dad's voice was rough in the early morning light. 'We missed you last night. Where were you?'

Finn glanced up at Joe Crowley. 'Out on the bike. Just . . . felt like riding, that's all.'

Joe frowned. 'You don't fool me, son. What happened?'

'I told you . . .'

'And I know you, Finn. Something happened.'

Finn shook his head, looking down at the object he'd been carving – a tiny wolf, its mouth open in mid-howl. He sighed, snapping his knife shut and stuffing both it and the wolf into his pocket. It was pointless trying to keep anything from his father, and actually, he probably needed to know about it. Some of it, at least. 'There was a hunt last night.'

'Not around here there wasn't. We'd have sensed it.'

'It was further south, near the road into town.'

'You saw it?'

'No,' Finn said. 'I picked up a girl on the road. She was running from them.'

Joe narrowed his eyes. 'What girl?'

Finn sighed, knowing what his father would say. 'The one from the mall.'

'And you just happened upon her at the right moment, is that right?'

'Yes. I kept my word. I didn't go looking for her. But I couldn't leave her there. You know that.'

Joe shook his head. 'Finn, you know what happened last time. You can't let this one get to you. Not again. You have to keep your distance.'

Finn shook his head. 'What if I don't want to? What if – what if we're here for a reason? What if this is a second chance?'

'We *are* here for a reason!' Joe said, his voice rising above the chatter of the early morning birds. 'But this girl isn't it! You know that.'

Finn upturned his coffee mug, tipping the dregs into the fire. 'I know what we're here to do,' he said quietly. 'I just don't see that it has to rule the rest of my life – or that it gives you a right to tell me how to live.'

'I'm just looking out for you, Finn.'

He shook his head. 'You can't, Dad. Not for ever. And this . . . this is too important to me. Try to understand that.' He turned his back and strode away towards his bike.

'Finn!'

Finn didn't answer. He slung a leg over the saddle and kicked the engine into life, its dull roar momentarily drowning out the dawn chorus. Then he headed into the early morning light, not even pausing to pull on his helmet.

The air was cold. It made Finn's eyes water, but he didn't slow down. He skidded through the trees, churning up snow in his wake as he headed for the road. Blood was pumping in his veins, fuelled by anger: anger at his dad, for saying what Finn already knew but didn't want to hear, anger that his life wasn't simpler, anger that he couldn't just walk up to the girl and ask her out like any other normal teenage boy would. He'd seen the look in her eyes; he knew she'd wanted him to kiss her last night as much as he had wanted to do it.

But his life wasn't normal. He wasn't normal, and no amount of wishing would make it so, and that was what had held him back. The fear of what had happened before happening again, the fear that if she ever found out she'd reject him anyway . . . The fear that his life, even now, was not his own.

It was this anger and fear that drove him on now, faster and faster, at speeds that were more and more reckless. But through the fear he'd made up his mind. He was going to talk to her again, no matter what his father had decreed. Finn had to talk to her again: he couldn't live in this world knowing that she was in it too, without being able to talk to her, see her, know her.

He heard the siren before he saw the flashing blue light. *A cop car*, Finn thought. *Oh great, that's just what I need right now.*

Finn briefly thought about kicking down and pushing the bike onwards even faster – but he thought better of it. That would cause more trouble for all the bikers, and would only distract from their task at hand – and his anger wasn't worth that. So Finn slowed, careful not to spin the back wheel the way he had the night before, and pulled to a stop at the nearest lay-by he could find.

Killing the engine, he pushed off the bike and leaned against it, waiting for the officer to approach. Finn recognized him as the same cop that had come up to talk to his dad the first day they arrived – Sergeant Wilson. He nodded a polite greeting but said nothing.

'Licence and registration, please.'

'Sorry, officer,' Finn said, as he handed over his documentation. 'I know I was speeding.'

'Damn right you were,' said Wilson, calmly. 'Any faster and your speedo would have burned right out.' He handed Finn's papers back before sticking his hands in his pockets. 'You're also not wearing a crash helmet. Where you off to in such a rush, so early in the morning?'

Finn decided to be honest. 'Into town, sir.'

'*Town.* Is that so? And what were you going to do in town, exactly?'

'I was heading for the bookshop. The lady there – Pam – I fixed her heating a few days back and I wanted to check that it was still holding up all right. Especially after last night – that was a cold one.'

The big officer stared at him impassively. 'You're polite for a biker, aren't you?'

'I was brought up right, sir.' Finn glanced at the ground. 'And not all bikers are out to raise hell.'

Wilson nodded. 'Your driving says otherwise.'

'Sorry, sir,' Finn said again. 'It won't happen again.'

'See that it doesn't.' Wilson paused before sighing. 'I'll give you the benefit of the doubt this time. I know Pam McCarron, and she has good things to say about you. But if I catch you driving like a maniac again, I'll see that bike of yours confiscated, understand?'

'Yes, sir. Thank you.'

'And, Finn . . . it is Finn, isn't it?'

'Yes, Sergeant?'

Wilson looked at him hard, and Finn had the impression that the gaze was boring straight down into his soul. 'Pam has a niece living with her. Faye McCarron.'

'Yes, sir. We've met . . .'

'Faye's good friends with my daughter, Liz. I want you to stay away from both girls, do you understand?'

Finn frowned. 'Faye and I are friends, and—'

'When Faye's dad's away, I keep an eye on her,' said Wilson, cutting Finn off with a steely look. 'And I can say for sure that you are exactly the sort of friend that Faye does not need, do you understand?'

Finn felt fury pricking in every pore, but he forced himself to keep his cool.

'Yes, sir,' was what he said.

Wilson eyed him again before nodding curtly and turning away. 'Right. I'm glad we understand each other.'

The cop car followed Finn's bike all the way to McCarrons'.

Chapter Nineteen

A Simple Investigation

The two girls carried on shopping, but Faye's heart wasn't in it. Every time she thought of that woman reflected in the mirror, she shivered. What was happening to her? First the terrifying chase through the woods, and now this? She wished her dad was around. Just talking to him would make her feel better, but there had still been no word from him. Even Aunt Pam was beginning to worry, and had said she'd try to track him down.

'Faye? Are you all right?' Liz asked. 'You've gone very quiet.'

Faye forced a weak smile and shrugged. 'I'm fine. Sorry, I'm probably just still tired from last night.'

Liz immediately looked guilt stricken. 'Are you still mad at me?' she asked. 'I'm so sorry for making you walk home, Faye. I still can't believe I did that.'

'No – no, it wasn't . . . You didn't . . .' Faye stopped. She didn't want to tell Liz that in the end she hadn't walked home, because that would mean explaining why. And Faye wasn't sure she wanted to tell Liz about the chase through the woods. That would make it all the more real, somehow . . . and she would prefer to think of it as all a bad dream. All except Finn's rescue, and that trip home on his bike. Her stomach still did backflips every time she thought of him touching her face . . . She cleared her throat. 'I just didn't sleep well, that's all.'

105

Liz narrowed her eyes and crossed her arms. 'I don't believe you. There's something you're not telling me.' Reaching out, Liz grabbed her hand and squeezed. 'Please tell me. We used to tell each other everything. Maybe I can help.'

Faye shook her head. 'I don't think anyone can help.'

'Then there *is* something going on!' Liz cried. She pulled Faye down onto one of the mall's benches. 'Come on, spill. A problem shared is a problem halved – or something like that. What's going on? You haven't been yourself all day.'

Faye took a deep breath. 'You're going to think I'm crazy,' she said.

Liz laughed. 'Come on, Faye. Out of the two of us, who's known to be the crazy one?'

Faye grinned. 'OK. Well, after I left the party last night, I didn't walk down the track. I took a short cut through the woods.'

Her friend looked horrified. 'Wasn't it pitch-dark?'

'It was pretty dark, yeah, but the moon was high . . . anyway, I wasn't really thinking straight. I just wanted to get home as soon as possible and I thought that would be the quickest way.'

Faye went on to tell Liz about being chased – her race through the woods, the wolves hunting her . . . Liz's eyes got bigger and bigger, and when Faye got to the part about falling onto the road, right in front of Finn, she let out a little scream.

'Ohmigod! You could have been killed! What did he do?'

Faye looked down at her wrist, playing with her new charm bracelet. 'He took me home, and told me not to go up there again.'

'So he knew what was out there?' Liz asked.

Faye nodded. 'I think he did, yeah.'

'My dad was right! He said those bikers were bad news!'

Faye shook her head. 'I don't know. Finn said he'd keep me safe . . .'

'Yeah – from *his* gang! They must have been the ones chasing you!'

'I don't think so – I only heard his bike out there. I don't think it was them, Liz.'

'Who else could it have been?'

'I don't know . . .' An idea struck Faye suddenly. 'But I have to find out. I have to go back up there and investigate. If there were wolves up there, they will have left traces! Let's go, Lizzie, right now. Come on – it's light, nothing will attack us during the day. It'll be perfectly safe. I can take pictures for photographic proof.'

'Faye, you're nuts!' Liz exclaimed. 'Didn't Barbie Finch tell you to stay away? And what about my dad? He'd go crazy if he found out I'd gone up there, especially if he knew about last night!'

Faye stood, her mind made up. 'You don't have to come, Liz. I'll completely understand if you don't. But I have to go. I have to.'

Liz stared at her for a moment before standing up with a sigh. 'And how are you going to get up there? Walk? Come on, I'll drive. Just make sure I'm home in time for dinner!'

Faye hugged her hard. 'Thank you!'

'I think this makes us even,' Liz muttered.

Liz half-expected to find nothing in the woods. She'd never say anything to Faye, of course, but she thought her friend had imagined the things she'd told her – it would have been easy to do, out there in the woods alone at night.

'How are you going to know exactly where you were?' she

asked, tramping through the snow as she followed Faye. They had parked on the road and were fighting their way up the embankment into the woods. It was cold, and already the light was fading from the afternoon sky.

'Well, I know that's the bend that Finn came around,' Faye said, pointing up the road behind them. 'So it must be about here that I fell down the slope. Start looking – even with this fresh snow, there has to be some kind of trace.'

Liz sighed as Faye began taking preliminary wide-angle shots of the area. She knew when her friend was engrossed in something, and there would be no getting away until Faye had found what she was looking for. It if existed at all. Liz just hoped it wouldn't take too long.

Something caught her eye and she stomped through the snowdrifts towards a bush festooned with icicles. Some of them were snapped and crushed. 'This is weird,' she called, over her shoulder. 'It looks like something has crashed into this bush and broken the ice.'

Faye came over to look, and grinned. 'Brilliant, Liz. We must be in the right place – I bet this happened during the chase.' After taking a picture, her friend knelt down in the snow and began digging.

'What are you doing?' Liz asked, confused.

'There must be wolf tracks around here somewhere! They have to be here, under the new layer of snow . . . Yes – look!'

Sure enough, Liz found herself looking at a paw print. She shuddered, 'Oh my god, Faye. I've never seen a paw print as big as that . . . It's huge!'

Faye stood up, and Liz saw the look of determination on her face as her friend scanned the area. 'OK. Let's keep looking. See if there's any more – I want to know if there really is a pack out here, or if it was just the two wolves I saw.'

Liz shivered, eager to get out of the woods, which had suddenly become a very scary place to be. 'Really? Do we have to? We found this, Faye, isn't that enough? I'd really like to go now . . .' Liz looked around her fearfully, convinced that something big with teeth was going to leap out of the bushes at any second.

Faye wasn't listening, instead walking deeper into the trees, searching the ground.

'Look at this!' she called a few moments later, snapping away with her camera.

Liz headed towards the spot Faye pointed at. It was a pile of bloody bones and a mass of fur, all in a heap. Liz was nearly sick right then. 'What is it?' she asked, with a hand over her mouth.

'A raccoon, I think. The head's over there,' Faye said, oblivious to Liz's discomfort as she nodded towards another bush. 'Can you check the slope again? I just want to take a few more pictures.'

Liz nodded, not trusting herself to speak. She was determined not to show Faye how scared she was. Her friend was always so strong, so confident. Nothing seemed to worry her. Liz often wished she could be more like that.

She walked back to the hill that led down to the road, imagining poor Faye alone in the dark, and shuddered. There were a few broken branches, but thankfully she couldn't see any more carcasses. Liz was about to turn back and shout up to Faye when something caught her eye.

It was hidden in the snow at the base of a tree, half-buried under a tree root, but it glinted when the afternoon sun hit it. Moving closer, Liz realized it was something silver. She reached down and picked it up. It was a tiny letter opener – pretty, with an engraved handle. A small, dark mark stained the blade, which was surprisingly sharp. Liz stared at it. Could that be dried blood? Liz pulled out a tissue from her bag and wiped it clean.

'Now, how did you get there?' she muttered under her breath. She looked back up the slope, but couldn't see Faye. 'Hey, Faye? Look at this—'

'Liz? Liz, where are you?' Faye's voice echoed from between the trees, cutting her off. 'I've just seen the time! Aren't you going to be late for dinner?'

Liz looked at her watch. 'Oh, no! You're right – God, dad and mom will kill me!' She shoved the letter opener into her bag, and struggled back up the slope.

Faye opened her mouth to say something, but stopped. Another sound penetrated the peaceful forest – motorbike engines revving in the distance. Faye turned towards the sound but Liz grabbed her arm.

'Time to go,' she said, firmly, afraid but determined to hide it. 'Right now.'

Chapter Twenty

Blowout

The sun was beginning to set as the two girls got back into the car. They couldn't hear the motorbikes any more, but Faye could tell that Liz was worried – though that could have just been because she was going to be in huge trouble if she was late home.

'Don't worry,' she told her friend as they pulled away. 'We'll be back in town in no time. You can tell your dad it's my fault you're late.'

Liz glanced over and smiled. 'It's fine. I should just make it. I'm more worried about—'

There was a sudden noise like a gunshot and the car swerved violently. Both girls screamed as it slid sideways, and for a second Faye was sure it was going to tip right over, trapping them both inside. Liz slammed on the brakes. The wheels screamed as they tried to get a grip on the icy road, but eventually the car skidded to a stop, bumping off the tarmac and into a thick bank of snow.

'What happened?' Faye asked, stunned, her hands still gripping the side of her seat.

Liz leaned against the steering wheel, breathing hard. 'I think we got a puncture. That was the sound of the tyre blowing. We must have driven over something really sharp.'

'Do you have a spare?'

111

'Yeah, but I've only ever changed a tyre once!'

Faye groaned. 'Can you call your dad? He'd come out and help, wouldn't he?'

Liz shook her head. 'Oh, he would – but I'd be grounded for at least a month! He'd want to know what we were doing out here.' She sighed. 'It's OK. I can do it . . . it just might take a while.'

'Can I help?' Faye asked as Liz opened her door. Outside, another snowfall was beginning, and the temperature was dropping fast. It was getting dark, too. Winter Mill always seemed to be dark these days, no matter what the time. Faye pulled her coat tighter around her.

'Yeah – can you hold the flashlight?'

The two girls climbed out of the car and stood staring at the ruined tyre. It was the front right wheel, and it was clear to see where the puncture had happened – a ragged hole about the size of a silver dollar where something had torn the rubber.

'What could have caused that?' Faye asked. 'It must have been something pretty big.'

Liz, already shivering, shrugged and went to get the jack and spare wheel out of the back. 'Right now, I don't care. I just want to get this thing changed before I freeze to death!'

Faye flicked on the flashlight, but as Liz prepared to put the jack under the car, a pair of headlights appeared round the bend. The car pulled to a stop behind them. Liz straightened up as the door opened, moving to stand next to Faye. She linked one arm through Faye's, and Faye realized Liz was shaking a little. They were obviously both still jittery after their almost-crash, because Faye's heart was hammering too.

'Are you two girls OK?' The rough voice was familiar, but it wasn't until the man stepped into circle of light cast by the flashlight that they realized who it was. Faye felt Liz's arm tense against hers.

'That's Ballard' Liz whispered into her ear. 'The man who works for Mercy Morrow. I saw him earlier today and he was horrible.'

'We're fine,' Faye said, in as firm and calm a voice as she could muster. 'We just had a puncture. Liz was about to change the wheel. Thanks for stopping, but we can manage.'

The big man glanced down at the ruined tyre and nodded. 'That's a nasty one. I can help.'

'No!' said both girls, in unison. Liz laughed nervously. 'No, really, Mr Ballard, it's fine. We – we were just going to call my dad. He's the local police chief, Sergeant Wilson. He'll come out just as soon as I call him, so—'

Ballard smiled, a curiously unpleasant gesture that curled his lip to show a set of yellowed, uneven teeth. 'Oh yes. Sergeant Wilson. I met him this morning, in fact. He gave me his card. I expect he's got plenty of other troubles to keep him occupied this evening. And since I'm here already, it would be silly to bother him, wouldn't it, girls?'

There was something about the way Ballard said the word 'girls' that made Faye shiver. It was like a cat preparing to play with a mouse – there was something sly and scary about it. But before either of them could say anything else to put him off, Ballard was on his knees in the snow, busily changing the tyre. They stepped back, wrapping their arms around themselves against the cold and watching Ballard as he worked. It was as if neither of them wanted to turn their backs on him, even for a moment.

Ballard was very strong; there was no doubt about it. Within moments he had the jack pumped up and was using his bare hands to twist the wheel from its housing. He slipped on the

113

new one and secured it. Faye glanced at her watch as Ballard finished up. It had taken him less than ten minutes. They should be grateful for his help, she knew – without him, she and Liz could have been there for hours. But all she wanted to do was jump in the car and get Liz to drive away as quickly as she could.

The man stood up, picking up the jack and the old wheel and slinging them into the back of the car. He brushed the snow from his knees and turned to the two waiting girls. 'There you go,' Ballard said. 'Done. No need to call Daddy, was there?'

Faye forced herself to move, squeezing Liz's arm as she did so. 'Thank you,' she said, with a smile. 'That's so great. We would have been really stuck without you, Mr Ballard.'

He stepped closer, towering over them, and smiled back. 'You're lucky that it was me that came along,' he told them, lowering his voice so that the sound of his words seemed to blend with the cold wind. 'There are all sorts of bad people around. You two girls should be careful. It can be dangerous out here.'

Chapter Twenty-one

Mirror, Mirror . . .

Liz dropped Faye off and then headed home, rehearsing what she was going to say to her father. Glancing at the clock on her dash, she realized that their trip into the woods and the puncture had cost her more time that she thought – she was an hour and a half late. She was in big, big trouble, for sure.

The first thing that struck her as odd when she pulled into their road was that the house seemed to be in total darkness. Usually there was at least one light on somewhere, and tonight it should have been blazing – especially with Poppy at home for the weekend. *Surely they can't all have gone to bed already? Though in a way, that would be good*, she thought. She could sneak in without her dad seeing her and get up early for school in the morning. Maybe a day's work would make him forget all about today?

Liz switched off the engine and climbed out of the car, shutting the door as quietly as she could. She headed for her front door and as she passed the downstairs window she glanced into the front room. And there, standing in front of the fireplace, was her dad. Liz could just make out his figure. He didn't seem to be moving. He was just standing there. Her heart sank. He was obviously waiting for her to come home. This was going to be worse than she thought. Liz tried to imagine how long she was going to be grounded for this time, and a horrible thought occurred to her. The Battle of the Bands was coming up! What if her dad decided she had to miss it as punishment? He knew how excited she was about it – she'd told him everything she knew that morning at breakfast, before he'd gone to the Morrow mansion.

Taking a deep breath, she unlocked the front door softly and walked in, heading straight for the front room – and her dad. *Best to get it over with*, Liz thought to herself. *And maybe I can explain. After all, I did have a puncture! I would have been home in time if not for that.*

He stood there with his back to her in the middle of the room and didn't turn round as she came in. *Ohmigod . . . he's really mad!* Liz thought. She could see his face reflected in the small mirror mounted over the fireplace but couldn't read his expression.

'Hi, Dad!' she said, putting on her brightest voice. 'You would not believe the evening I've had! I know I'm late, I'm so sorry – I hope you guys didn't wait too long before you ate? I tried to call, but I think there's something wrong with my cell – or maybe this weather has broken one of the masts? Anyway, I couldn't get a signal.'

She paused, waiting for him to say something, but he still didn't turn round. She rattled on.

'Anyway – look, I know you're probably mad, but before you start yelling, just listen for a second. I got a puncture! It was awful – really scary. I don't know what caused it, but it was a true blowout – we could have had a terrible accident! But I did what you taught me to do in that kind of incident, and we were fine. But there was no way I could drive on the tyre, so we had to change it. And I remembered everything you taught me, as well! How cool is that? I managed to change it all by myself! Well, Faye helped a little,' Liz added, suddenly wondering if it

116

was just too implausible to suggest that she'd done it all herself. But she didn't want him asking too many questions – and if her dad believed that she'd managed to solve the problem herself, Liz hoped he'd be too pleased with her for that to ask just where she'd been.

Sergeant Wilson still didn't move. Liz stepped forwards, wondering if he really could be that mad. Then she realized that he didn't have his head bowed, as she'd first thought. Sometimes he did that – if he was thinking hard about something, he'd stand there with his arms crossed, staring at the floor. He was staring at his reflection in the mirror.

'Aren't you proud of me?' she said, trying to get him to respond. 'Isn't that great? So anyway, that's why I'm late. So I hope you're not too mad. Because it really wasn't my fault and I wouldn't have been able to do anything about it. Even if I'd left earlier. Not that I left late. The place . . . where we were. OK? So please don't ground me. And if you do . . . please don't make me miss Battle of the Bands. It's, like, the biggest thing to happen here in decades. Please, Dad? Please?'

Sergeant Wilson still didn't answer, and Liz began to wonder if he'd actually heard any of what she'd been saying at all. He was still staring into the mirror. And then, as Liz looked closer, she realized that he wasn't really staring, as such. He was watching something. His eyes moved around the glass as if following something that was happening inside it.

Liz looked, trying to work out what he was searching for. And then she saw something. Something dark, like a shadow. It moved from one side of the mirror to the other quickly, so quickly that if she had blinked, she would have missed it.

She gasped, and her dad finally moved, turning round. Liz looked at his face, but his eyes were glazed over as if he was focused on something very far away.

'Dad?' she asked, shakily. 'What's the matter?'

He ignored her, brushing past her as he stepped out into the hallway. Liz was suddenly very cold.

'*Dad?*' Liz asked again, panicked. This was so unlike her father. 'Dad? What's going on? Where's Mom? And Poppy?'

'It's late,' he said. His breath made clouds in the icy hallway. 'It's time for bed, now.'

Liz stood at the bottom of the stairs, shaken. She watched her father disappear into his bedroom and shut the door. And then, though she could hardly believe her ears, she heard him lock it behind him.

Chapter Twenty-two

Here Comes the Sun

A few days later, it actually seemed as if things might be getting back to normal. For the first time in weeks, Faye woke to clear skies and a warm sun. Looking out of her window, she couldn't remember the last time the streets of Winter Mill had not been piled with fresh snow. The thought that the strange early winter snap might be over lifted her spirits, and she got ready for school quickly. She stopped for a breakfast of coffee and toast with Aunt Pam before pulling on her coat and heading out, carrying the large pile of books she had to return to the library.

The turn in the weather seemed to have affected the rest of the town too – people waved and smiled at each other, or said a chirpy hello as they passed. Faye felt happier. There was surely a rational explanation for everything that had happened over the past few days. Just because she couldn't explain it didn't mean there was something scary and strange going on. And whatever was happening in the woods – whatever creatures were haunting it right now – there must be a perfectly reasonable explanation for that, too.

Liz was waiting for her on the Winter Mill High steps, looking great, as usual. She'd borrowed some more of Poppy's boho clothes and was mixing them in with all the new items she'd bought from MK. Faye was always amazed at how Liz managed to come up with a gorgeous new outfit so easily – she loved coming up with new looks herself, of course, but it seemed like second nature to Liz.

As she got closer, Faye saw that her friend was staring into the distance, a faintly worried look on her face.

'Hey!' she called, as she got closer. 'Everything OK?'

Liz smiled when she saw her, and they walked into the school building together. 'Oh, yeah. It's just my dad. He's being really weird.'

Faye winced. 'Oh, no. He hasn't grounded you for Sunday, has he? I thought you said that so far he hadn't mentioned it at all.'

'He hasn't! That's what's so weird.'

'You're complaining that he hasn't grounded you?' Faye teased. 'Has someone done a body swap with my Liz? Who are you and what do you want?'

'I know, I know,' Liz laughed. 'But seriously, I don't know what's with him at the moment. He's hardly talked to us all week.'

'You didn't manage to find a way of telling him about the wolf, then?'

Liz shook her head. 'I tried, but it's hard to find a way without letting on that we both went up there. And to be honest, I'm not even sure he'd listen. Sometimes it's like we're not even there. I think Mom is worried too.'

'That is a bit weird,' agreed Faye. 'But maybe he's just tired? There's been a lot going on recently. I think the snow has got to people a bit. Especially with that poor guy dying in it out in the woods. You don't really think of snow as being dangerous, but it is. And we've been surrounded by it for weeks now. Your dad's probably been preoccupied with all of that, hasn't he?'

'Yeah, I'm sure you're right,' decided Liz. 'Anyway, like you said – if it means I'm not getting punished for something, why am I complaining?'

120

'He'll snap out of whatever it is soon enough, you'll see.'

Liz nodded. 'You're probably right. Which means I should commit as many teenage misdemeanours as I can right now!'

Faye shook her head with a smile. 'Look, I've got to go hand in these articles. I wrote up all our findings in the one about the woods. It might get me into trouble, but I think it's worth it. And I finally finished the Mercy Morrow one last night, as well. It's so late – Ms Finch is going to kill me!'

'Nah,' said Liz, waving her hand dismissively, 'She'll be fine. She's the softest teacher in school. I'd better get to class, though. I'll let Mr Petrus know where you are. Or do you need help with all those?' Liz asked, nodding to Faye's books.

'No, I'm fine. I'll be along in a minute.'

Faye headed for the school newspaper office, which was up a level, near the science labs. It was unusual for Faye to be late delivering a piece, but then it was unusual for her to be nervous about handing in what she'd written, too. Faye had done as Ms Finch had asked, and produced a bio article on Mercy Morrow. Even though she hadn't really wanted to write it, Faye had figured that it was a good exercise in journalism anyway. After all, she wouldn't always be able to choose her assignments. But she'd also done a longer, in-depth piece on what had been happening in the woods, from the bikers' arrival to her more recent discovery of the animal carcasses. She'd left out the bit about her being chased – for one thing it was too personal for an objective newspaper article, and for another she didn't want anyone to know she'd been up there at night, especially after being told to avoid the place. She also didn't want to get Finn into trouble. Faye still wasn't sure what the rest of the Black Dogs' involvement in all this was, but she was convinced that Finn had nothing to do with any of it.

Faye was about to shoulder open the newspaper room door

121

when someone beat her to it from the other side. Jimmy walked out, a perplexed look on his face.

'Morning, Jimmy,' Faye greeted him. 'How's things?'

Frowning, he shut the door carefully, pulling her to one side. 'Ms Finch is in a r-really odd m-mood today,' he whispered.

'What do you mean?'

Jimmy shook his head. 'I mean *o-odd*, Faye. She's usually so . . . b-bubbly, even first thing in the morning – but today, she's like a b-brick wall. I t-tried to talk to her about this week's issue – I think we need to include a b-big feature on the Battle of the B-Bands; competitor profiles, judge b-bios, stuff like that – b-but she j-just clammed up. Do you know if something's h-happened?'

'Nothing that I've heard about,' Faye said quietly. 'She's probably just got a headache or something. Or she's in a bad mood.'

Jimmy raised his eyebrows. 'Since w-when have you known Ms Finch to b-be in a b-bad mood?'

'Never,' admitted Faye. 'Well, I'll try to find something out. I've got to go deliver these articles anyway.'

'G-good luck,' Jimmy whispered, opening the door for her before he headed to class.

It was dark inside the office. The blinds on the windows were still shut, and none of the lights had been switched on. Faye could see her teacher sitting at her desk in front of her computer.

'Uh, morning, Ms Finch,' Faye began, as she walked towards the desk. 'I've got two pieces for this week here. I'm really sorry they're late. I hope you like them.'

There was no response from the teacher. She seemed engrossed in whatever was on her computer screen. Faye thought that maybe she was reading – as the newspaper editor, there was a lot to get through on top of her regular marking duties each week. She put down her books and took her papers out of her bag.

'I worked really hard on the second one,' Faye added as she got closer. 'I know you told me not to write it, but I think it's a really important story, and I hope you'll at least—'

She stopped. Ms Finch's computer was not turned on. The screen was blank, just reflecting the edges of the windows behind them where the blinds had not shut out all the morning light.

'Ms Finch?' Faye whispered. 'Are you OK?'

The woman didn't answer. Her eyes were set and glazed, and maybe it was the lack of light in the room, but to Faye they seemed darker than usual. It was as if the light in them had turned into something hard and black.

Suddenly scared, Faye dropped her assignments on the desk and backed away. 'I – I'll come back in recess, Ms Finch,' she said. 'I can see you're busy . . .'

Faye scooped up her books and made it to the door before Ms Finch's voice sounded behind her. Except it wasn't Ms Finch's voice, not really. It had something hard and closed about it, like her eyes.

'I thought I told you to stay out of the woods, Faye.' said the voice.

The skin on the back of Faye's neck prickled with fear. Instead of answering, she opened the door and rushed through it, pulling it shut behind her. She stood in the light of the corridor, waiting for her heart beat to calm, and as she did so she looked out of the window.

The clouds had closed over the sun again, and it was snowing.

Chapter Twenty-three

Unexpected Chemistry

Catching her breath and pushing her fear away, Faye set off down the corridor. Her head was full of questions that she knew no one could answer. She was so wrapped up in what had just happened with Ms Finch that she wasn't paying attention as she turned the corner. Someone walked right into her, sending her pile of books flying and almost knocking her over in the process.

'Whoa!' Lucas Morrow reached out, grabbing Faye's arms to stop her from falling.

'Hey! Watch it!' she yelped, wrenching herself free.

Lucas held up his hands. 'Sorry, but you're the one who wasn't looking where they were going, Flash,' he said, bending to help her pick up the strewn books. 'Where are you off to so fast?'

'Class,' Faye said. 'Come to think of it, isn't that where you should be right now?'

Lucas grinned, handing her a book and reaching for another. 'Just on my way. Although I'll be late now, so you owe me.'

'I owe you?' she said, raising an eyebrow. 'That's rich.'

Lucas straightened up with a cheeky smile. 'No, that would be me. Is that why you hate me? Because I'm sooooo rich?'

Faye crossed her arms and shook her head at him, amazed. 'You are *not* rich,' she told him, trying to keep a straight face. 'Your mom is. And I don't hate you. I don't hate anyone. I think you've hurt Liz's feelings, though.'

Lucas was looking at a flyer that he'd picked up from the floor. It had fallen from one of Faye's books. He looked up, puzzled. 'Really? What did she say?'

Faye sighed, realizing that anything she told Lucas would probably embarrass Liz. And, after their last stupid fight over him, she wasn't going to risk upsetting her best friend again. 'Nothing, it doesn't matter. I'm sure she's fine.'

Lucas held up the flyer. It was an advert for the Battle of the Bands night. 'Are you going to go to this, Flash? Could be fun.'

Faye snatched it out of his hand, mildly annoyed. 'You know, Lucas, I don't think I've actually seen you attend a class yet. And this is the only time I've seen you pick up a book. Is fun all you're interested in?'

'No,' Lucas said, reasonably, apparently amused by her exasperation. 'But I also don't see what the use is in being bookish all the time. Lighten up. It'd do you some good.'

'I have plenty of fun!' said Faye. 'And I am *not* bookish!'

Lucas raised his eyebrows, pointing to the books still on the floor. 'Just how many of these were you carrying?'

'I – I have to go to the library at lunch!'

The boy crossed his arms, an infuriatingly amused smile on his face. 'I believe you just made my point for me.'

Faye sighed in defeat. 'So, are you going to go?'

'To the Battle of the Bands?' Lucas grinned. 'You interested in knowing my social timetable?'

'If I know it, I can avoid you, can't I?'

'Aw, don't be like that. You'd like me if you got to know me. Sure, I was thinking of going. It'd be . . . fun if you did too. So how about it?'

'Are you asking me out?' Faye said, genuinely shocked.

'Is there something strange about that?'

126

'What – other than the fact that I just told you you've upset my best friend?'

Lucas shrugged. 'I don't think I did. And anyway, I didn't know one ruled out the other.'

Faye shook her head and began to gather up the last of her books. 'You know what, Lucas? That's probably why you don't have any friends.'

He was silent for a moment, before stepping away and crouching to retrieve the last volume. 'Well,' he said, quietly, 'when you move around as much as I do, it's kind of hard to make any.'

Faye straightened up, feeling a sudden pang of guilt. She hadn't meant her quip about his lack of friends to come out quite the way it had. It couldn't be easy moving to a new place where you knew no one. And it wasn't as if anyone but Liz had really made an effort to get to know him. Yes, people talked about Lucas and his mother all the time, but it was always about how much money they had, or what they were doing here, or their huge house. She wondered if anyone had actually asked Lucas about himself since he got here. Faye sighed. As usual, she hadn't paid attention to Aunt Pam, who was always right. She'd judged Lucas without knowing him. But she couldn't date him. She didn't want to, for a start. And then there was Liz . . .

Lucas stood up and held out the book. As Faye reached out to take it, their fingers brushed together. Lucas trapped hers beneath his, and Faye was stunned to feel her heart stutter and her cheeks burn. She glanced up at Lucas, surprised to find his blue eyes full of a warmth she hadn't seen there before. Then he glanced down at the title of the book and grinned, entirely too cheesily for Faye's comfort.

'Chemistry one-oh-one,' he said, voice still soft. 'I think

there's some chemistry between us, don't you, Flash? There must be – after all, you're blushing . . .'

There was sudden movement at the end of the corridor, and Faye saw Liz and a group of their friends heading towards them. Afraid that Liz would see the two of them together, she snatched the book out of Lucas's hand, stuck it on top of the pile beneath her chin and hurried away, her cheeks still burning. *What are you blushing for?* She shouted at herself, silently. *It's Lucas Morrow! What about Liz? What about Finn?* Faye was shocked and horrified by her reaction to his touch, which she certainly hadn't intended. What did it mean? She couldn't like him . . . she couldn't! Yes, she was beginning to realize Lucas was far nicer than she'd first thought, but that didn't mean anything . . . Did it?

'Faye, where have you been?' Liz asked as Faye joined the gaggle of girls – and Jimmy, who was tagging along behind as usual. 'You've missed the most important conversation of the day: who's going to win the Battle of the Bands?'

'I'm really hoping I've got a shot,' said Rachel Hogan, one of Liz and Faye's oldest friends, 'but I'm terrified I'm going to catch a cold with all this awful weather and ruin my voice! Can you imagine how terrible it would be if I couldn't sing on the night?'

'You'll be fine,' Candi Thorsson told her, threading an arm through Rachel's as the group started off again. 'Just keep drinking honey and lemon – and wear a scarf!'

'Why don't you get a pair of Uggs?' Liz suggested. 'They look so cool, and they're warm, too!'

Faye followed, putting on a smile and trying to join in the chatter. But she knew that Lucas was still standing there, watching her. She glanced back before turning the corner and saw him smile.

Chapter Twenty-four

Home Time

Lucas stood outside the school gates, watching the kids stream out and head home as he waited for Ballard to pick him up. He'd spent most of the day thinking about his encounter with Faye that morning. She was so cute when she was annoyed, and he'd been surprised – and pleased – that she'd blushed when their fingers touched. There had to be something there, didn't there? He sighed. Girls were so hard to figure out.

Ballard's black car rolled to a stop in front of him, but Lucas didn't rush to get in. Ballard hated to be kept waiting, and right now, anything Lucas could do to push his buttons was worth it. Lucas was still angry about their encounter over the old biker jacket. He'd thought about telling his mom as he'd threatened, but decided against it. For whatever reason, Ballard was Mercy's most trusted lackey at the moment, and Lucas knew she wouldn't take her son's side about something so trivial.

Lucas pulled open the front passenger door and slid in – another thing that annoyed Ballard. He preferred him to sit in the back, but Lucas was in the mood to stir things up. Ballard didn't say anything, or even look at him. He just pulled away.

'I think you're going the wrong way,' Lucas said as Ballard turned into the street heading for town. 'Losing your marbles, maybe?'

Ballard ignored him, but Lucas was persistent. 'Where are

we going, Ballard? I've got homework to do; I don't need a magical mystery tour.'

The big man curled his lip in a silent snarl. 'We're picking up your mother,' Ballard said shortly, and he didn't speak again.

Lucas sighed, leaning back into the plush leather seat. The car was pristine, as if it had never been used before. He wondered what Ballard kept in the glove compartment, and reached over, flipping it open. He felt Ballard glance at him, but Lucas ignored it. Inside the compartment was nothing but a manual for the car. He snapped it shut again and drummed his hands on the dash instead – another thing sure to annoy Ballard.

Lucas looked out at the shops that lined the town's streets. They were all small, the sorts of places that sold gift items to tourists but nothing really useful.

They coasted to a stop outside McCarron's Bookstore, which made Lucas sit up with interest. McCarron? *That can't be a coincidence*, he thought. *It must be owned by Faye's family . . .*

The store had two large glass windows set either side of a quaint wooden and patterned-glass door. Hanging over it on a string was a small model of what looked like a dog. Lucas realized it was actually a wolf. He wondered why it was there – it seemed out of place beside the hanging baskets full of evergreen shrubs and blooming red winter poinsettia.

Then a movement inside the shop caught his eye. One of them was his mother, and since there didn't seem to be anyone else in the shop, he figured the other woman must be the owner. Was it Faye's mom?

Somewhere a dog was barking furiously. It seemed to be coming from inside the shop, and he saw his mother bend down to swat something away. Then she turned and headed for the door, the other woman following her all the way, dipping out of sight every few steps as if she was trying to scoop something up from the floor. The door opened and his mother stepped out – and at her heels was a small but extremely furious dog. It barked and snapped, baring its teeth and lunging at Mercy's heels as she tried to get away from it.

Lucas wound down his window. 'I'm sorry,' the shop owner was saying, over the noise of the angry animal. 'Jerry's usually very friendly – I don't know what's gotten into him.'

'If you're going to have a creature like that loose in your shop,' he heard his mother say icily, 'then you should learn how to control it. The thing's practically feral.'

'I'm sorry,' the woman repeated. 'Like I said—'

The dog lunged again, and his mother stepped backwards, onto the little step outside and directly beneath the wolf model, brushing it with her hair. As Lucas watched, it seemed to freeze for a second, before slowly turning again – but in the opposite direction. He blinked, unsure of exactly what he'd seen. Then a gust of wind rattled along the street, shaking the hanging baskets and setting the little model spinning.

Mercy kicked at the dog before turning on her heel and sweeping towards the car. She opened the back door and climbed in, the little dog still going crazy, trying to bite her with every step she took. It yelped and danced backwards as the car door almost slammed on its nose.

Lucas turned and looked at Mercy, who was rearranging a few stray strands of hair with one immaculately manicured hand.

'What on earth was that about?'

His mother smiled tightly and shrugged. 'Some people just don't know how to control their dogs. They shouldn't be allowed to have pets.'

Lucas saw his mother glance in the rear-view mirror, sharing a look with Ballard that he didn't understand. Then she looked out of the window.

Lucas was about to turn away too, when he noticed something in her hair. It was a thin streak of pure black, as if something had stained it right down to the root.

He couldn't be sure, but it seemed to be exactly where the little model of the wolf had touched.

Chapter Twenty-five

Jimmy

Standing on the school steps, Jimmy watched as Lucas Morrow got into the car and he felt a sharp pang of envy as it pulled away. Lucas didn't even have to drive himself home! Jimmy, on the other hand, didn't have a car, let alone someone to take him home in it. Which meant another long, cold and wet walk back from school.

He hung back from the first surge of kids leaving Winter Mill High, waiting until he saw Liz Wilson emerge from her last class. Every time Jimmy saw her, his heart skipped a beat. But she'd always given him the brush-off, which didn't surprise him in the least – Liz was one of the prettiest girls in school, and he was the undisputed King of Geek. But the other day, at the mall – she'd actually talked to him. She'd smiled at him, in fact. So maybe Faye was right. Maybe he just needed to have a bit more guts around girls, and they'd notice him.

Which is why he'd decided to try talking to her again. Sure, it had taken him a couple of days to pluck up the courage, but he was ready now. He'd wait until she walked past, and say . . .

'H-hi, Liz! H-how was your d-day?' Jimmy called from a few paces away.

Liz didn't answer. She was sending a text, one hand working her phone, the other reaching up to push a stray strand of long dark hair back under her cute woolly hat. Jimmy was stuck in a moment of indecision. Should he try again? She might not have heard him . . .

'Hey, Liz! Wait up!' There was another shout from further along the corridor. She turned to see who it was, smiling and waving as the owner of the voice snaked through the knots of kids towards her.

Jimmy scowled. It was Hart Jesson, one of the boys from the school basketball team. He was tall, muscular and tanned, and as far as Jimmy was concerned, he had the IQ of a lower primate. He sighed as Liz and Hart headed down the steps and out of the school gates together. They were probably off to meet a group of other kids at Griffin's. The most popular kids sometimes went there after school if they had a light homework day. He'd never been, even though Faye had asked him along a couple of times. He'd known he wouldn't fit in, so what was the point? He'd just sit there silently like an idiot, or else he'd start talking about something no one was interested in and bore them all to death.

Jimmy shouldered his backpack and trudged out of the school gates. It was going to be a miserable walk home. They'd actually had some sun during the day, which had been great at the time. But it had also started to melt the top layer of snow, turning the sidewalks into wet piles of dirty grey slush that soaked his feet after just a few steps.

Reaching the crossroads, Jimmy turned away from the town, starting his long daily trudge up the hill. His family home stood in an isolated section of the forest on the edge of the Morrow mansion's land. Originally built as a farmhouse by his great-grandfather, it was one of the oldest buildings in Winter Mill. The family history that went with Jimmy's home meant his parents would never leave it, but Jimmy often wished they'd sell up and move closer to town. It was a beautiful place to live, tucked away among the trees. But sometimes, just sometimes, it would be nice to live a bit closer to someone else.

He'd been walking for a while when he heard the sound of a car behind him. Turning, he noticed it was the same one he'd seen Lucas jump into after school. *Odd*, he thought, *they must have gone into town first. Who knows, maybe they'll give me a lift . . .*

Jimmy was out of luck again. Instead of slowing down, the car speeded up, taking advantage of the long, empty road. As it passed him, its tyres threw up a tidal wave of snow water that drenched Jimmy, soaking him to the bone.

'Oh! Oh, yeah, that's j-just – that's j-just g-great!' Jimmy spluttered, wiping his face and looking down at his wet clothes. He still had at least another mile to walk, and the cold was beginning to bite.

Shivering, Jimmy glanced away from the road, into the trees. He could take a short cut – if he walked through the forest, rather than on the road, he'd save at least fifteen minutes. But it was getting dark and just a few days ago Sergeant Wilson – in front of both of Jimmy's parents – had told him not to go into the woods until further notice. The officer had told them about some poor guy – a vagrant, most likely – who had been stuck out there in the snow and frozen to death overnight. Jimmy shuddered at the thought of it. What a horrible way to die.

But right now, Jimmy was *so* cold. And he wasn't some sick old hobo – he knew where he was going. And who would know, anyway? Making up his mind to take the short cut, Jimmy struck out among the trees, pleased to see that under their thick canopy, the snow had remained firm.

He hadn't got far before he heard rustling behind him. At first he thought it was the evening wind stirring the trees, but then he heard it again, and again. Suddenly scared, Jimmy turned, relieved when he saw nothing behind him.

You're just spooked, he told himself. *You're hearing things. Stop worrying. There's nothing there!*

Jimmy carried on walking, picking up the pace, stepping over the uneven forest floor as quickly as he could. Up ahead he saw the light at the end of their garden path, and smiled to himself.

There. Home. Nothing to worry about. Nothing at all . . .

But then something made him turn his head. He didn't hear anything – something was just there, in the corner of his eye.

Two yellow eyes stared at him from the darkness. They didn't blink. They hung there, watching him, and Jimmy stared back, his mind blank. For a moment he was rooted to the spot – he tried to make himself run, but he couldn't move. His skin was icy cold, but he couldn't even shiver. All he could do was stare into those horrible, evil-looking eyes, and hold his breath.

Then the eyes moved, slinking forwards out of the dark leaves and into the meagre light. It was a great grey wolf, its cruel face scarred, its wide mouth open. Saliva dripped from long, sharp yellow teeth. The wolf snarled at Jimmy, hackles raised.

Forcing himself to move, Jimmy turned, yelling, 'M-Mom! D-Dad!'

He tried to run, but his feet felt like lead. He managed to take one step, but the creature pounced. Jimmy felt its claws in his back, knocking him forwards. His head cracked hard against a tree trunk before he crashed to the ground, stunned.

The wolf sank its teeth into his leg, Jimmy screamed, still trying to get away. He couldn't feel anything, even though his mind was telling him that his leg should hurt. His heart was pounding in his chest. Home was just a few yards away. He just needed to—

The last thing he saw was a pair of black boots as someone stood over him. Then everything spun away into darkness.

Chapter Twenty-six

Hopes and Fears

Faye couldn't believe it. She waved her copy of *The Miller* at Liz as they sat eating lunch together in the school cafeteria.

'My article has been almost completely rewritten!' she said. 'And it's been cut in half – look! Ms Finch made the piece about Mercy Morrow twice as long and hacked out all the important parts of what's going on in the woods. Can you believe it?'

'Well,' said Liz, eating her pasta, 'she did tell you she didn't want you to write that piece in the first place, didn't she?'

'Well – yes,' admitted Faye. 'But – I don't know – I guess I thought that when she read it, she'd see that something needed to be said about it all. What we found up there, Liz . . . If there are wolves back in the Winter Mill forest, surely people need to know? At the moment the students think they shouldn't go into the woods because of the weather, not because they might ended up being hunted by a wolf! And now the piece doesn't even mention the bikers at all. '

Liz put down her fork and grimaced. 'You know, Faye, I've been thinking. Those paw prints could have just been from a dog, couldn't they?'

Faye stared at her friend. 'Liz – come on. You saw the size of them! And I told you what I heard when I was being chased.'

'I know, I know,' Liz nodded, making a face. 'And it's not that I don't believe you – but Faye, it was at night, and you were

137

on your own in the dark, in the woods. You don't think ... I don't know, maybe that your imagination was playing tricks on you?'

'No!' Faye exclaimed. 'Liz – you saw what I did up there!'

Liz sighed. 'I know. But come on, you're the smart one. Are you telling me that everything we saw couldn't be easily explained?'

Faye shook her head. 'Liz. I swear this isn't me imagining things. Something's going on.'

'Well then, what do you think it is?' Liz asked. 'All we know is that there might be some wolves in the woods and there's a bunch of bikers camping up there, in the snow, because they're obviously crazy.'

'There was the horn, as well,' Faye said, slowly. 'Didn't I tell you? When I was being chased that night, I thought I heard a horn.'

'What, like a car horn?' Liz asked, puzzled.

'No. I'm not sure what it was – but I think it was to do with the wolves that were chasing me. I think it was controlling them.'

Liz took a mouthful of her lunch and chewed thoughtfully for a moment. 'So you think someone is, what – keeping wolves as pets, or something?'

Faye sighed. 'I don't know. Maybe.'

'Who would do that?'

'I don't know, Liz, I really don't,'

Liz nodded. 'What about the bikers?'

'Liz . . .'

'Don't pretend you didn't think of them first! And if what you say is true, it has to be them, doesn't it? They're camping in the woods, and all this strange stuff started happening when they turned up.'

Faye shook her head, adamant. 'No. Finn rescued me from them. Why would he do that if it was his gang chasing me?'

Liz shrugged. 'Well, if you don't think it's them, who do you think it is?'

Faye shook her head. She had no idea. Liz was right, the bikers were the obvious answer. But she didn't want it to be them. She didn't want Finn to be involved . . .

'I'll just have to keep investigating,' she said, determined.

After school, Faye and Liz stayed behind for a Prom meeting. It was still weeks away, but the students all wanted this year's Halloween ball to be Winter Mill High's best yet, so preparations were starting early. The meeting went on quite late, so it was already eight o'clock when Liz dropped Faye off at home.

The bookstore was long shut, but Faye could see a lamp burning downstairs as she unlocked the door. Aunt Pam was at the desk in the store's little back room, surrounded by piles of open books. Jerry jumped up from his bed and ran over as Faye came in, and she bent down to pet the little dog as she said hello to her aunt.

'Hey,' said Pam, attention still on her books. 'Did you have a good day at school?'

Faye moved to the desk, sitting on a nearby chair and leaning her elbows on the old wood. 'Not really,' she said, but decided not to say more.

Aunt Pam stood up, a sympathetic look on her face, and moved around the desk to give her niece a hug. 'I'm sorry,' she said, 'but try not to worry.'

Faye assumed that meant there was still no word from her father. 'Nothing from Dad?'

'No, not yet.'

Faye nodded as her heart sank. 'When should we start to worry? It's been weeks, now.'

Pam squeezed Faye gently before letting her go. 'I'm sure everything's fine. You know what he's like when he gets stuck into a dig. But if you like, tomorrow I'll put in a call to the consulate in Tanzania. I'm sure they'll be able to track him down.'

Faye smiled. 'Thanks, Aunt Pam. So, what's all this?' she asked, waving at the books in front of them.

'Just some local research – about the area, and the history of Winter Mill. Did you know,' she went on, getting the faraway look Aunt Pam always got when she was intrigued by something, 'when the first settlers got here, they tried to tame the local wolf pack? They actually thought they might be able to domesticate them. I suppose they thought they could use them like huskies.'

At the mention of wolves, a shiver ran down Faye's spine. Had Aunt Pam read her mind? Why was she researching that particular subject all of a sudden? She forced her voice steady as she asked, 'But it didn't work?'

'Of course it didn't!' exclaimed Aunt Pam. 'Wolves aren't at all like dogs – they're far more independent. Far more intelligent – no offence, Jerry, dear,' she added, looking over the counter to the little Jack Russell. 'No, they have their own complicated social structure, more like humans than dogs. That's why the native peoples stuck with huskies in the first place. Far more manageable.'

'So what happened? To the settlers that tried to tame the wolves, I mean.'

Aunt Pam looked over her glasses at Faye. 'The wolves turned on them. Tore them to pieces. It took another ten years before the settlement really established itself here. People were too scared.'

Faye shivered. 'That's horrible!'

'It is,' agreed Pam.

Faye wondered whether now was the time to confide her suspicions. Aunt Pam was always so cool about stuff . . . But the last thing she wanted was for her aunt to ban her from her investigation in the woods, which she'd probably do if she knew there were dangerous creatures out there.

'What brought on all this research, anyway?' Faye asked.

'I had that Morrow woman in here yesterday,' said Aunt Pam, and Faye was surprised to see her face darkening. It was unlike her aunt to dislike anyone, let alone someone she didn't know.

'Mercy?'

Pam made a disparaging sound. 'I doubt she has much of that!' She shook her head with a sigh. 'There's something about her that worries me. I can't work out what it is – but Jerry can feel it too. I've never seen him go for someone the way he went for Mercy Morrow.'

'Is that why you've put the new amulet up?' Faye asked, talking about the small wolf hanging over the store's door. Her aunt was fascinated by folk art, especially charms and talismans. 'I don't think I've ever seen that one before.'

Pam smiled. 'Yes – to be honest, that's one of the reasons I started thinking about wolves in the first place. Finn gave it to me – the young biker I told you about?'

At the mention of Finn, Faye felt herself flush. 'Yeah,' she murmured. 'Yes, I remember . . .'

'He told me he'd made it himself,' aunt Pam went on. 'It's for protection, apparently, although he didn't say from what. I thought it was beautiful, so I put it up. That boy's got so much talent. He really should enrol in Winter Mill High if he's going to be here for a while. The amulet doesn't seem to have

141

protected the whole town though, does it? Not with what's happened to poor Jimmy.'

Faye felt her blood turn to ice. 'What do you mean? What's happened to Jimmy?'

Aunt Pam looked at her in surprise. 'What do you mean?' she repeated. Faye – you don't know?'

Faye swallowed hard, shaking her head.

'I thought . . .' Pam shook her head. 'I'm so sorry, Faye – when you said you'd had a bad day, I assumed that's what you meant . . . Jimmy never went home after school last night. He's been missing since then.'

Faye put a hand over her mouth. 'Jimmy's missing?'

'Yes. I really don't know what Mitch Wilson is playing at. He should have been all over that school this morning, trying to find out what he could from you kids. But you haven't seen him?'

Faye shook her head. 'No. Liz didn't know anything about it either – she would have said something. I noticed he wasn't there, but I just assumed he was ill!'

The shadow on Aunt Pam's face grew darker. 'Those poor Paulsons. They must be worried sick.' She sighed heavily. 'There's something very strange happening in this town, Faye. I don't know what, but it's nothing good.'

They both jumped at a loud knocking at the front door.

Chapter Twenty-seven

Guess Who's Coming to Dinner?

'Who on earth could that be, at this hour?' said Aunt Pam, looking at her watch. 'It's almost eight-thirty!'

'Don't answer it,' Faye said, catching hold of her aunt's sleeve as she stood up.

'I've got to. What if it's Mitch Wilson, finally here to talk to you about Jimmy?'

Faye realized she was right, and followed Pam out of the little room and towards the front door, with Jerry following at her heels. Through the textured glass, they could see a large shadow – someone standing on the steps outside. Faye was shocked to see Aunt Pam look around, before picking up the heaviest book she could find.

Her aunt grimaced as she saw Faye's expression. 'Just in case,' she whispered. 'You can never be too careful.'

Faye wondered if there had been more to her aunt's run-in with Mercy Morrow than she'd let on.

Taking a deep breath, Pam reached out and unlocked the door, pulling it open with a bold flourish.

Finn stood on the doorstep, clad in his biker's leathers, a black patterned bandana wrapped around his neck against the fresh falling snow. He looked at Pam, and then at Faye standing behind her, and then at the book Pam was brandishing in her hand.

143

'I'm sorry if I disturbed you both,' he said. 'I just wanted to check on your heating. You know, make sure it's still working properly. It's such a cold night. And to return this.' Finn held up a copy of '*The Motorcycle Diaries*' by Ernesto Guevara. 'I've read it already – it's brilliant.'

'Oh,' said Aunt Pam, the relief clear in her voice. 'Oh, Finn, it's you. Come in, come in – get out of the cold.'

Finn did as he was told, still looking at the book in Pam's hand. 'I really don't want to get in the way,' he said.

'No, no, not at all. I was just helping Faye with her home-work on, on . . .' Faye watched as Aunt Pam, flustered, checked the title of the book she was holding. 'The, um, *Ancient fishing habits of the Basque people of northern Spain*.'

Finn looked amused. 'Right. Guess school's changed a bit since the last time I went.'

'Yes, well,' said Faye's aunt. 'I'll pretend I didn't hear that. You know what I think about your schooling.'

Finn grinned. 'Yes, I do. Which is why you'll be pleased to know that I dropped off my enrolment papers at Winter Mill High this morning.'

'Finn! That's wonderful news!'

'You're going to be a student?' Faye exclaimed, surprised.

Finn looked at her, his eyes full of his smile. Faye felt her heart stutter as he shrugged. 'Well, your aunt said I should, so . . . I start next week.'

'That's – that's great,' Faye nodded, her mind whirling. She'd be seeing him every day, then. He might even be in some of her classes . . .

'Why don't you stay for some dinner, Finn?' suggested Aunt Pam, her words cutting through Faye's thoughts. 'I was just about to go and get it ready. I made lasagne, and we've got plenty of salad.'

Finn looked a little surprised by the offer, but was obviously tempted. He glanced at Faye, as if wanting to check it was OK with her before saying yes.

'Oh, you definitely should stay,' Faye said, though she felt herself blushing. 'Aunt Pam's cooking is the best.'

Finn smiled again, and her heart turned over. 'In that case,' he said, 'I will.'

Dinner was far more relaxed with Finn there than Faye expected. He was eager to help Aunt Pam prepare the food, and Faye wondered how long it had been since he'd had a proper meal, instead of one cooked on the road.

'So,' he said, once they were all seated and eating. 'I've been seeing posters around town for this Battle of the Bands night. It seems kind of cool.'

'Yeah, I'm looking forwards to it,' said Faye. 'We've got some really good musicians at Winter Mill High, so it should be a good night. I know at least four groups of my friends are entering.'

'Have you got a favourite?' Finn asked. 'You know, someone you want to win?'

Faye shook her head. 'No. It'll just be a fun night, that's all.' She laughed. 'It's not often we have something like this come here! We're pretty quiet, usually.'

'Not right at this moment,' Aunt Pam interjected. 'What with the bikers, this awful weather, that poor man freezing to death and that Morrow family – and now poor Jimmy . . .'

Faye sobered at the thought of her friend. Finn looked between them both with a frown. 'Who's Jimmy?' he asked.

Faye sighed. 'A friend of ours. He works with me on the school paper – he's missing. Didn't get home last night. No one knows where he is.'

Finn paused, his fork halfway to his mouth. 'Anyone know where he was last seen?'

Faye shook her head. 'No. But he lives up on the edge of the mansion estate – in the woods.'

Finn was quiet for another moment, thoughtful. Then he smiled. 'I'm sure Jimmy's fine. If you like, I'll have a look around up there. I know the woods pretty well now.'

Faye smiled, gratefully. 'That would be fantastic. The police don't seem to have done anything at all.' She shook her head. 'Things have been really strange around here recently. But usually, nothing much happens at all.'

Finn smiled. He was doing a lot of that this evening. Faye liked it – his face was softer when he smiled. Then she realized she was thinking about him again, and blushed, looking down at her almost-empty plate so that he wouldn't see.

'I like this place,' Finn said, softly. 'I thought I didn't at first, but it's great. It's quiet. The people care about their town, and their neighbours. And it's . . . beautiful.'

As he said the word 'beautiful', Finn looked right at her, and Faye felt her breath catch. Was he talking about her? She felt her face burn red, but this time she couldn't bring herself to look away.

Aunt Pam cleared her throat and began tidying their now-empty plates. Finn flushed slightly, breaking eye contact and standing up quickly to help.

'The forest, I mean,' he added, sounding slightly flustered. 'The woods are just beautiful.'

'Oh yes, they are,' Faye agreed, a little too quickly. 'You should see them in the summer too, when all the flowers are out . . .'

'Well now, since I did all the cooking, I'm going to leave you two to wash up,' Aunt Pam announced. 'I shall leave you both

146

alone and go back to my reading.' She shot her niece a grin that made Faye groan with silent embarrassment, especially since Finn had seen it too!

Faye waited before her aunt had disappeared downstairs before she risked looking at Finn again. 'Sorry,' she said. 'She's just—'

'She's great,' Finn told her.

Faye smiled. 'Yeah, she is. Without her – I don't know what I'd do.'

They stood in silence for a second, and after a moment Faye realized they were staring at each other again. She shook herself, moving to pick up one of the dishes left on the table.

'So,' she said, searching for something to say that wouldn't cause either of them further embarrassment. 'You're a biker. How did that happen?'

Finn turned on the tap and leaned over the sink. 'Well, my dad's always been one. He's been on the road as long as I can remember.'

'What about your mom?'

Finn shrugged. 'She died when I was very small – so small that I don't even remember her. I lived with an aunt for a while, but she had her own family, you know? And I was never any good at school. So I guess it just made sense to follow him as soon as I could. I was pretty young. Most bikers don't move around as much as the Black Dogs do, but it's really all I've ever known. It feels . . . normal.'

'You didn't like school?' Faye asked, picking up a dishtowel and standing next to him to dry.

Finn shrugged. 'I just never fit in properly. I'm better with my hands than my head.'

Faye glanced at his hands. They were large and tanned, and looked as if they'd seen a lot of rough work. A sudden memory

147

flashed in her head, of Finn running his fingers down her face. . .

'Hey,' he said, in a low, soft voice. 'Penny for them?'

Faye looked up. He was very close, looking at her with warm, dark eyes, and her heart nearly thumped its way right out of her chest. Blushing furiously, she shook her head, grabbing something without checking and running the cloth over it vigorously. 'Oh, nothing, it's – ow!'

Finn dropped the bowl he'd been washing and grabbed her hand as a tear of blood began to flow from her palm. What she'd picked up was a knife. 'Idiot!' Faye berated herself. 'I'm so clumsy!'

'No, you're not,' Finn protested, his two wet hands cupping her injured one. 'You were just . . .' He tailed off, and when she looked up she saw his eyes were laughing. 'Well, maybe just a little bit . . .'

She laughed, and he reached out to run the tap again. He pulled her closer to clean the wound, and Faye found herself pressed against him, their legs close together. Finn turned off the tap and dried her hand before pulling his bandana from his neck and winding it around her hand.

'There,' he said softly. 'Good as new.'

'Thanks,' Faye whispered. She didn't want to move, and as they stood there, he slid one arm lightly round her waist. She looked up at his face, just inches away, and was hardly able to breathe. Finn looked down at her, his thumb gently stroking her back where his hand held her to him. For a second he seemed to hesitate, but then something sparked deep in his dark eyes. He leaned in, his breath mingling with hers as their lips almost touched . . .

'Hey, you two!' Aunt Pam's voice called from the bottom of

148

the stairs, loud enough to make them spring apart. 'There's some ice cream in the freezer if you want dessert.'

Faye glanced at Finn, but he avoided looking at her, turning away instead. He was breathing hard, his shoulders bunched as he leaned against the sink.

It took Faye a moment to find her voice. 'Um, thanks, Aunt Pam!' she called as loudly as she could manage.

The uncomfortable silence stretched between them. After a few moments, Finn reached out and picked up another dish, but he didn't look at her again. Faye kept her distance, mind whirling.

They didn't have dessert.

Chapter Twenty-eight

Wanted: The Perfect Outfit

'So, do you reckon this is going to be mainly poppy, or mainly rocky?' Liz asked, staring at her open wardrobe.

The two girls were trying to decide what to wear to the Battle of the Bands night. Faye had headed over to Liz's early to get ready, but now neither of them knew what outfits to choose.

'I think there will probably be a mix of both,' Faye said, with a sigh. Liz looked over as Faye held up the clothes she'd brought with her – a favourite pair of jeans and a cute blue T-shirt. Liz thought her friend looked great, but Faye wasn't so sure.

'I think that works really well,' Liz told her, 'but if you want to borrow some of my stuff, do.'

'Really?'

'Of course! But you have to tell me what to wear, because I think my head will explode if I try to work it out for myself.'

'What about that punk print top you got online?' Faye suggested. 'Have you even worn it yet? That's really cool, and no one else will have anything like it.'

Liz clapped her hands together. 'Oh my god, Faye, you are so right. See, this is why we are such good friends. You always know what to do!'

Faye pulled out a pale pink shirt and held it up to her chest. With another sigh, she hung it back in the closet and picked out something else, pulling a face as she looked at herself in the mirror.

'You know,' Liz told Faye, 'you should just wear what you're comfortable in. That blue top you brought along is great.'

'But it's boring!' Faye protested. 'I'm tired of people thinking I'm bookish and that I don't know how to have fun!'

Liz raised her eyebrows. 'Do people think that?'

'I think some people do,' Faye mumbled. 'Let's face it, Liz, I'm a bit of a boring geek.'

'You are not,' cried Liz. 'Look, you can never go wrong with jeans, and that top has great potential. All you need to do is funk it up a bit.'

'What, with accessories?'

'Yes – and make-up.' Liz went to her dresser and picked up a handful of brightly-coloured bottles. 'I bought these the other day – they're the latest colours.'

Faye took what Liz held out to her. 'Wow. These are great. I love the yellow nail varnish.'

'The fluoro-green eyeshadow is awesome, too,' Liz pointed out. 'And it'll really contrast with that top, especially if you sweep it right over your eyelids and then mix it with the turquoise eyeliner.'

Faye grinned. 'I've never tried make-up like this before.'

Liz shrugged, 'Well, you wanted a change – go for it. You'll look great!'

Faye began to paint her nails as Liz looked at herself again in the mirror. This was such a crucial night in the school calendar, she was determined to look amazing.

'Is your dad still acting weird?' Faye asked, as Liz began to choose a pair of heels to go with her outfit.

'And then some,' Liz said, shaking her head. 'It's actually getting kind of scary. I think Mom's trying to pretend there's nothing wrong, especially since Poppy went back to college, but something's definitely not right. This morning I tried to ask him about Jimmy, and I swear he just spent the whole time staring into space.'

'He didn't tell you anything?'

'No – I couldn't get anything out of him at all.' Liz sighed. 'I can't stop thinking about Jimmy, Faye. It's horrible. How can someone just . . . vanish? Here in Winter Mill?'

'I know. I keep wondering if there's anything we can be doing to help find him.'

'Yeah,' Liz agreed. 'There must be something. Maybe we can make some posters and start putting them up all over town? I mean, I know we're not supposed to go up to the woods, but someone might have seen something somewhere, right? Do you think Ms Finch would let us use the newspaper equipment?'

Faye frowned. 'Usually, I'd say yes. But honestly? She's another one who's acting really weirdly at the moment. Aunt Pam says something is happening to the whole town. And she had an argument with Mercy Morrow. I actually think she's scared of her.'

Liz snorted. 'Sometimes I think it would have been better if the Morrows had never turned up at all.'

Faye looked up at her friend. 'Are you still upset about Lucas?'

Liz waved her hand dismissively. She was determined not to dwell on him. 'Oh, not really. Anyway, let's not talk about the Morrows any more. I'd rather spend my energy talking about Jimmy.' Liz had actually been thinking a lot about Jimmy since she heard the news. It was strange – she hardly noticed him when she knew he was there, but the idea of him not being around at all . . . for some reason, it seemed wrong. It wasn't just that something awful might have happened to him, which was really horrible to think about. Jimmy was a part of their lives, Liz had realized – a part of her life. As geeky as he was, things wouldn't seem right if he wasn't around. And Liz kept thinking about the little conversation they'd had in the mall right after her fight with Faye. Jimmy had been so sweet . . . Liz shook herself. 'I guess we can ask around about him tonight.'

Faye nodded, starting on her other hand. 'Yeah, that's a good idea. And Finn said he'd have a look around in the woods, see if he can find any sign of Jimmy up there.'

'Wait a minute – Finn?' Liz repeated, shocked. 'The biker boy? When did you see him?'

'He, uh – he came for dinner a couple of nights ago,' Faye said, and Liz watched as her friend's cheeks turned pink. 'It was sweet, actually. He came to check that the heating was still working. And Aunt Pam has been lending him books to read. She asked him to stay for dinner, so he did.'

'God. I would have thought she'd know better,' Liz said, shaking her head. 'I wouldn't have even let him in!' She hadn't missed the flush on Faye's cheeks as she'd talked about Finn. It really worried Liz – she didn't want her best friend getting into trouble with the wrong kind of guy. Faye was usually so smart, but the bikers and the mystery of what was happening in the woods really seemed to have caught her attention. Liz was worried for her friend.

'You've got Finn all wrong,' said Faye, quietly. 'I think he's a good guy. Anyway, he said he'd look for Jimmy, and that can't be bad, can it?'

Liz shrugged, reluctantly. 'I guess not.'

Faye's phone jingled as a text arrived. 'Darn it,' she said, holding up her wet nails. 'Can you get that for me?'

Liz pulled Faye's phone out of her bag and examined it.

'There's no name,' she said, with a frown. 'And whoever it is isn't in your contacts.'

'Probably because it's my old phone,' said Faye. 'I dropped my new one in the woods. What does the text say?' Faye asked.

'It says, *Meet me by the stage door 7pm tonight*. That's it.'

Chapter Twenty-nine

Let Battle Commence!

The Battle of the Bands competition was being held inside Winter Mill High. The students and teachers involved had spent the past week preparing for the event, decorating the gym where the main stage had been erected. Everyone seemed excited about it – after the weeks of constant snow, it was a chance to enjoy some colour and fun.

It had taken Faye and Liz so long to decide what to wear that their original plan of getting there early had gone out the window. Instead, they actually had to hurry so as not to miss the first act.

'We're going to be late,' Liz exclaimed, as the two girls pulled into the school's parking lot.

'Don't worry, we won't miss anything,' said Faye, looking around at the streams of chattering people walking up to the school gates. 'See, there are plenty of people still on their way, like us. They'll want a full audience before they start the show, won't they?'

'Yeah, but I wanted to get a really good spot,' Liz moaned. 'Now we'll be squashed in at the back, or something.'

Faye shook her head, smiling as she opened the car door. 'It'll be fine. Stop worrying! And anyway, it was worth being late – you look great.'

Liz got out and looked down at the outfit she'd finally

chosen. She looked at Faye, and sighed. 'You know, here I am worried about how I look and who's going to win this competition . . . and Jimmy's somewhere out there, lost . . . or . . . or worse. It just doesn't feel right.'

Faye walked round the car and gave Liz a hug. 'I know. I feel guilty too. But us staying at home isn't going to help him. Maybe if we're here, and ask everyone plenty of questions, we might find something out that can help.'

Liz nodded. 'I know. You're right. I just don't understand why we're the only ones who seem to care that he's missing. Look – everyone else is acting as if nothing's wrong at all.'

Faye had to agree. Around them, students were laughing and joking, excited about the evening ahead. She also had to admit that the usually boring high school building looked amazing. It was lit by multi-coloured laser lights and there were streamers everywhere, billowing into the air on plumes of smoke from little machines.

She felt Liz tug at her sleeve, and turned to see her friend nod towards a car parked in a shadowy part of the school's parking lot. It was Mercy Morrow's servant, Ballard. He was just sitting there, and he seemed to be looking right at them. As both girls watched, Ballard smiled his creepy smile at them.

'He's watching us,' Liz hissed, with a shudder. 'I don't like it.'

Faye couldn't stop the shiver that ran down her spine, but forced herself to shrug as they turned away. 'He's probably here to wait for Lucas. Just ignore him.'

'I wish we hadn't let him help with the tyre,' Liz muttered. 'I don't want him to think we owe him anything. I feel like he could tell my dad at any moment.'

Faye squeezed Liz's arm. 'He won't do that. Why would he?

Anyway, don't think any more about it tonight. We're here to have fun!'

'We've got to find out who this mystery texter is first,' Liz reminded her. 'Come on, let's find the stage door.'

They walked round the corner, to where a team of roadies were still busy hauling equipment from trucks into the school. It was gloomy, but Faye could see someone leaning up against the wall, silhouetted against the light spilling out of the stage door.

'Do you know any of the roadies?' Liz asked in a hushed voice.

Faye shook her head. 'I don't think so. None of them look familiar.'

Liz pointed at the person leaning against the wall. 'I guess that must be who sent the message asking you to meet them here, then.'

The light was so dim that it was hard to work out who the person was – but then, as they got closer, Faye realized it was Lucas Morrow! She cast an anxious look at Liz, worried about what her friend would think. She didn't want Liz to think she'd given him her number.

'Lucas?' she asked, as he stepped forwards out of the shadows.

'Hi, Faye. I wasn't sure that you'd come. How are you?'

'Fine . . . but how did you get my number? I don't remember giving it to you . . .'

Lucas shrugged. 'I asked your Aunt Pam. She said you'd lost your phone somewhere.' He looked suddenly anxious. 'You don't mind, do you?'

Faye shook her head, although inside she was feeling pretty confused. She didn't know why Lucas made her feel so unsure of herself. She should just be able to ignore him, or just treat him like a friend, for Liz's sake at least, but there was something about him that always turned her head around.

Liz spoke up, breaking through Faye's little reverie. 'Do you want me to go?' she asked, 'I can wait inside, or—'

'No,' said Faye and Lucas, both together, glancing at each other with a slight laugh.

'No,' Lucas said again, smiling at Liz. 'I really just wanted to make sure you were here – both of you, actually.' He looked back at Faye, his eyes warm. 'But especially you, Faye. You see – and Liz already knows this – but you're the one that inspired me to sing in this competition, Faye. And I really wanted you to hear me.'

Faye didn't know what to say. She felt her face burning red as Lucas carried on staring at her. 'Wow – that's ... that's amazing.'

'Not really,' he muttered. 'But I hope you like it. Because I'm singing it for you.'

Suddenly footsteps sounded behind them and they all turned to look at the person who appeared around the corner.

'Finn!' Faye exclaimed, surprised, instinctively stepping back from Lucas. 'What are you doing here?'

Finn walked towards them until his face was in the light, and Faye felt her heart jump. Finn glanced at Lucas, and the smile that had been on his lips faded away into suspicion. Faye was suddenly reminded of the last time she'd seen him – she'd been in his arms, and he'd been about to kiss her. But after Aunt Pam's interruption, Finn had been quiet and distant, leaving as soon as he'd finished helping her wash up.

'Hello, Faye,' he said, quietly. 'You look great. So do you, Liz.'

'What are you doing here?' Lucas asked, roughly.

'Yeah,' Liz added. 'You're not a pupil at this school.'

Finn smiled grimly. 'I am, actually. Signed up last week. I start classes on Monday.'

Lucas made a disgusted sound in his throat. 'You've got to be joking. Well, as long as you're not in any of mine.'

Finn stepped forwards, obviously angry. 'What's your problem?'

Lucas shrugged, a smirk on his face. 'Oh, I don't know. Just can't help feeling that you'd be bringing the tone down, somehow.'

Faye and Liz looked at each other, feeling the tension between the two boys. 'Look, you two don't know each other,' Faye said. 'I'm sure if you—'

'I don't need to know him,' Finn growled, still staring at Lucas, 'to know that he's trouble.'

'I'm trouble?' Lucas laughed. 'That's definitely a joke, coming from you. Don't you live in a tent, or something?'

Finn took another threatening step towards Lucas, but Faye pressed a hand to his chest, holding him back. 'Finn, please don't . . .'

'Look, I have to go, anyway,' said Lucas. 'The competition is about to start and I have to change. Faye – I'm first up. Don't miss it, OK? Please.'

Faye looked over her shoulder. 'I promise,' she said.

Lucas flicked a triumphant grin at Finn before turning on his heel and heading inside.

'Come on, Faye,' Liz said, 'let's go inside. You don't want to miss Lucas's performance!'

Finn stopped Faye before she could answer. 'Faye. Just talk to me for a minute. I really wanted to see you. Please?'

'Faye,' Liz warned. 'Come on, let's go. You're supposed to be taking photographs of all the acts, remember?'

Faye looked between both of them, desperate to talk to Finn, but unwilling to make Liz angry. From a little way behind them, she heard a single, dry cough; they all turned to see Ballard standing half in shadow, watching them. His hands were in his pockets and his face was in darkness, but Faye was sure she could see his eyes, clear as day.

'Faye,' Finn said again, softly. His voice was anxious, and she looked up to see his gaze fixed on Ballard. 'I really need to talk to you. It's important.'

Faye stared at him. She'd only met him for the first time a few weeks ago, and they'd spent so little time together. And when they had seen each other, she'd found it so difficult to work out exactly what Finn felt about her. Sometimes it seemed as if she were the only thing he was interested in, but then all of a sudden, he could change and be so distant that it he didn't even seem know she was there. Yet here he was, right now, begging her to choose him over her best friend in the world, and Faye wanted to be with him so much it hurt.

Liz threw up her hands. 'You know what? If you want to hang out with him, be my guest. But I'm not getting into trouble again because of some college dropout who lives in a tent. Got it?'

'Liz, wait!' Faye shouted after Liz as she marched away, but her voice was lost in a wave of music that surged out of the building as the gig began. Faye tried to reach her friend before she ran up the school steps, but in an instant they were surrounded by students, all desperate to get inside before the contest began. Faye pushed forwards, trying to find Liz, but someone grasped her hand, pulling her back. She turned to see Finn behind her.

'Faye, wait. I've got some news. About—'

The crowd swallowed them, sweeping them up the steps and into the school gym before either of them had time to get out of the way. Then the music changed, and Faye realized that the competition had started. She scrambled to get her camera out of its case – she'd promised Jimmy she'd get good pictures of all the contestants for his piece in *The Miller*. It didn't seem right to let him down, especially now.

The stage was in darkness, but someone was up there, playing the guitar better than Faye had ever heard anybody her age play before. It couldn't be Lucas, could it? If it was, he was amazing. She recognized the song as an acoustic version of 'Use Somebody' by Kings of Leon. She saw Liz, her head bobbing up and down among the crowd. She tried to move forwards through the noisy students, still holding onto Finn's hand.

And then the performer on stage started to sing, and everyone in the crowd fell silent.

Chapter Thirty

True Colours

Lucas's singing was incredible. Right from the first line of the song, his voice filled the gym, and everyone was totally transfixed. Faye saw Liz turn her head, looking for her. When their eyes met, Faye realized that Liz was so caught up in the amazing music that she'd forgotten her earlier anger. Faye was relieved – she really didn't want another fight with her best friend. Liz pushed her way over. No one minded – everyone was too busy listening to the performer on stage.

'That can't really be Lucas, can it?' Liz asked, when she was near enough. 'He's amazing!'

Faye shook her head. Liz was right – the singer really was incredibly talented. It was too dark for her to take pictures, though – she needed to get closer to the front of the stage.

Finn's voice whispered in her ear, very close, and Faye realized that they were still holding hands. Finn had laced his fingers through hers as if he didn't want to let go

'Faye,' he said, his breath tickling her ear, making her heart jump. 'I've really got to talk to you. It's about your friend Jimmy. I know—'

At his mention of Jimmy, Faye tried to lean closer to hear what Finn had to say, but his words were drowned out by the growing noise of the crowd and the performer on stage. Finn leaned down, so close that his lips brushed against her ear as he tried to tell her something, but Faye still couldn't hear what he was saying.

At that moment Lucas reached the song's chorus – and as he did so, all the lights on stage exploded into life. Flashes of white and blue lit up the background as the performer was illuminated in a bright pool of incandescent light. The crowd shouted in delight as the singer was revealed amid the fluorescent glare.

'Oh my god,' squealed Liz, 'Faye! Look! And he's singing this for you!'

Lucas stood comfortably in front of the microphone as if he belonged on the stage, his voice rising above the shouts of the audience. He was dressed in pale-blue jeans and wore an elaborate, but old, leather jacket. He turned, and Faye saw that It bore a large emblem on the back, one that she was sure she'd seen before, but couldn't place where. She glanced up at Finn, who was staring darkly at the figure on stage, and it suddenly came to her – it was a Black Dog biker jacket. She'd seen all the bikers wearing it that day in the mall.

'Finn,' Faye shouted. 'Isn't that—'

There was no way that Finn was going to be able to hear her while Lucas was still performing. The crowd were going wild. As the song reached a crescendo, the lights flipped up, raking the gathered students with colour as everyone rocked along to the music.

'Finn,' Faye shouted, over again, the noise. His gaze was fixed on Lucas, and he looked more angry than she'd ever seen him look. Faye raised a hand to his cheek, trying to get him to look at her.

At Faye's touch, Finn jumped, his head snapping towards her. Their eyes met, and his anger dissolved into something else, something so powerful and raw that it turned her insides

166

to lava. He turned his cheek into her hand where it still rested against his face, pressing his lips into her palm. They were pressed together in the crowd, staring at each other as if there was no one else in the room.

The song came to an end, and the crowd exploded in rapturous applause. Faye thought Finn was about to lean towards her when Lucas's voice boomed out from the stage.

'Thanks everyone! Glad you liked it,' he yelled, over the still-echoing applause. 'That one was for Faye McCarron!'

At the sound of Lucas's voice, Finn looked once more towards the stage. His anger returned, and he pulled away from Faye.

'Finn,' she called after him, as he began to push his way towards the exit. 'Finn, wait!'

He didn't stop. Faye followed him before he could vanish into the crowd.

The crowd was still cheering as Lucas left the stage, pulling his guitar strap over his head as he went. His heart was pounding – if this is what it was like to perform for people, no wonder everyone wanted to be a rock star! It was amazing . . . the crowd had gone crazy for him. For him – Lucas Morrow! He grinned to himself, rubbing one hand through his hair. He could get used to that, for sure! He just hoped that Faye had loved it, too. He'd looked for her in the crowd, but couldn't see her amid all the other figures. The room had been packed!

Lucas saw Ballard waiting by the stage door and held out the guitar.

'Time to go,' the servant said, as he took the instrument.

'Not yet! I want to see some of my competition.' Lucas was about to head for the auditorium, but Ballard gripped his elbow.

'I said, time to go. Your mother is waiting for you.'

Lucas narrowed his eyes and stared at Ballard, but knew

better than to argue. Lucas hung back as the next contestant began to sing. Through the curtain, he saw that it was the girl called Rachel that Liz had told him about. He smiled to himself – definitely no competition for him there. Actually, he kind of felt sorry for her, having to go on straight after him!

He headed out of the door, following Ballard across the parking lot, wondering what his mother wanted. He really would have liked to stay and hang out a bit. Maybe he could come back later . . . Lucas was almost at the car when he felt a strong hand on his shoulder. He spun around. It was the dark-haired biker guy of about his own age, the one who had butted in earlier, before the show – with a thunderous look on his face. He'd seen him around town, with his crew of thugs. Then Lucas saw Faye and Liz run out of the school and down the steps.

'Finn!' Faye shouted, sounding worried. 'What are you doing?'

Flash was still hanging out with this guy? A wave of anger tinged with envy washed over Lucas. He pulled away.

'What do you want?' Lucas asked. 'I'm busy.'

'Where did you get that jacket?' Finn demanded, through jaws clenched in anger.

Lucas smirked. 'Why, you planning on buying one? Not sure you could afford it.'

He turned towards the car, but Finn stopped him, grabbing him by the arm. 'It's a biker jacket. As worn by the Black Dogs, and *only* the Black Dogs.'

Lucas wrenched his arm away. 'So?'

Finn stepped forwards again, right up in Lucas's face. 'So you're not a member. You can't wear it.'

Lucas stepped back as he looked his attacker up and down. 'What's it to you, biker boy?' He asked. 'Afraid I might take your place?'

168

Lucas saw the flash of anger in Finn's face as he grabbed his collar, dragging Lucas forwards until they were nose to nose. More and more students were gathering round, excited by the prospect of a fight. Lucas realized that the music inside the school had stopped, probably because most of the audience had suddenly left and were now standing around them, waiting to see what was going to happen.

Out of the corner of his eye, Lucas saw Ballard waiting outside the school gate. With him was the policeman that had come to visit the house – Liz's dad, Sergeant Wilson. He was just standing there, doing nothing as Ballard spoke into his ear.

Finn shook him, hard. 'I want that jacket back,' he said, with a snarl. 'Take it off.'

Lucas struggled to free himself, pulling backwards and then barrelling forwards, shoving the boy hard in the chest with his shoulder. Finn overbalanced, falling heavily to the ground.

Breathing hard, Lucas leaned over him. 'It isn't yours. I found this in my house. Why don't you just back off?'

Finn was back on his feet in an instant, so fast Lucas wasn't even sure he'd seen him move. 'You're lying,' his voice a low, slow growl. '*Take it off*. Before I make you.'

Lucas made a derisive sound in his throat as he shrugged off the jacket. 'You really want it that much, huh? Well, it's kind of rotten, so I guess it'll suit you. It's pretty dirty, too. Here, let me give you something to clean it with.'

Lucas spat on the battered leather before tossing the jacket to the ground. He saw the fury on Finn's face. Before Lucas could step back, the biker was on his feet. The punch came out of nowhere, a fast uppercut that connected hard with Lucas's jaw and smashed his teeth together, throwing him backwards.

169

Stunned, Lucas crashed against the car. He saw Finn raise his arm again, and pushed himself off the car, ready to level his own blow.

Finn stepped forwards for another shot. Lucas tensed, prepared for it. But then . . . nothing happened. Lucas blinked. It was as if someone had freeze-framed the scene. Finn stood with his arm raised, his hand clenched into a fist. Next to him stood Sergeant Wilson. In a flash, the policeman had reached out and grabbed Finn's hand in midair. Finn's muscles were bunched hard, trying to free himself, but Sergeant Wilson was obviously stronger. So strong, in fact, that he didn't even need to try. There was something very strange about the way the policeman was standing. His body looked relaxed, as if he was asleep. His face was calm – blank, even. He stared at Finn with expressionless eyes. And then, without warning, he twisted the boy's arm back, flinging him against the car with a crunch, as easy as someone would toss a ball to a dog. Finn's face twisted in pain.

'Dad!' Liz shouted, obviously horrified.

The policeman didn't seem to hear, leaning heavily on Finn as he pulled out a pair of cuffs and fastened them tightly around the boy's wrists. Lucas looked at Sergeant Wilson's face, and felt a needle of cold fear thread through his veins. There was no emotion in the man's eyes. In fact, there was no sign of life at all. It was like looking at a deep, still pool of water – empty and fathomless.

'Sergeant Wilson,' Faye began. 'Please don't arrest Finn, he was just—'

Wilson didn't listen, or speak. He marched Finn in front of him, through the gathered crowd. Liz followed, touching her father's arm, trying to get him to stop. The policeman shook her off, sending his daughter crashing into Faye.

They were almost at the police car when Lucas saw Finn twist round, shouting for Faye.

'I know where your friend is,' he shouted. 'Faye, I know where Jimmy is!'

Chapter Thirty-one

The Mill

Faye helped Liz up. Her friend was shaking. Faye was trembling, too. She'd never seen Sergeant Wilson like that before. He was never violent – he never needed to be. He was too good a police officer for that. Around them, the rest of Winter Mill High's students were heading back into the Battle of the Bands, discussing what had happened. Faye spotted the jacket that had caused the fight still lying on the ground, and went to pick it up.

'We have to follow them,' Liz said, her voice rough.

'I'm not sure that's such a great idea,' said Faye.

'Once we're at the police station, Dad will talk to me,' Liz insisted, though she sounded as if she was trying to convince herself as much as anyone. 'And didn't Finn say that he knew something about Jimmy? If he knows where he is, we should find out, shouldn't we?'

Faye couldn't argue with that. They headed for Liz's car. Faye saw Lucas standing alone, nursing his jaw, and she realized that Ballard was gone. Faye didn't feel as if she could just leave him there.

'Are you all right?' she asked.

Lucas eyed her warily. 'I'll be fine. Nice friends you have, Flash.'

Faye ignored the comment. 'Where's Ballard gone?'

Lucas shrugged. 'No idea. You couldn't give me a lift home, could you? I don't want to call my mom . . .'

Faye looked around. Liz was already backing the car out of their space. She shook her head. 'Look, Lucas, I'm sorry . . . but I have to help Finn.'

Lucas looked hurt. 'Right,' he said.

'He says he knows where Jimmy is,' said Faye, trying to explain. 'And . . .'

'Don't worry about it,' Lucas told her, obviously hurt.

'Lucas? Are you all right?' The voice came from behind them, where a crowd of students was still milling around, chattering about what had just happened. It was Rachel Hogan, looking worried. 'Look, let me take you home – I've got my car here.'

Faye saw Lucas's surprised look. 'Oh – that would be really great. Thanks.'

Liz pulled up beside them and hooted. 'Come on, Faye! Let's go!'

'I'm really sorry, Lucas,' called Faye, as she ran around the car, but he was already walking away with Rachel.

Faye slammed her door shut and Liz tore out of the parking lot in pursuit of her dad's squad car. They headed for the police station, which was on the town's main street. The sidewalks and roads were quiet – there didn't seem to be anybody about, even though it wasn't really that late. It made Winter Mill look abandoned and creepy, and Faye shivered miserably. Aunt Pam was right. There was something very strange going on in their town.

'Look,' Liz pointed, cutting through Faye's unhappy thoughts. 'Ballard's following my dad, too!' The two cars ahead of them passed through town. 'Dad's not stopping at the police station,' Liz said with a frown. 'Where's he going?'

174

They followed Sergeant Wilson through the central cross-roads and into the old section of town. Faye thought that they were going to stop at one of the houses along the road. Instead, they carried on to the town limit, making a sharp left and heading up the hill into the dense pine forest that surrounded Winter Mill.

'I think Dad's going up to the Old Mill!' Liz muttered, as they watched the two cars ahead of them pull onto an old, disused road.

'But why?' Faye asked. 'There's nothing up there. It hasn't been used for decades! Why would he take Finn there, instead of to the police station?'

'I don't know,' said Liz, helplessly. 'I don't know why any of this is happening. It's all crazy. The bikers, the stuff going on in the woods, Jimmy going missing . . . and now this. Faye, what on earth is happening to us? What's happening to my dad? Back there . . . I've never seen him like that. He looked so weird. And the way he treated Finn . . . and now, not taking him to the police station? What's going on?'

Faye didn't have an answer. They drove in silence, and as the track became even narrower Liz slowed down even more. She turned the car's lights off.

'Liz! What are you doing?'

'They'll see us coming if I don't!'

'But there's no light! We'll crash! Pull over. Let's walk the rest of the way – that way they won't hear us, either.'

Liz nodded and stopped the car in a hollow of earth that looked as it if might once have been designed to let two carts pass each other. The snow was deep enough to rise over the car's hood. The two girls slipped out as quietly as they could, stepping in the tyre tracks left by Sergeant Wilson and Ballard.

Ahead of them, the Old Mill loomed out of the darkness, its

milling tower making it look like some ancient castle. Faye shivered. She'd never liked this place. Her dad had brought her up here once on one of his local-history tours. When she was little, he'd loved taking her out on pretend archaeological digs around Winter Mill, teaching her about the history of the area. Faye had usually loved it – learning about how to excavate delicate artefacts had been fun, even if what she found were usually just fragments of dinner plates. Faye had to swallow a sudden lump in her throat at the thought of her dad. She wished he was here for her now, instead of somewhere so far away he couldn't even call.

But *this* place – as soon as she'd seen it, Faye had been filled with a horrible sense of foreboding. Her dad had told her it was one of the earliest buildings in the district. It had first been built as a loggers' rest, and then later, when the town was bigger, it had milled wheat into flour for everyone who lived there. But now it was abandoned, decrepit, its tower a half-destroyed wreck. Faye didn't understand why they didn't just pull the whole ugly thing down.

She and Liz slipped off the tracks and into the trees once they got closer, using Liz's little keyring flashlight and the glow from the moon on the snow to light their way. There was no sign of either car, and Faye figured that both Ballard and Sergeant Wilson must have driven right into the mill. Faye hadn't wanted to say anything to Liz earlier, but during the fight she could have sworn she saw Ballard telling the policeman what to do. Faye didn't like to think of Mitch Wilson being on the wrong side of the law – he'd been like a second dad to her since she was a baby. But things didn't look good.

'What are we going to do now?' Liz mouthed. 'We can't just walk in there!'

Faye looked around. In the gloom she could just make out a

176

gap in the mill's wooden walls, just peeping out of the snow. It would mean they'd have be in the drift to see what was going on, but the only other option was to climb up to one of the broken windows, which would make far too much noise. Faye pointed and Liz nodded. Together, they crept towards the opening, kneeling down so they could see what was happening.

Inside, the mill was dry, but dark. Faye could just make out the two cars, parked side by side. Suddenly, there was a loud crack, and a light burst into life. They both jumped, clinging on to each other. After a second, Liz realized what it was.

'It's a flare,' she said into Faye's ear. 'Dad lit a flare.'

The luminous green glow lit the large space inside. It was empty, apart from a few stacks of logs and old, broken wooden crates. Ballard was holding a heavy rope. As they watched, he dragged a chair to the centre of the floor. Sergeant Wilson opened the back of his squad car and forced Finn to get out. Faye pulled her camera out from beneath her jacket and angled it up, trying to get a clear shot of what was going on.

'What are you doing?' Liz hissed.

'What if we need evidence?' Faye whispered, making sure the flash was off as she grabbed a couple of shots.

'Evidence of what?' Liz asked.

Faye didn't want to think about that.

Chapter Thirty-two

Bound

The two girls watched as Sergeant Wilson and Ballard tied Finn to the chair. Finn struggled and yelled, but he was no match for the two men, even when Sergeant Wilson removed the cuffs. Ballard tied the boy's legs and hands together, then twisted the rope around Finn's neck, forcing his head back, and securing the end to the chair.

Ballard turned to Sergeant Wilson. 'Get out. *Now*.'

Liz's dad didn't even hesitate. He walked to his car, slid into the front seat, started the engine and backed out.

'I don't understand,' Liz said. 'Why is Dad taking orders from that horrible man? What's happening to him? We should go after him!'

Faye squeezed her arm as they watched the police car disappear down the narrow track. 'We have to stay here,' she told Liz. 'We can't leave Finn alone with Ballard.'

Liz looked miserable, but nodded. Through the window, they saw Ballard lift his hand and hit Finn, hard, across the face. The boy's head smacked back against the chair, and the girls heard him groan.

'You think you can interfere with our plans, do you, Finn?' Ballard said, his sinister voice amused. 'How long will it take you and your kind to learn you will never win?'

Finn lifted his head, twisting it from side to side to loosen the

179

rope. He coughed, turned his head, and Faye was shocked to see blood on his lips.

'We haven't lost yet,' Finn managed. 'And you know we won't go down without a fight. I've seen worse than you come and go.'

Ballard was circling Finn, the way an animal might stalk its prey. 'But you will go down, boy. Look at you. How long has this battle been going on? You never change. And you *never* learn. I've been waiting for one of you to slip up, do something stupid. And what you did in that school yard – that was stupid. Drawing attention to yourself. To all of us . . .'

Finn coughed. 'What do you want?' he rasped. He seemed to be finding it hard to breathe. 'Stop playing games. I've got better things to do.'

'I'm going to give you a choice,' Ballard bent over Finn, his voice echoing in the eerie emptiness of the old mill. 'Because I'm generous that way, and because I want to send a message. Your kind may have hindered us before, but that's not going to happen again. So here we are, Finn. You can join us. Or I can kill you, here and now. I can end your pathetic little life once and for all, because I'm tired of your arrogance.' Ballard straightened up. 'I'm going to give you five minutes of quiet time alone to make your decision. Make sure you choose wisely. Or your long life might just be at an end . . .'

Ballard walked away, laughing cruelly as he went. As the girls watched, he slid open the old main doors to the mill and went into the snow, closing them behind him.

Faye turned to Liz, her teeth chattering from crouching in the snow. 'We've got to get Finn out, right now,' she said.

'We can't do that on our own!' Liz protested. 'Come on – let's go back to town and get help.'

'And what if Ballard kills him before we can get back?

Whoever we ask for help is just going to call the police and you know that's not going to help! Your dad is the only policeman on duty and he's the one that brought Finn here in the first place! Come on, Liz – we've got to try.'

Liz shook her head before shrugging helplessly. 'OK. OK, let's do it. But we have to be quick, before Ballard comes back.'

Faye checked the gap they'd been looking through again. They should be able to fit through it, especially if they dug out a little of the snow as they went. She just hoped there weren't any rusty nails or nasty spikes of rotten wood hiding underneath. 'I'll go first. Just be careful.'

Faye began to squeeze through, wriggling her shoulders to fit through the narrow gap. In less than a minute she was on the floor the other side. 'Come on,' she hissed to Liz, who was still hesitating, 'Hurry up!'

At the sound of her whisper, Faye saw Finn turn around, obviously shocked to see her. She ran to him, kneeling behind the chair to help him as he struggled against the ropes.

'Faye, you shouldn't be here,' he said. 'You've got to go before Ballard gets back. He's dangerous. Please, Faye . . .'

'Not without you,' she said, struggling with the heavy knots with cold-numbed hands. Faye glanced over her shoulder to see Liz making her way down too. 'Quick!' she called to her friend. 'Help me with these.'

They managed to get Finn's legs untied, but they couldn't get his hands undone.

'We'll get it off later,' Liz said, urgently. 'Let's just get out of here.'

Finn glanced at the gap they'd squeezed through. 'I'll never get through there without my hands free. And I won't be able to run fast enough, either.'

Faye glanced at the mill doors. There was no sign of Ballard

181

yet, but they were running out of options. 'I need something to cut the rope. Do you carry a penknife?' she asked Finn, but he shook his head.

'Wait!' said Liz. 'Wait – I do. Sort of, anyway.' She rummaged in her bag, and a second later pulled open the little silver letter opener. 'I think one side is sharp enough!'

Faye reached for it but then stopped, her hand in midair. She stared at the letter opener, pale-faced. It was familiar. 'Where did you get this?'

Liz shrugged. 'I found it – that night we went up to the woods and found the wolf tracks and stuff. It was just lying in the snow, all dirty. Why?'

Faye took it, holding it in the palm of her hand. 'It's my dad's,' she whispered. 'He takes it everywhere with him. It used to belong to my great grandfather.'

'What? It can't be.'

'It is. It's got a crack in the handle. I'd recognize it anywhere. Why didn't you tell me about the knife, Liz, why didn't you show me?'

'I – I forgot about it. We were late, and then we heard the bikers, and then we had the blowout, and—'

'Girls,' Finn interrupted. 'Can we please do this later?'

Faye shook herself. 'Right . . . right. Hold on . . .' She went to use the knife on the rope, but Finn backed away.

'Is that silver?' he asked, looking warily at the letter opener.

'Yes – why?'

'Just don't touch my skin with it, OK? I'm – I'm allergic. Very badly allergic.'

Faye nodded. Finn held out his wrists behind him and she slid her fingers between his skin and the knot. Finn was warm, and she could feel his pulse, throbbing against her hand. Trying to ignore how close they were, Faye worked the

182

letter opener into the ropes and began to saw through the fibres.

'It's taking too long,' hissed Liz, watching the door. 'Hurry up!'

Faye wrenched at the rope, watching it fray. Just a few more moments, and . . .

'Well, well, well,' said a sour voice behind them.

All three of them spun to see Ballard, watching them with a vicious look on his face. 'Just look what the dog's dragged in.'

Chapter Thirty-three

Yellow Eyes

Finn pulled his hands away from Faye and strained against the half-cut rope. Faye watched as his muscles bulged in his arms, the rough threads cutting at his skin. The rope broke suddenly, and he was free. He stood in front of the girls, holding his arms out to shield them from Ballard. The older man walked towards them slowly, his hands behind his back and an unpleasant smile on his face.

'Let them go,' Finn said. 'You don't need them. It's me you want.'

Ballard opened his cruel mouth and laughed, slowly. He brought his arms forwards. On both hands he wore heavy silver knuckledusters, which he must have retrieved from the car.

'Now, Finn,' said Ballard, very softly. He carried on walking towards them, slowly. 'Where would the fun be in that?'

Finn lunged, hoping to take him by surprise, but Ballard was ready. As Finn went for his legs, the man took a step back, bracing himself to take his weight. Then, as he made contact, Ballard placed his hands on Finn's shoulders and flipped him backwards, sending him head over heels across the floor. He crashed into a stack of old wooden boxes, crushing them into splinters that peppered the air with lethal shards. He heard the girls shriek, but swallowed the pain, determined not to let Ballard think he had the upper hand.

'Come on, boy,' Ballard taunted. 'Can't you do better than that?'

Finn sprang to his feet, worried about Faye and Liz. He pushed them into a corner, where they would be at least partially sheltered by a heavy wooden beam. It'd also give him a chance to keep Ballard away from them. Turning back as Ballard lunged, he threw a punch that struck Ballard's shoulder and spun him round. Finn added a kick that forced him to the floor, though Ballard was back on his feet before Finn could land another. He caught Finn's foot and turned it over sharply, flinging him into the air. Finn twisted himself to land on his feet. He attacked Ballard again, punching a blow into the older man's ribcage, but it didn't even seem to register. Ballard struck back, scissoring his arm into Finn's throat and leaving him gasping for breath.

Before Finn could recover, Ballard lifted him, bodily, snarling as he smashed the boy against the wooden wall. He slammed a silver knuckleduster against Finn's throat, pressing it into his Adam's apple. There was the sharp crackle of searing flesh, and a plume of steam rose from his skin. Finn screamed as the silver burned him, an ungodly sound that went on and on, turning into a long, moaning howl.

Through his pain, Finn heard Faye scream, and knew that in the next few moments, she'd know exactly what he was. Anger coursed through him, filling him with a fury that seemed to burn in his very soul. Anger at Ballard, for forcing him out, anger at the woman that had made him this way, anger at the world. He'd wanted to keep this aspect of himself away from this girl. He'd wanted her to think him whole, normal. Finn hadn't wanted her to know what he was, what he could become . . . Was that really so much to ask? Was it?

Finn struggled against Ballard, but could not free himself,

the silver draining his strength even as the rage within grew. He searched out the girls, knowing that as soon as he met her eye, Faye would see that he was no longer the person she had thought he was. Finn looked at Faye, and through the pain and the blood rushing in his ears, he registered her shock.

'Run,' he rasped, his words distinct despite his agony. 'Run. *Now.*'

His eyes were yellow. Terror flooded through Faye as she watched Finn convulse. She could hear screaming, and only realized it was from her own mouth when Liz grabbed her arm, screaming too.

'We have to get out of here!' Liz yelled into her ear. 'We have to—'

Faye grabbed Liz's hand and together they ducked out of their corner and made for the door. Faye was shaking so badly that she stumbled, almost dragging Liz down with her. She heard Finn – or whatever he really was – scream again, an echoing, animal sound. They had almost made it to the door when she tripped over something and fell, plunging to her knees. Liz tried to pull her up, but as Faye looked over her shoulder, she froze in horror.

Ballard had dropped Finn, and the biker now knelt on all fours, shaking his head like a dog. He opened his mouth wide and howled. Finn threw his head back, and Faye could see the scar where Ballard had hurt him with the knuckleduster. Except that it wasn't a scar – it looked like a split in his skin, as if the silver had torn Finn apart. The tear was growing, spreading. It ran down his neck to his chest and up into his hair. Faye watched as Finn wrenched off his shirt. She could see the wound spreading, spreading, rupturing his torso, his back, his arms. The single wound became many as Finn's skin seemed to melt away, showing a layer of thick, grey fur sprouting beneath.

He howled again, and Faye saw his face begin to change. The eyes she knew as Finn's had been replaced by hard, glaring yellow discs. His mouth and nose were stretching, transforming into a dog's snout, sprouting more thick fur. Faye could see teeth, long, vicious and dripping with saliva and felt her skin prickle with terror. That couldn't be Finn, could it? It couldn't be!

She looked at Liz, still gripping her hand, and saw her friend's mouth stretched in a horrified O.

The Finn she knew was almost completely gone. In his place was a huge grey wolf. It shook its head, spraying saliva left and right. It flexed its muscles, long legs ready to spring into action, growling, angry, nose wrinkling with fury as it bared its teeth. Even Ballard was backing away. But then, just as the wolf was about to pounce, it turned its head, looking directly at her. Faye almost screamed again, but then she realized it was trying to tell her something. Finn was trying to tell her something. The wolf was looking at her, but for a split second, Faye felt as if she was looking into Finn's eyes, and she could hear his voice as clearly as when he'd stood before her after saving her in the woods.

'*You don't have to be afraid,*' he was saying. '*Not while I'm here. Never while I'm here.*' Then the wolf looked away, focusing on Ballard.

But Faye didn't know if she could believe him. That night, in the woods . . . had it been Finn? Had it been Finn chasing her, after all? Faye jolted herself into action, pulling Liz across the floor. They heard a human scream as they reached the door, but Faye didn't dare look back. The two girls plunged into the snow, struggling into a run. Every second, Faye expected to hear another howl behind them, or the sound of powerful paws thudding across the snow. She was taken back again to that chase through the woods, when she'd been convinced her life was in danger. Now she realized she'd been right, and a sick knot of terror tied itself around her gut.

'There!' shouted Liz, through gasping for air. 'There, look – my car!'

They collided with it and Liz pulled out her keys, fingers shaking so hard she couldn't fit the right one to the lock. Faye wrapped her hands over her friend's, steadying them enough to unlock the door. They flung themselves inside, breathing hard. Liz slammed down the locks and started the engine, pulling away so fast that the wheels spun against the snow. They roared down the track, slipping and sliding but too desperate to get away to drive carefully.

'A werewolf,' Liz stammered, through violently chattering teeth. 'That . . . that *thing* . . . is a *werewolf.*'

Faye shook her head, wanting to deny what she'd seen, but couldn't find words. Her whole body was quaking. She shut her eyes, but couldn't block out the image of Finn's skin tearing apart like paper.

'What do we do?' asked Liz, in a harsh, shocked whisper, finally pulling the car over. 'Faye, what should we do? We can't call the police. I can't go home. Dad—' she sobbed, a huge intake of breath. 'Dad's part of it. I don't know why, but he is. I can't . . . I can't go back.'

Faye reached out, taking Liz's hand and holding it firmly. They sat like that for a few minutes, trying to calm down.

'What about Jimmy?' Liz said, suddenly. 'Wasn't Finn saying something about Jimmy?'

'Yeah,' Faye nodded. 'He said he knew where he was.'

Liz pulled her hand away and gripped the steering wheel hard. 'Do you think they've got him? That thing . . . Finn's . . . gang? The bikers – or the werewolves, whatever they are? Faye, have they got Jimmy?'

189

Faye nodded, shutting her eyes. 'I think they might have. Liz – you were right . . . you were right about Finn . . .'

Liz turned to her friend. She was still shaking, but when she spoke, her voice was calm. 'We have to go get him. We have to get Jimmy.'

'I'm not sure . . .' Faye began.

Liz looked at her, a determined look overtaking the fear. 'I'm not leaving him with those monsters, Faye,' she said. 'Only we know what they are. Only we can do anything about it. We have to save him.'

Chapter Thirty-four

Family

'You know what?' Liz muttered, as she eased the car up the track towards the Mathesons' cabin. 'I'm getting really tired of being in these woods at night.'

Faye nodded. 'You and me both.'

Liz pulled to a stop before they reached the turn off to the cabin, taking a deep breath and leaning on the steering wheel. Faye watched as her friend took several deep breaths. Faye was still shaking herself, her body cold from shock and fright. She stared out of the woods, feeling sick at the thought that they had to go in there, in the dark, after what they'd seen. An image flashed through Faye's mind, of tearing skin and dripping teeth. She shuddered.

'All right,' said Liz. 'Do you think you can work out where the biker camp is?'

'Well, I've never been there . . . but I think it must be some-where around here. After the party Finn found me not far from the Mathesons', and Jimmy's house is up here too.'

Liz nodded. 'Well, I guess there's only one way to find out, isn't there?'

Faye shook her head. 'Are you sure you want to do this?'

'No,' Liz said with brutal honesty, 'but we have to.'

Despite everything, Faye smiled. Liz seemed to have dis-covered a hidden store of courage from somewhere. She

wondered how much it had to do with Jimmy being in danger
. . . But she thought it best not to ask.

They had stopped at Liz's to grab dark coats and flashlights
– the house had been dark and quiet, and there was no sign of
Sergeant Wilson's car. Liz led the way into the cold, snowy
woods, shining her torch at the ground to light their way.
Neither of them talked as they walked. Faye was still going over
and over that moment when Finn – the wolf – had looked at her.
She didn't want to believe it, but there was no escaping the
truth. Finn was a werewolf, and most likely responsible for the
events that had swept these woods and her town.

A werewolf. In Winter Mill. It seemed unbelievable, and yet
Faye had seen it with her own eyes. She had a sudden memory
of something Aunt Pam had told her – about the first settlers in
the area being torn apart by wolves – and shuddered.

'You OK?' Liz whispered.

'Yeah,' Faye answered. 'Just trying to take it all in. It all
seems so insane.'

'It *is* insane!' Liz said, swinging the flashlight from side to
side. 'Maybe this is why Dad's acting so weird. Maybe Ballard's
a secret agent or something, and they're working together to get
rid of the bikers.'

Faye shook her head. 'Ballard doesn't seem like much of a
good guy to me.'

Liz shrugged. 'I bet you have to fight really dirty to beat
these werewolves. Why else would Dad be acting the way he
is?'

'Maybe. But—'

Liz stopped, holding up a hand. She flipped off the light.
Ahead of them, the faint glow of a fire lit the forest, and the girls
could make out the murmur of voices.

They crept forwards slowly until they could see the camp.

Crouching behind a snow-covered bush, they watched as the bikers moved about. They'd chosen a small clearing where the trees were much more sparse. The camp was bordered in all directions by the forest and, as with everywhere else, there was snow on the ground. But the bikers had swept most of it aside before they pitched their tents – huge piles lay in drifts around outside of the camp. In the centre was a large fire, burning fiercely. Around it was a collection of small tents, given extra protection from the elements by tarpaulins, which had been stretched between the trees. Another tarp was stretched over the bikes, which stood on the other side of the camp. Faye counted five – Finn's was nowhere to be seen.

As they watched, the tent closest to the fire opened and one of the bikers stepped out. Through the opening, Faye could see a figure lying on a low camp bed.

'Look,' whispered Liz. 'That's Jimmy!'

Wrapped in a heavy wool blanket, Jimmy lay still, his eyes shut. Even from where they were, Faye could see that his breathing was shallow, and he was very pale.

'What are we going to do?' Faye asked. 'We can't just walk in there and get him. He doesn't look well – he probably can't walk on his own!'

Liz frowned. 'How about if you create a distraction? You've outrun them before. You can . . . I don't know, throw a stone or something, and then make a break for it. They'll follow you, and I'll go in and pull Jimmy out.'

'I don't know . . .' said Faye, terrified of being chased again, especially now that she knew what would be hunting her. 'I'm so scared, Liz. I just don't know if I can do it . . . Maybe we can wait until they're all asleep?'

'Won't they have superhuman smell?' Liz objected. 'They're like dogs. They'll smell us coming. Oh – but wait!' Liz's face

193

brightened. 'The silver really hurt Finn, right? Look!' Liz pointed to her ears. She was wearing little silver studs. 'I can throw these! They'll be like . . . like grenades!'

Faye shook her head. 'Liz, don't be ridiculous. Didn't your dad give you a pepper spray, or something?'

'Oh.' Liz looked sheepish. 'Yeah . . . He did. You're right. That might work better.'

'You think?'

'Of course,' said another, deeper voice behind them, 'you could just ask us if you can visit your friend . . .'

Both girls leaped to their feet, spinning round to see the lead biker – Joe Crowley, Finn's dad, standing there. Then, as the girls watched, they saw more bikers emerging from the woods. Faye looked about, and realized they were surrounded.

Liz went for her purse. 'Stay away!' she gasped, rifling through her bag. 'I'm armed! I will defend us! I've got – I've got pepper spray!' Liz pulled something out and held it in front of her. It was a hairbrush. Faye felt herself turn cold with fear as the men pushed forwards.

Joe began to laugh, and the other men followed suit. 'My dear,' he said. 'I know we are a scruffy bunch, but there's no need to threaten us with death by grooming.'

'Just . . . just stay away,' said Liz, almost sobbing as she struggled to find the spray.

'But you came to find us,' Joe pointed out. 'There must have been a reason.'

'Jimmy,' Liz blurted. 'You've got our friend, Jimmy. What have you done to him?'

The big biker stepped closer to Liz, stilling her hands and putting one arm round her shoulders. He looked over at Faye. 'Jimmy's fine. He was sick, so we took care of him.'

194

'Is he – have you made him one of you?' Faye asked, finally finding her voice. 'Is he – is he a werewolf?'

Joe smiled. 'Why don't you come see for yourselves?'

Jimmy could hear noise, but it seemed very far away. He turned his head, and felt something soft against his face. His throat was dry, and he realized he wanted water. He was hot. Opening his eyes, Jimmy blinked, trying to focus. He was in a tent, beside a blazing fire, the flames flickering indistinctly. Something appeared, hovering over him. He looked up, and realized it was Liz. She looked worried, and beautiful. Jimmy wondered if he was dreaming. He tried to speak, to say her name, but his mouth was so dry that it came out like a growl.

Liz leaped away as Jimmy growled, putting her hands up to her mouth. 'Oh my god! He's a dog! You've turned him into one of you!'

Joe Crowley laughed gruffly. 'He just needs some water – someone get the boy a drink!'

'We don't want anything from you,' said Liz, scared but defiant. 'We're going to take him to a hospital, right now.'

Joe shook his head, taking the cup offered to him by one of the other bikers. He crouched down beside Jimmy and lifted him up with one hand, holding the cup to his lips with the other, helping him drink.

'Slowly now, Jimmy,' he said. 'Don't gulp it, son, or you'll choke.'

Liz frowned as she watched Jimmy drink. He didn't seem scared of Joe at all – and Joe actually wasn't being that scary. He was really being very kind. It reminded her of how her dad looked after her when she'd been sick as a little kid. Tears pricked at Liz's eyes when she thought of her father. Would he ever be that kind again?

Joe looked up at Liz and nodded towards the blanket covering Jimmy's leg. 'Take a look for yourself. There isn't a doctor alive will know what to do with that.'

Liz hesitated before moving forwards again and pulling back the blanket. She gasped. The wound was open and raw; large teeth marks had been left in his leg, seeping with black pus. It was all she could do to stop herself throwing up right then.

'What happened to him?' Liz asked, swallowing her bile and putting the blanket down, gently.

Joe frowned, attention on Jimmy. 'Something bit him.'

Liz gasped. 'You did this! You, or one of your men. We – you—'

'It wasn't us,' Joe told her calmly.

'But you're—'

'We stopped what attacked him.' The biker straightened up. putting the cup down where Jimmy could reach it. 'And now we're trying to help him.'

'He's really sick,' whispered Faye. 'Really, really, badly, by the look of it. We have to get help. I'm going to call an ambulance!'

At her words, Jimmy struggled where he lay, trying to sit up. Liz put a hand on his shoulder to make him stay still. 'N-no . . . no . . .' he muttered faintly, his voice still hoarse. 'Y-you c-can't . . . y-you m-mustn't . . . E-everyone in the t-town c-could be h-hers by n-now. T-there's n-no one . . . n-no one you c-can t-trust . . .'

Joe nodded wearily. 'He's right. You can't.'

'Jimmy?' Liz asked. 'What do you mean? I don't understand. I don't understand any of this! What do you—?'

There was a sudden commotion in the undergrowth and Finn stumbled into the circle of light cast by the campfire. He was shirtless, shivering in the cold. Purple bruises covered his face and torso, and blood poured from cuts on his arms and face. The burn on Finn's neck was red-raw. The bikers ran to him as he stumbled towards the fire. Liz saw a flash of anger pass over Joe Crowley's face as he strode towards his son.

'Finn? What happened? Who did this to you?'

'Ballard,' Finn managed, as he crumpled into a heap. 'It was Ballard.' He looked up, and Liz saw his gaze drawn towards her friend, who was standing beside the entrance of the tent. 'Faye,' Finn said. 'Faye, are you—'

His question was drowned out as the other bikers crowded around him, all speaking at once. They were all angry, demanding to know what had happened.

'Why did he do this?' Joe asked. 'What did he want?'

Finn shook his head. 'He offered me a choice. Join them, or die. I think . . . I think this time is different, Dad. I think . . . that maybe this time, we won't be able to stop her . . .'

Joe turned to the rest of the gang. 'Go. Now – find him! We need more information. Bring him back here, alive if you can.'

In a moment, the clearing was filled with terrifying howls. Liz watched in fear as, outside the tent, silhouetted against the fire, every one of the bikers except Finn and Joe began to transform. Faye stumbled backwards, scrambling into the tent to get away as the air was filled with the sound of ripping skin and gnashing teeth.

Liz heard herself scream, and tried to turn away from the sight in front of her. They'd be torn to shreds, she was sure of it, just like they'd tried to do to Jimmy. She shut her eyes screamed, and screamed, until Liz felt something brush against her hand.

Looking down, she saw Jimmy's fingers laced through hers, his blue eyes watching her gently.

'D-don't b-be afraid,' he whispered, with great effort. 'It's OK. E-everything w-will b-be OK.'

The werewolves ran into the woods, leaving a strange kind of peace behind them. As Joe went to help Finn, Liz leaned close to Jimmy, who had closed his eyes again, though he still held her hand. Faye crouched beside them, white and shaking.

'Jimmy,' she said, shaking him gently. 'We've got to go, Jimmy. We're not safe, we have to get you out of here . . .'

'If you take him, he'll die,' Joe said, over his shoulder, as he wiped away the blood from Finn's cuts.

'Just stay away from us,' said Faye, in a trembling voice. 'We'll fight if we have to.'

Joe glanced up at her, shaking his head. 'We're not the bad guys here. There's someone far worse for you to worry about, Faye McCarron. Believe me.'

Chapter Thirty-five

Midnight

Lucas woke with a start. It was the middle of the night, and his room was freezing cold. His breath traced patterns in the frigid air as he sat up, shivering.

He climbed out of bed, pulling a blanket around his shoulders. The house was silent – no, not just silent. It sounded empty, void. Dead, like the dark spaces behind an unknown door in an unknown house. He shuddered.

Lucas opened the door of his room and peered out. The corridor stretched into inky blackness, pierced only by the light from his room. He slipped quietly into the hallway beyond.

He'd expected it just to be his room that was cold, but the rest of the house was freezing too. Lucas walked towards the balcony that overhung the central staircase, feeling his toes getting colder and colder with every step. The heating must have gone off, and maybe the power. That would explain why all the lights were out. Ballard usually left at least one burning on each floor. He crept forwards, feeling a twinge in his shoulder from the bruise he'd got in the fight with Finn. Lucas rotated his arm, slowly, trying to ease the muscle.

Reaching the balcony, Lucas looked over the railing and noticed a faint glow coming through the semi-open door of the living room. Maybe his mother had told Ballard to light a fire –

199

she always was a light sleeper, and the cold had probably woken her up as well.

Lucas hesitated, torn. He liked the idea of sitting in front of a roaring fire right now, but if it meant having to be in the same room as his mother, and possibly Ballard ... Although Lucas had been waiting to talk to *him* all evening. Lucas wanted to know where Ballard had rushed off to and why he hadn't stayed to make sure he was all right, for a start. He also wanted his guitar back – the last he'd seen of it was Ballard carrying it to the car. But Lucas had waited up for hours, and there'd been no sign of Ballard returning home.

If they were down there now, together, Lucas had no doubt that Ballard would have told Mercy about the incident at school earlier. His mother hated him drawing attention to them, despite the fact that she herself was endlessly photographed in all the celebrity gossip magazines. He suspected she just didn't like people to be reminded that she was old enough to have a son. Sometimes Lucas thought Mercy would have preferred not to have a child at all.

On the other hand, his feet were beginning to ache with the cold, and the warmth would help his sore shoulder ...

He'd got halfway down the stairs when he heard a muffled, but horrible scream. It came from the living room. Lucas froze, hanging on to the railing. The scream was followed by a loud, angry voice. It was his mother's.

'How dare you?' Mercy shouted. 'You fool. You could have ruined everything! Do you know how long this has taken to plan and execute? Do you? *DO YOU?*'

There was another scream, as if his mother's words were causing somebody physical pain. Lucas's heart shuddered fearfully in his chest, but he carried on down the stairs, overtaken by a compulsion to see what was happening. The temperature dropped even further, getting colder still as he crept across the entrance hall.

'This is unacceptable,' Mercy raged. 'This is one too many mistakes!'

Lucas had heard Mercy angry before, but never anything like this. The sound of her fury chilled the blood in his veins. He wanted to see who she was shouting at, but the door of the room wasn't open quite far enough. He reached out, intending to push it just a little bit more. His fingers touched the handle, but Lucas immediately jerked them back. It was icy cold – no, it was colder than cold. It was freezing, a cold so deep that it was painful to touch. He looked at his hand, shocked to see that his fingers were marked where he had touched the handle, tiny pieces of his skin torn off by the cold metal.

'Do you have anything to say?' his mother's voice barked, and Lucas ducked down behind the door. Had she seen him? Through the keyhole, Lucas saw a familiar figure kneeling on the floor in front of his mother, trembling hands clasped together.

'Please . . . please, my lady . . . I am sorry . . . It won't happen again. It was just – the boy, Finn . . . I thought . . . he is determined, this time. The girl . . . she is too much like . . . like her. If he would join us willingly . . .'

It was Ballard. He was grovelling at her feet. Lucas felt his mouth drop open in surprise. *What did that biker guy have to do with Ballard and his mother?*

'Silence!' Mercy screamed, raising her hand.

Ballard jerked up as if held by an invisible rope, his chin quivering as his head snapped back on his neck. He whimpered in pain.

'You miserable, disgusting worm,' Mercy sneered. 'I have *allowed* you to serve me, and this is how you repay me? You

201

could have ripped asunder everything I have worked to achieve.'

'Please, my lady,' Ballard begged again. 'I thought—'

'Enough!' she roared. 'That girl is marked, as is Finn. You knew that. That's all you needed to know!' Mercy turned her hand as she spoke, and Lucas watched as Ballard twisted in agony. 'Now you must pay for your stupidity.'

'No . . . No . . .' Ballard pleaded. 'I've learned my lesson . . . Please don't . . .'

'Stop snivelling, Ballard. Rejoice that you may still serve me.'

Mercy clapped her hands together, and the servant collapsed in a heap on the floor. He howled once, and then dissolved into pathetic, whimpering sobs. Lucas watched as his mother took a step backwards and then held up her hands. The sight of them filled Lucas with terror.

Mercy's fingers were – *growing*. He heard knuckle-cracking pops as each digit stretched until they looked twice their normal length. His mother's nails became talons, cruel and sharp.

Then, as Ballard lay moaning on the rug in front of the fireplace, Mercy began to chant.

'To-than-dek, par-than-dek, kan-than-dek . . . '

It was no language he had ever heard before, but the words made his skin crawl. He was so scared that he couldn't move, but stayed there, crouching beside the door, watching through the keyhole. His mother repeated the phrase, over and over, her voice becoming louder and louder. She slowly raised her un-natural hands, chanting all the time, until they were held high above her head. On the floor, Ballard was writhing, screaming, hands over his ears as if trying to block out the words. Lucas felt the ground begin to shake beneath his bare feet. He wanted to run, but something made him stay still. If he mother saw him now, if she heard him running away . . .

202

The furniture in the entrance hall began to rattle as if an earthquake was building below the mansion. Lucas could feel the tremor deep in his chest.

He heard a sound behind him and glanced over his shoulder, but the second his head was turned there came an almighty scream, so soaked in terror that Lucas was almost sick with fear. The living-room door snapped shut, but he could still hear the scream. It felt as if it would go on for ever but, as suddenly as it had began, it stopped. Just as quickly, the quake ceased. Silence fell.

Lucas tried to calm his frantic heart. Footsteps echoed from inside the living room. Scrambling to his feet, Lucas leaped behind one of the hallway's large chairs. Mercy threw open the door. Her lips were set in a line, and her eyes were still full of fury. She swept to the front door and flung it open, stepping out into the cold night. It slammed shut behind her with a resounding bang.

When it seemed safe, Lucas got up from his hiding place and moved slowly into the living room. It was empty. Ballard was nowhere to be seen. There was no other way out of the room, and Lucas had not seen him leave. Apart from that, everything seemed normal. Nothing had moved. The temperature was rising again, thanks to the fire crackling peacefully in the grate.

Lucas walked over and stared into the fire, trying to work out what had just happened. Something made him look up. There, on the old glass, were two large handprints, as if their owner had pressed his hands to the mirror.

Chapter Thirty-six

The Truth

Faye stared at Joe Crowley in shock. She, Jimmy and Liz were sitting beside the roaring campfire, Liz anxiously holding Jimmy's hand.

'Mercy Morrow?' Faye repeated. 'No way.'

Joe nodded. 'It's true. She's why we're here. And she's the one causing havoc in Winter Mill, not the bikers.'

'But you're the ones who are werewolves,' Faye pointed out, boldly. Her fear had lessened – sitting here, beside the fire, she didn't feel in danger. There was something about Joe that was reassuring, not scary. And as for Finn . . . Faye looked at him now, and couldn't imagine ever being afraid of him.

Joe took a clean cloth and a bowl, filling it with water from a pan that had been heating over the fire. Faye watched as he prepared to tend to his son's injuries, and something inside her trembled as she saw Finn wince in pain. She remembered that moment in the Old Mill, when even as a wolf, Faye had thought she had known what he was thinking.

'I can do that,' she found herself saying, standing up. 'You can tell us your story.'

Joe glanced up at her, then back at Finn, apparently reluctant. In the end, though, he stood, and held out the bowl of water and cloth.

'Are you sure you're ready to hear it?' the big biker asked.

'It's not pretty, and it won't be easy. But whatever Mercy has planned, we're going to need all the help we can get.' Joe glanced over her shoulder at Liz and Jimmy. 'And I'm beginning to think that means the three of you.'

Faye looked over to Liz, who was still holding on to Jimmy's hand. Her friend shrugged. 'Maybe knowing what's going on will let us help Jimmy,' Liz said, softly.

'We want to know,' Faye told Joe. 'After everything that's happened – everything we've seen . . . We need to know.'

The biker looked at her for another moment before nodding slowly. 'All right. In that case, I'm going to make some coffee and find you all some blankets. I think you'll need both.'

Joe disappeared into one of the tents as Faye knelt down beside Finn. He was bruised and bloodied, a nasty cut running from his shoulder to his chest.

'Aren't you scared of me?' Finn asked, gruffly, after a moment.

Faye shook her head, but found she couldn't quite manage to look him in the eye. 'Back there – I was, just a little,' she admitted. 'But that night in the woods – you told me I didn't need to be afraid with you around. And I . . . still believe you.'

Finn's neck still bore the burn mark where Ballard had pressed his silver knuckleduster hard against his flesh. Faye reached out, tracing her fingers over the edge of the damaged skin. Finn flinched slightly, and she jumped, pulling her hand back.

'Sorry,' she whispered. 'I—'

Finn grabbed her hand and held it, tightly. Faye looked at him for the first time, and felt her heart jump at the pain in his dark eyes.

206

'Don't be,' he told her, softly. 'Faye, I—' He trailed off, before starting again. 'You came after me. I can't believe you came after me. It was so dangerous, but – thank you.'

Faye looked at her fingers, tangled with his. Could she really have seen what she saw in that old building? The boy sitting before her now was so perfect, so ... beautiful, even. How could he have such an ugly creature inside him, ready to spring out at any moment?

She pulled her fingers away, gently, and dipped the cloth in the warm water before pressing it to his cut. Faye concentrated on what she was doing. Neither of them said anything, but she could feel Finn's heated gaze on her face.

'Why didn't you tell me?' Faye whispered, eventually. 'About ... About what you are?'

Finn shook his head. 'How could I? It's not the sort of thing that comes up in normal conversation. And ...'

He stopped. She looked up at him. 'And what?'

It was Finn's turn to reach out, and Faye held her breath as he lifted one finger to gently trace the curve of her jaw. Finn shook his head again. 'I didn't want you to know. With you ... I just wanted to be this me. Not ... some awful creature, something that would scare you, or disgust you.' He dropped his hand and looked away with a frown. 'I'm sorry.'

Faye watched the sadness on his face, and felt tears prick at her eyes. She blinked, and brushed her hand over his chest. Finn turned to look at her, and she tried to smile.

'I'm not disgusted,' she whispered. 'It's just ... going to take a bit of getting used to ...'

Finn's eyes grew even darker, and for a moment Faye thought he was going to say something else. But then the crunch of footsteps told them that his father was returning.

Joe handed out blankets and poured them coffee before

207

settling down beside them. Then he took a deep breath, and began to speak.

'My story begins about three hundred years ago,' he said, staring into the fire. 'My family were Romanies, from eastern Europe. We lived on the road, travelling from place to place. I've always been an expert with wood – I can carve it, whittle it, build with it.' He looked at his son. 'It's one of the good things that Finn had inherited from me. In those days, wherever we went, townsfolk would flock to buy my furniture or to ask me to repair their houses for winter. That's how I met Mercy Morrow. She came to my caravan. She'd heard I could carve the likeness of any animal, and she wanted a figure of a wolf.' Joe looked down at his huge black boots. 'She was the most beautiful woman I had ever seen in my life. She still is. And her beauty is a curse on all mankind.'

Faye stared at Joe in disbelief. 'Three hundred years ago?' She looked at Finn, who didn't meet her eye. If his dad was three hundred, what did that make him? Faye turned back to Joe, not sure she believed what he'd said. Sure, his face was lined, but he didn't look much older than her dad. Joe's eyes, though ... now that Faye looked at them, they seemed older than the rest of his face, somehow. They looked as if they had witnessed much, but told nothing.

'I fell in love with her,' Joe continued slowly. 'Right there and then. That was my first mistake. My second was to follow her home, and enter her house.'

'What happened?' asked Liz, who had been listening, wide-eyed.

The biker gave a grim smile. 'She enchanted me. Not just me, but my family. Mercy Morrow enslaved us all, taking part of our humanity and replacing it with the wolf. We became part-men, part-beast, bound to do her will and to act as she ordered.

Those were terrible years of bloodshed, hunger and pain.'

'I don't understand,' said Liz. 'Why did Mercy want you as werewolves? What did she want you to do?'

'We hunted for her,' Joe sighed. 'We were part of her wolf-pack – I was, in fact, the leader. You see, Mercy Morrow is far older than the oldest thing you can imagine. She has stalked the countries of the world for thousands of years, always keeping her beautiful human form, and she has no intention of passing on. She and her kind spent all their time finding ways of cheating death and extending their youth and beauty.'

'But how?' asked Faye. 'How does turning people into wolves do that?' She looked over to Jimmy, who was trying to stay alert as Joe spoke. 'Is that what they were trying to do to Jimmy?'

'There is an . . . underworld,' Joe explained. 'It's called Annwn. It is full of everything you fear most – of creatures ancient, eternal and cruel. Nothing can defeat them – all we can hope is that none of us or the ones we love end up in their domain. Here, on Earth, we are lucky – they cannot survive in our world. But there, in Annwn, they are full of power. Mercy and her kin found a way of communicating with them.'

'But why?' Faye asked.

'Because they knew that they could give the inhabitants of Annwn what they wanted – human emotion. Human life. Imagine never being able to eat, ever, and then tasting something for the first time. Wouldn't you want more? That's what Mercy's people did,' said Joe. 'They introduced the evil spirits of Annwn to the idea of humanity, and they craved more. So much more, in fact, that they would take any they could get, though the purer and rarer the emotion, the more they would pay. Fear they enjoy – that's what the hunt is for, to terrify the prey. But love – true, eternal, unselfish love – that's one of the rarest emotions there is. Nothing can simulate it. No one can make someone else love another person, not with potions or trickery or even with the strongest magic. True love, real love, grows suddenly, unasked for and unexpected. That' – the biker added quietly – 'is what Mercy took from me. And in return, Annwn keeps her young and beautiful.'

Faye stared into the fire, trying to take it all in. It just seemed too fantastical to be true, and yet Finn's father seemed deadly serious. She finished washing the blood from Finn's chest and picked up her tin mug of coffee, wrapping her fingers around the heat as she tried to make sense of it all.

'But you're not under her spell any more?' Faye frowned, wondering whether they could really trust Joe. He seemed sincere, and she wanted to . . . but he was a werewolf, after all. But then, so was Finn, and Faye knew, now, that she could trust him with her life, if she needed to. Finn must have got that from somewhere, mustn't he?

Joe took a mouthful of coffee, shaking his head. 'Some of my brothers loved the hunt. They embraced the wolf, wholly. I never did. I hated making others feel fear, and maybe that allowed me to keep a tiny piece of my humanity. That and the fact that for the first time in a long, long time, Mercy felt love for someone other than herself. For me.'

'Mercy was in love with you?' Liz asked.

He nodded, glancing away. 'I don't know why, but yes. I became more than just another person to be used. She trusted me. And then . . . then something changed. I could work against her, just a little. I suppose her love for me lessened her grip on my soul. Real love cannot help but be selfless, after all. So I began to learn, as much as I could, about her magic, about how she bargained with Annwn.'

'Why?' Liz asked. 'What good did that do you?'

'It meant I knew what to offer them. Something greater than anything Mercy's kind had exchanged before. And that was enough to free me – and those that wanted to come with me – from the curse.' He sighed. 'We knew it would be difficult, but we craved freedom – to live our lives as best we could under our own hand, despite the creatures she had made us. And to do no more harm to the innocent.'

Faye felt a cold shiver rattle its way down her spine. 'What did you give them?' she asked, eyes fixed on Joe's face. 'What did you give Annwn?'

Joe smiled, grimly. 'All of Mercy's kin,' he said, softly. 'I twisted one of her bargains, just a little. The spirits of Annwn grasped as many of her family as they could, and dragged them down into Annwn. I hid, and listened to the screams. They were the most terrified sounds you could ever imagine. Mercy survived, but alone. And in return Annwn freed me of her power. Though they didn't take the wolf from me. Or from any of us.'

'So . . . so Mercy's the only one of her kind left?' Faye asked.

'Yes.' It was Finn that spoke this time, the flickering fire casting long shadows across his face. 'But she's determined to get her family back.'

'She keeps trying,' Joe agreed. 'She keeps finding different bargains to make with Annwn. So we track and follow her, wherever she goes, trying to save as many as we can.'

'One day we'll find a way to stop her, once and for all,' Finn muttered.

'Yes,' said Joe, seriously. 'And that day is almost upon us. She's planning something – something bigger than ever before. We must stop her, or we will all pay the price.'

Chapter Thirty-seven

Man in the Mirror

Lucas stared at the handprints on the mirror and realized with horror that they were pressed to the inside of the glass, not the outside. They were too big to have been left by Mercy – they were far more likely to be Ballard's. But he was nowhere to be seen. The room was empty, the house silent except for the crackle of the fire in the grate.

He stepped closer to the reflective surface, gazing into its depths. For a moment Lucas felt as if he were falling from a great height, down, down, down, deeper and deeper into the mirror. He reached out to steady himself, gripping the edges of the ancient frame. The feel of the carved wood jolted him back to earth, and Lucas blinked. He saw something skitter along the edge of the mirror, spider-like, a motion that made his skin crawl.

Suddenly, Ballard's face was in front of him. Lucas leaped backwards, terrified. Ballard was inside the mirror. His eyes were baleful, horrified. He looked this way and that, searching for something.

'Help me,' Ballard begged, his eyes finding Lucas, his voice distant and pleading. 'Please. Let me out. Let me out . . .'

'I don't . . . what . . . I can't . . .' Lucas stammered, shaking.

'Please,' Ballard said again. 'It's so cold, so cold . . . I've learned my lesson. I've been here so long . . . Too long . . . it feels like for ever.'

'Ballard,' Lucas said, trying to shake off his fear. 'Ballard, I don't know how to help you. I don't know what's happening . . .'

'Mercy,' whispered Ballard, his figure wavering in the reflection. 'My lady can help me. She . . . she can release me . . . Please . . . So cold . . . So—'

Ballard's words melted into an unearthly scream, his mouth stretching wide in fear as the sound went on and on. Lucas stumbled backwards as from even deeper inside the mirror, a gnarled arm reached out of a well of deep blackness. Its bony fingers reached up to grab Ballard and the man screamed again as he tried to twist out of its grasp.

Lucas watched in horror as the arm dragged Ballard down into the deepest recesses of the mirror; into a featureless, swirling void. Ballard shrank until he was nothing but a tiny, writhing figure. And then, with a final echoing scream, he was gone.

Lucas stood, breathing hard, staring at the vacant mirror. His own trembling face looked back, pale and wide-eyed.

Then, he made up his mind. Whatever his mother was, whatever she had done – he had to know. Lucas had no idea when she would return, but right now, the house was empty. If he was to act, it must be this instant.

The door to his mother's bedroom was unlocked, as Lucas knew it would be. Mercy never locked her doors – she didn't believe she needed to, and before now, Lucas would never have dreamed of ransacking his mother's private rooms. But now, his fear had been replaced by anger and a desperate need to know. Somehow, Lucas realized he was closer to the truth about his life than he had ever been before. All the constant moving

214

around, the strange companions, the everlasting money that Mercy never seemed to earn . . .

He pushed open the door. His mother's room was opulent, decorated in rich colours and expensive fabrics. Across the huge four-poster bed and on the floor lay furs – to Lucas, they looked real.

In the bay window was a desk. It was old – another piece of furniture that Lucas remembered from his childhood. It had followed them around like the mirror, but he could never remember seeing inside it. Its surface was a large slab of deeply patterned wood and beneath this were four drawers with worn, ornate handles. Lucas tried them all in turn, but they were locked.

He rummaged around in the papers on top of the desk, but there was no sign of a key. Looking around quickly, he saw his mom's make-up dresser on the other side of the room. What he needed was a nail file, and sure enough, his mom had several.

Sliding the thin blade into the first lock, Lucas twisted it hard. He heard a soft 'pop' as the metal sheared, and then the drawer sprang open. He pulled it out, looking through the objects his mother had locked away. There was nothing significant – what looked like some dried flowers, a lock of hair and two old books. Lucas flicked through these, but found nothing interesting inside. They were old and fragile, printed roughly in a language he didn't recognize, and someone had signed both at the front. He moved on to the next drawer, finding more of the same, and then the third.

His hands froze on an old, yellowed envelope, stuffed with photographs. Lucas pulled them out, settling on the edge of his mother's chair and laying them, one by one, on the desk in front of him. The photographs were all old – some of them looked like they were from the dawn of photography. The people in them wore elaborate gowns and suits, bowties and top hats. Some of them were so old it was hard to make out the people's faces. Lucas leaned close, tracing his eyes over the brown images. He wondered if these were relations of his, like a photographic family tree. And then he realized something.

He would swear that his mother was in every single one of these pictures.

Her face stared serenely from each image – in some, she was with a single other person, usually a good-looking guy. In others, she was with a group of people, most of whom seemed to be looking at her, adoringly.

Lucas sat back, his heart and mind racing. How could these old photographs feature his mother, who couldn't be more than forty? She looked exactly the same in each picture. That just wasn't possible. And why did she have them at all? He thought back to that screwed-up image of Faye he'd found, tucked away in that old jacket.

'They've got to be fakes,' Lucas muttered to himself. 'Digital manipulations. Maybe . . . maybe they were taken at one of those funfairs where you can dress up.'

But even as he said it to himself, Lucas didn't believe it. There was something horribly real about each picture, from the colour and the fading to the ragged, dog-eared edges. He pulled out another one, and held it up to the light. His mother stood in the background, a cold smile frozen onto her hard, beautiful face. But it wasn't her that had caught his attention. Beside her, tranquil, equally beautiful, was another girl. He'd seen her before, and he'd thought about her often . . .

It was Faye McCarron. It had to be – it couldn't be anyone else. But she was dressed in old clothing again, a high-necked lace collar and dark, full-length dress, and the photograph was as old as the others. And she was standing with his mother.

216

Lucas stared at it, growing colder and colder. None of this made sense, but now at least he knew who could help him. Shoving the rest of the photographs back in the drawer he slammed it shut.

If Faye was in the picture, she must know what was going on.

Chapter Thirty-eight

Secrets

'But how does it work?' Liz asked, looking at Jimmy's pale face as she held his hand. 'I mean, I get the bargaining thing. But how does Mercy contact Annwn without having to go there herself?'

Joe stood, stretching as he finished the last of his coffee. 'She has the Black Mirror, the oldest in the world. She's owned it for centuries. It was taken from an ancient castle in the eastern-most part of Romania. Mercy discovered that it was a connection to Annwn – a passageway between the two worlds.'

'It's why the weather's been so cold around Winter Mill since she arrived,' Finn added quietly. 'The Black Mirror doesn't just suck in whatever offering Mercy gives it. It takes whatever energy it can get. It's like a sinkhole, leading to Annwn. And right now, she's drawing more power than she ever has before. This is the worst I've ever seen it.'

'Doesn't that make it incredibly dangerous?' Faye asked.

'Oh yes,' said Joe. 'Not even Mercy can control the Black Mirror. All she can do is possess and use it. Long ago her kin developed complicated methods of their own to limit the physical contact they have with both the victims and the mirror.'

Liz felt herself shudder. Just a couple of days ago she'd thought Mercy and Lucas Morrow were the most perfect two people she'd ever seen. Now every time she thought about either of them, it felt as if someone was walking on her grave.

'What are we going to do?' she asked. 'If she's so powerful, what can we do to stop her?'

Joe smiled. 'We're working on it. Somehow, there's a way, and we'll find it.'

She nodded, looking down at Jimmy and biting her lip. He seemed so pale. 'What about Jimmy? What's happened to him?'

'He got caught up in one of her hunts,' Joe explained. 'I'm hoping we stopped them must in time.'

'What do you mean, just in time?'

Joe sighed. 'Usually, when a hunt attacks it is to feed, or to gather new members. We stopped them from feeding, but . . .'

Liz put a hand over her mouth in horror. 'Oh my god. So he *is* going to turn into a werewolf?'

'That's what we're trying to stop,' Finn told her, gently. 'It's looking good so far, but he does still have some of the wolf in him. That's why he looks so bad right now.'

Liz felt her eyes filling with tears as she looked down at Jimmy. 'Are you sure we shouldn't take him to hospital? What did he mean, when he said they could all be hers by now?'

'Mercy doesn't just take victims outright,' Finn explained. 'She uses her powers to control them, too. She enchants people – controls them by affecting their minds, their judgement. Then she can use other mirrors, standard ones, to give them instructions, or to nudge their thinking in whatever direction she wants.' He shrugged. 'It's amazing how many mirrors you look in every day without realizing.'

Liz looked at Faye. Her friend was shaking her head, and Liz knew exactly what she was thinking. That all of this was crazy, unbelievable. And yet, after everything both of them had seen recently, how could it not be true? She remembered the night of

Candi's party. Had Liz been quite . . . herself? She reached out a hand and touched Faye's. Faye turned to look at her, lacing her fingers through Liz's and squeezing her hand gently.

'Pretty wild, huh?' Liz said.

Faye nodded. 'Oh, yeah.'

'What are you going to do?'

'I'm going to help them,' Faye told her, firmly. 'Mercy has to be stopped, and if there's no one else to do it . . .'

Liz nodded. 'You're right. We have to help them.' She looked at Joe. 'You will look after Jimmy, won't you?'

The big biker nodded. 'Of course we will. And you too, Liz.'

'Me?'

Joe glanced at Finn, who nodded. 'We think your dad – Sergeant Wilson – may have been turned by Mercy,' Joe explained, quietly. 'She always targets the most important people in town as soon as she arrives. I'm sorry. I think it'll be safer if you stay here, with us, at least right now.'

'But . . . but what about my mom?' Liz asked, in a whisper. 'She – she's still there, with him . . .'

Joe nodded. 'Don't worry. She's not a threat to Mercy, so she'll be safe enough. But Mercy must know by now that you helped Finn, Liz. That makes you a target. In fact, your mom will be safer with you out of the way.'

Liz nodded, feeling a numbness in her chest, spreading from her heart. She blinked, tears blurring her vision. 'He has been acting very strangely recently. And – and we've got this big mirror. In the living room. I found him, a week or so ago, just standing in front of it. Staring.'

Joe sighed. 'Had he spent any time with Mercy before that?'

Liz felt the tears slide down her face, and nodded again. 'Yes. He'd been to see her, earlier that day.'

She felt Jimmy's hand move, and looked down to see that his

eyes were open. He was watching her with concern, and offered a smile. 'Don't worry,' he said, hoarsely. 'They'll help him if they can. And I'll look after you while you're here. Promise.'

Liz smiled back, and nodded, trying to be brave. 'OK,' she whispered. 'OK, Jimmy. I'll stay right here.'

Faye watched Liz and Jimmy. For a second, they both seemed oblivious to everything else around them, and Faye felt a pang of loneliness. She wished she had someone like that, someone that could make the rest of the world and all its troubles fade away, if only for a moment.

'You should go home though, Faye,' said Finn's soft voice, behind her. 'Pam will be worried.'

She tore her gaze away from her friends and stood up, nodding. 'Yeah, you're right.'

'I'll take you,' said Joe, getting to his feet. 'It won't take long.'

'No, Dad, it's fine – I'll go.' Finn got up. He looked a little stiff, but otherwise OK.

Joe shook his head. 'I don't think that's a good idea, Finn. You need to recover – that was quite a beating you took.'

'I'm fine. It's just a few scratches.'

'Even so, I don't think—'

'Dad,' Finn interrupted. His voice was calm and low, but brooked no argument. 'I am taking Faye home. I won't be long.'

Joe narrowed his eyes and looked at Finn for a second, before nodding. 'All right. Just be careful. Understand?'

Faye caught a look between Finn and his father that suggested Joe was talking about more than just the journey into town, but she didn't know what it meant.

She went to Liz, and the two girls hugged tightly. Faye still didn't like the idea of leaving her best friend alone with these

. . . werewolves. She couldn't even believe she was using that word!

'Are you sure you're going to be OK, staying here?' Faye asked Liz in a low voice.

Liz nodded. 'Really, Faye, I think we have to trust them. And I feel safe with Joe. Don't you with Finn?'

Faye smiled. 'Yeah. Yeah, I do.'

She knelt down to give Jimmy a gentle hug while Finn got her a helmet ready.

Her friend still looked weak, but less pale than a few hours earlier. Though that may have had something to do with the way Liz was insisting on holding his hand.

'I'm relying on you to take care of her, you know,' she whispered. Jimmy grinned back, nodding.

Faye was tired, but once she was on the back of Finn's bike, her arms wrapped around his waist, exhilaration took over. They careered through the woods, bumping smoothly onto the road in moments. Below them, the lights of Winter Mill shone brightly, and Faye wondered how something so terrible could be happening here, in her peaceful little town.

Finn slowed as he reached the town centre, careful not to wake any of the inhabitants as he turned towards McCarron's Bookstore. Faye could see a light burning upstairs, and hoped that Aunt Pam hadn't stayed up, waiting for her and worrying.

They slid to a stop, the engine idling as Faye swung her leg over the bike and jumped off. Finn watched as she pulled off her crash helmet. She handed it to him with a smile, but he didn't return the gesture. He was staring at her again, in that way he had – like he had the very first time they'd met, in the mall, and every other time they had seen each other, too. Her heart turned over, but it also ached. There was something heart-breakingly sad in Finn's gaze. It didn't ease the loneliness that

223

Faye was feeling – it just made it worse. He hadn't tried to kiss her again, and it didn't look like he was going to now. He was just looking at her, as if trying to sear every detail of her face into his mind. Faye felt something inside her tugging her towards him, a tie she couldn't cut alone.

'Don't,' she whispered. 'Please.'

'Don't what?'

'Don't look at me like that. You're always staring at me, as if – I don't know – as if you're seeing more than me. I can't—'

Finn looked away sharply. 'I'm sorry. I just . . . it's difficult. Every time I look at you . . .' He tailed off, shaking his head. 'Never mind.'

'No – I want to know. Tell me.'

He shook his head, as if trying to find the words. 'Every time I look at you, it's like seeing the picture of someone I haven't seen for a very, very long time,' he said, so softly that Faye had to lean forwards to hear him. They were very close, and his breath danced along her cheek as he spoke. 'Except, you're not just a picture. You're real. You're real, Faye, you're right there, and you look so much like—'

Faye realized she'd been holding her breath as he spoke. Their lips were so close, they were almost touching, and all she needed to do was move in, just a fraction, and they would meet. 'Like who?' she whispered, half wanting to know, the rest of her wanting him to shut up and kiss her.

Finn hesitated. 'Someone I . . . Someone I cared about. A lot. She—' He stopped again, leaning back suddenly and squaring his shoulders. 'Sorry. I . . . I didn't mean to . . . You should get inside, where it's warm.'

Before Faye could say anything, he kicked the engine into gear. The noise of the bike filled the quiet air as Finn roared off into the night.

224

'Wait!' Faye called after him. 'Wait, I—'

It was no good. He'd already gone. Faye stared after Finn for a few moments. The adrenaline of the bike ride and their half-conversation drained away suddenly, leaving her exhausted. Pulling out her keys, she moved to the shop door and unlocked it, rubbing a hand over her tired eyes as she stepped inside.

But as she went to shut it behind her, a foot pushed into the gap, forcing it open.

Chapter Thirty-nine

Sleepover

It was Lucas. He was breathing hard, as if he'd been running, and he looked scared. Faye tried to ram the door shut, but he wouldn't move. Faye was terrified – after everything she'd just learned about his family, about how dangerous his mother was . . . and now he was here.

'Go away!' Faye hissed, looking around frantically for something that might work as a weapon.

'I've got to talk to you!' Lucas begged. 'Please, Faye. Please let me in.'

'I don't want to talk to you,' she told him, trying again to shut the door.

'Faye . . . don't . . .'

They struggled, the door between them, but Lucas was far stronger. He pushed hard, forcing Faye back, until the gap was big enough for him to step through. The door slammed shut after him. Faye backed away, putting distance between her and Lucas.

'Get out,' she said, petrified now, wishing desperately that her dad were here to help her. 'You're not welcome here. You . . . whatever you are.'

A flicker of confusion, followed by a flash of anger, passed over Lucas's face. 'What do you mean?' He asked.

'I know what you are,' Faye said, trying to keep the tremor

out of her voice. 'You, and your evil mother. I know what you do to people. What you've done.'

'What do you know about my mother? Or perhaps I should ask, how long have you known her, Faye?'

It was Faye's turn to be confused. 'What? What are you talking about?' She suddenly realized how pale Lucas was. He looked scared, his hands shaking slightly.

Lucas snatched something from his pocket, holding it up for her to see. It was an old photograph, lined and creased.

'This is you,' he said, his voice full of accusation. 'This is you, and I want to know who you are and what this was doing in my mother's desk drawer.'

Faye stared at the picture in Lucas's trembling hand. She felt the colour draining from her face, like liquid being poured from a bottle. It wasn't her. It couldn't be her. And yet . . . and yet it looked like her. It looked exactly like her. She shook her head in incomprehension.

'This is you,' Lucas said again, taking a step forwards. 'I know it is. And you're obviously into the same kind of thing my mother is – so explain it to me. What's going on? What – what is that mirror thing?'

The mention of the mirror snapped Faye back to the present. She looked up at Lucas, shocked. 'I'm nothing to do with your mother! How could you think that? How could you think that I would do . . . that . . . to people? How could you?' she spat, furious and horrified in equal measure. 'How could you think I would be that evil?'

There was a second of silence as they both stared at each other. Then something crumbled in Lucas's eyes. He blinked, looking away, and put one hand up to his face.

'This is a nightmare,' he muttered. 'I don't know where to go. I don't have anyone I can trust. I don't know what's happening. Everything ... everything's falling apart. And I don't know why.'

Faye watched him with a frown. He wasn't acting the way someone with unlimited, ancient power should. Lucas seemed lost, unsure of himself.

At her silence, Lucas shook his head again, turning back to face her but not looking her in the eye. 'Look,' he said. 'I thought – I thought we were getting to be friends. Weren't we? And ... and I've got to find out what's going on. My mother – she's ... doing something. I don't know what it is, but I think it's why we came here, and I know it's not good. And this is the second picture of you that I've found in our house, Faye. That's got to mean something, hasn't it?'

Faye still didn't say anything. Was this a trick? Had Mercy sent him? Or was this real, and Lucas really didn't have any idea what was going on?

'I like you, Flash,' Lucas continued, quieter now. 'You're the only one who hasn't been interested in our money, or my mother. And ... and you're cute.'

At that, Faye felt the colour rush back to her cheeks with a vengeance. She looked away as Lucas carried on talking, feeling her heart stutter just as it had when their hands had touched as Lucas helped pick up her scattered books. Faye didn't know why he had this effect on her – but she did know that it was nice to have someone be honest about how they were feeling for a change. Unlike Finn, who made every nerve in her body buzz with excitement, but always seemed to be leaving her standing on her own.

'If you know what's going on, please tell me,' he begged. 'I don't have anyone else to ask. Faye, I don't even have anywhere else to go.'

She stared at him for another moment. Then she nodded,

slowly. 'Yeah,' Faye said, with a slight smile, 'you wouldn't believe the day I've had, either. Why don't we make some hot chocolate? Then we can talk, OK?'

Lucas sat at the McCarrons' kitchen table, trying to take in everything that Faye had just told him. He stared at the mug in his hand, watching the thick hot chocolate swirl gently inside. He wished it was hot enough to burn him – anything to take his mind off what she had asked him to acknowledge.

Across the table, he felt Faye's eyes watching him. 'I know it's hard to believe,' she said, softly. 'And I'm sorry. But I swear it's true, Lucas.'

After a moment he nodded, and took a swallow of his drink even though he could no longer really taste it. The sweet chocolate turned bitter in his mouth.

'It's not really that it's hard to believe,' he muttered. 'I just don't . . . don't want to believe it. She's my mom. She . . .'

He trailed off, and was surprised to feel Faye's fingers brushing over his own, where they were bunched on the table between them. Lucas looked up, finding her eyes full of sympathy, and thought again about how pretty she was.

'I'm sorry,' he said.

'What for?' she asked, removing her hand.

He shrugged. 'For having an evil mother. For not realizing it sooner . . . And, I guess, for fighting Finn, earlier. If he's a good guy in all this, I mean. Despite the weird werewolf stuff.'

Faye smiled. 'Well, the first two things really aren't your fault. And the third . . . it's hard to know what Finn's thinking. He doesn't say much. And the bikers all think you're part of Mercy's circle, so he was as willing to fight you as you were to fight him. So I don't think you need to apologize for that. You were amazing, by the way.'

Lucas looked up, not understanding what she meant.

'At the Battle of the Bands, I mean,' Faye clarified. 'The way you sang, and played that guitar. You're really, really talented, Lucas.'

He smiled. 'Thanks. Music means a lot to me. And I've had a lot of time to practise. Even though Mom's always taken me everywhere with her . . . I guess I've always spent most of my time alone.'

Faye nodded. 'I'm sorry.'

Lucas laughed, though it sounded harsher than he really intended. 'Don't be. After all, if she'd been more interested in me, maybe I'd be as evil as she is by now.'

'I don't believe that,' Faye said, softly. 'You're a good person, Lucas. Will you help us?'

'Help you with what?'

'I don't know,' Faye admitted, with a sigh. 'Joe's determined to stop whatever she's planning. And I think we – and the bikers – will need all the help we can get. Whatever that turns out to be.'

Lucas smiled, shrugging slightly. 'Hey. If it helps you out, Flash . . . anything. OK?'

He was pleased to see a faint blush tint her cheeks again, and had to stop himself reaching out to brush her hair out of her eyes. There was just something about her . . .

'Do you want to stay here tonight?'

He blinked. 'Uh . . .' Lucas was surprised, and hesitated – not because he didn't want to stay, but because he was suddenly afraid of what his mother would do when she found out where he was.

'There's a couch downstairs,' Faye added, in a rush, her blush deepening. 'It's really old, but it's comfortable. Then tomorrow, we can work out what to do. You should probably meet Joe and the others.'

231

Lucas recovered himself quickly. 'Right. Got you. Yes – thanks. The couch will be great.'

He rinsed off their mugs as quietly as possible while Faye got spare bedding together. She showed him where the couch was, anxious about making him as comfortable as possible. Lucas smiled as she bustled around. He couldn't remember the last time he felt . . . cared for. It was a good feeling.

'Thanks,' he said again, when Faye finally stopped fussing. 'For everything, Faye. I mean it. Without you . . .'

They were standing quite close together. She shook her head. 'You're welcome. I'm sorry . . . well, about everything, really.'

Lucas nodded, not really knowing what to say. They stared at each other for another moment, until he couldn't help but reach out and push a strand of hair out of her eyes, running his fingertips over her forehead and down her cheek. Her skin was warm . . .

Faye jumped at his touch, catching her breath. 'I . . . I'll say goodnight then.'

He smiled. 'Goodnight, then.'

Lucas watched as Faye fled to the door. Just before she went up the stairs, she glanced back to look at him.

It was dark outside McCarron's bookstore, the street full of deep shadows. Standing on the sidewalk opposite, Mercy Morrow watched through the lit window as her son pulled down the shop's blinds. Her face was creased in fury, her eyes full of anger. Stretching out her hand, she found the railing of the house behind her. Her knuckles burned white with cold as her fingers gripped it, harder and harder, tighter and tighter . . .

There was the sound of screaming metal and a loud crack as the rail turned to ice.

Chapter Forty

Healing

Finn made his way back to the camp, kicking himself. His dad was right – he shouldn't be alone with Faye . . . when he was, she was all that he could see, and all that he wanted. But it wasn't that easy – for him, it was never going to be that easy, and spending time with her just made everything worse. His heart beat a fast, painful rhythm as he remembered how close they'd been, and how warm her breath was as it floated across his cheek. And despite his best intentions, he kept hearing a small, insistent voice at the back of his mind.

She knows, it whispered, as he tried to silence it. *She knows what you are, and she still . . .*

Finn shook his head, pushing the thought away.

The other bikers were out on patrol when he got back to camp. They'd called in to report that there was no sign of Ballard anywhere – he must have gone back to the mansion before they'd had a chance to catch him. They thought there was a good chance there would be another hunt, though, so they were staying on alert.

'I'm going to go out and join them,' his dad said, as they chatted quietly beside the still-burning fire. 'I was just waiting for you to get back. I don't want to leave these two here alone.'

Finn looked over his dad's shoulder, to the tent where Jimmy still lay. Beside him, curled up under a thick blanket, was

233

Liz. They were both fast asleep, Liz with one arm flung out across Jimmy's chest.

'How's he doing?' Finn asked, softly. 'Do you think we managed to stop it in time?'

Joe shrugged. 'I'm hopeful. He's a stronger kid than he looks. There might be some lasting side effects – but I don't think a full wolf will rise in him.'

Finn found himself relieved. He'd known none of these people long, but he cared about all of them. They hadn't asked for any of this, and he was determined to do everything he could to keep as many of them safe as possible.

'Will you be all right here?' Joe asked, pulling on his jacket as he prepared to go out on patrol.

He nodded. 'I'll be fine. You go.'

In truth, Finn was happy to see his father leave. He wanted some time alone after his ride with Faye. He watched Joe roll out on his bike and then pulled over one of the old camp chairs they'd brought with them. Pouring himself a coffee from the pot the bikers always kept brewing, he sat and stared into the fire, trying to calm his scattered emotions, trying to work out what he should do. Finn prided himself on always doing the right thing – or at least, trying to. He'd seen what harm powerful people could do if they used that power in the wrong way. He never wanted to be like that. He never wanted to hurt anyone, especially not someone like Faye.

He rubbed a hand over his face. The thing was that trying never to hurt anyone else usually ended up with him being the one that was hurt. And right now, not being with Faye, even if it was the right thing to do – well, that hurt him more than anything had for a long, long time.

'Are you thinking about Faye?'

The quiet voice made him jump. Finn looked up to see

234

Jimmy standing over him, looking more than a little shaky.

'Hey!' he said, standing up himself. 'You shouldn't be up!'

Jimmy waved his concern away. 'I'm fine. Feeling better all the time.'

Finn pulled up another chair and Jimmy sank into it gratefully. 'I've seen the way you look at her,' he said, quietly, as Finn sat back down. 'Have you told her?'

Finn shifted uncomfortably in his seat. 'Told her what?'

Jimmy raised a knowing eyebrow. 'You know what I mean.'

He took a mouthful of his coffee and shrugged. 'It's not that simple,' Finn muttered.

Jimmy nodded. 'The centuries-old werewolf thing is a bummer.'

Finn laughed under his breath. 'Yeah, you could say that.'

'I've known Faye my whole life,' Jimmy said. 'And she's been through a lot – her mom dying, her dad being away most of the time. And she's always managed to deal with it. She'll deal with all this, too. And what you are.'

Finn finished his coffee and put his mug on the ground, leaning forwards to rest his elbows on his knees. 'Maybe,' he said softly. 'But she deserves better.'

He watched Jimmy glance back towards Liz, who was still fast asleep. 'Funny,' he muttered. 'I was thinking the same thing earlier.'

'You know what?' Finn said, realizing something. 'You haven't stuttered for the whole of this conversation.'

Jimmy looked back at him, surprised. 'You're right. I don't even feel like I'm going to stutter.'

'How do you feel otherwise?'

'OK.' Jimmy shrugged. 'Kind of weak.'

Finn picked up his tin mug and played with it for a second. Then, without warning, he flicked it towards Jimmy, heading

235

straight for the boy's face. Quick as a flash, Jimmy brought his hand up, punching into the tin mug so hard that it almost plunged into the fire. Finn reached out, catching it before it reached the flames. He looked at the mug and grinned, holding it up for Jimmy to see. There was a shape in the metal – an imprint of Jimmy's knuckle.

'Let me see your leg,' Finn said, already knowing what he would find. Jimmy unwrapped his bandage to show the wound, which seemed to be healing. The black infection was beginning to disappear, replaced by new, healthy pink flesh. Finn smiled. 'I think you're going to be OK. Looks like you got the good bits of the wolf.'

Jimmy wrapped his leg back up again, grinning briefly before a serious expression settled on his face. 'And what about you?'

Finn looked away, into the fire. 'I'm fine,' he said. 'I'm always fine.'

Chapter Forty-one

Teamwork

Faye walked to school on Monday morning – she'd talked to Liz on her cellphone, and her friend had said she was going to go home to get a change of clothes and would meet Faye at Winter Mill High. Faye had been able to hear the tremor in Liz's voice as she talked about going home, but her friend had been adamant that she'd been fine going alone.

'It'll be quicker if it's just me,' Liz had said. 'I'll be in and out. Hopefully they won't even notice. As far as mom's concerned, I've been at your place all night.'

Still, Faye was relieved when she turned into the school's gate and saw Liz across the busy parking lot. Her friend started walking towards her, but then stopped dead. Faye wondered what had made her hesitate, and then realized that it was probably the fact that Lucas Morrow was walking beside her, bold as brass.

'Faye!' Liz hissed, shooting a horrified glance at Lucas. 'What on earth are you doing with him?'

Faye looked at Lucas, whose face fell. She'd been worried about him the night before. He had been anxious and troubled, even though he'd promised to help them. This morning, Lucas had seemed a little better – not happier, exactly, but more composed. He'd seemed more worried about having to borrow some of her dad's clothes – Lucas really hadn't been impressed

237

by the tweed slacks Aunt Pam had thoughtfully picked out for him. Liz's reaction wasn't what he needed right now.

'Don't worry, Liz,' she said, as her friend reached them.

Liz grabbed her sleeve, pulling her to one side. 'What do you mean, don't worry? Don't you remember what we've just found out? Lucas . . . he's . . . he's—'

'Nothing to do with what his mother's up to,' said Faye firmly, finishing Liz's sentence.

'And how do you know that?' Liz asked. 'Oh – let me guess. He told you so?'

'Liz, don't.'

'Don't what? Have you gone completely mad? After everything we saw yesterday, everything we learned?'

Faye sighed. 'Liz. Liz, just listen to me. Please? Just for minute.'

Liz shook her head and crossed her arms. But she set her lips in a straight line, raising an eyebrow as she waited for Faye to speak.

'Do you trust me?' Faye asked, looking her friend in the eye.

'What?'

'Come on, Liz. We've known each other since we were small. Do you trust me?'

Liz sighed. 'You know I do.'

'Then trust me, right now. I'm telling you, Liz, Lucas is OK. All right?'

They stared at each other for a moment, before Liz rolled her eyes and shrugged. 'Fine. But—'

'Look, we'll explain, I promise,' Faye interrupted. 'But it'll have to wait until recess or we'll be late for school. We can't do anything out of the ordinary right now.'

Liz shook her head. 'Forget school, Faye. Look around you. What do you see?'

Faye looked at the students in the parking lot, and saw what Liz meant. No one was talking. They were all just moving about, silently. It looked as if they were sleepwalking, except everyone's eyes were open. It was distinctly creepy, and it made Faye think of that weird moment in the Miller office with Ms Finch. It was also freezing, even colder than it had been just a few days previously. She shuddered.

'What's going on?' Faye asked. The school bell rang and all the students instantly turned towards the school's main doors.

'They look as if they're hypnotized, or something,' said Lucas, in a whisper.

'I think they are,' Liz whispered back. 'My dad's like this. I mean, he's talking, still . . . but it's not normal. And my mom . . . my mom's just sitting there, staring at the mirror. It's just like Joe said. Faye, I'm scared. What are we going to do?'

Faye watched as the last of the students disappeared into the school, leaving them alone in the schoolyard. 'We can't stay here,' she decided. 'Come on – we've got to go.'

Lucas looked around as the three of them walked the streets of Winter Mill. It obviously wasn't just the school kids who were affected. Everyone they passed seemed to be acting exactly the same.

'This is horrible,' Lucas muttered, as he watched a young woman mechanically wheeling a pushchair along the snowy street. 'What's happened to them?'

'Your mom, that's what,' Liz told him shortly.

'Are you sure?' Lucas asked, upset. 'I mean, look at them. It's the whole town! How can she have done this?'

'She controls people through mirrors,' Faye told him quietly.

'Mirrors?' Lucas repeated faintly, thinking about the image of Ballard, trapped behind his mother's favourite looking-glass.

'Yes. Joe says there's a really old one that she contacts Annwn through. The Black Mirror.'

Lucas stopped so suddenly that the two girls carried on walking for a few steps before they realized he wasn't with them.

Faye turned round with a frown. 'Lucas? What is it?'

'The Black Mirror?'

'Yes. That's what it's called. It's hundreds of years old.'

Lucas nodded. 'I've seen it. I think so, anyway. It's at the mansion. I . . . it's really weird. But I didn't . . . I didn't know . . .' He shook his head. 'Last night – I believed you, but I was still hoping. You know? And now . . .' he pointed at another one of Winter Mill's residents, walking past them, oblivious. 'Now it just seems . . . I don't know . . . real. And I don't want it to be.'

Faye walked towards him and rested one hand on his arm. 'I know, Lucas. I know.'

Liz walked over too, looking at him seriously. 'You really didn't know anything about this? About what your mom really is?'

Lucas shook his head. 'I swear I didn't.'

'And you're going to help us? No matter what?'

Lucas nodded. 'I promise.'

Liz took a deep breath. 'OK. Then you're going to help us get into my dad's home office.'

Liz's house looked exactly as it had when she'd left it that morning. The windows were dark, the curtains still pulled. When she pushed open the front door, everything was quiet. She glanced at where her dad's boots usually stood, but they weren't there. Good. That meant he wasn't home.

There was no sign of Liz's mom, either. Liz checked the house from top to bottom, but she was nowhere to be found.

'She must have gone to work after all,' Liz whispered, as she waved Faye and Lucas in. 'Come on. We'd better be really quick.'

'How are we going to get in?' Faye asked, once they stood outside the solid office door. 'We can't just force the door – he'll know straight away.'

'I've got a penknife,' Lucas told them. 'I can probably pick the lock.'

'You know how to pick locks?' Liz asked, shocked.

Lucas nodded, attempting a small smile. 'When I was a kid, Mom's bodyguard used to lock me in my room at night. Just don't tell anyone, OK?'

Sure enough, Lucas made short work of the door. It opened with a sharp click. All three of them looked round as if Mitch Wilson might have sneaked up on them while their backs were turned, but they were alone still. Lucas stepped back to let Liz push open the door.

'OK,' Faye said, looking around the neat room. There was desk with drawers, two filing cabinets and a bookcase. 'Where should we start?'

Lucas and Faye took a filing cabinet each, leaving the desk to Liz. They searched in silence for several minutes, the room filled with the sound of rustling paper.

'What are we looking for, exactly?' Lucas asked, opening another drawer. 'All I'm finding here are bills and receipts.'

'Same here,' said Faye. 'These all look like notes from old police cases.'

'I think we'll know it when we see it,' Liz said, softly. 'It's just going to be something out of the ordinary. Something about what's been happening around here, maybe – this all started with that body in the woods, so maybe that. Or something about his visit with Mercy? Maybe he wrote notes about that and it'll tell us something about how she—'

She stopped, and the other two looked up. 'Liz?' Faye asked. 'What is it?'

Liz straightened up from where she had been bent over one of the drawers. She turned slowly. In her hands was a small silver box. It was covered in intricate engraving.

'Have you seen that before?' Lucas asked.

Liz shook her head. 'Never.'

Faye took a deep breath and let it out, slowly. 'OK. Let's look inside.'

They knew they'd found what they were looking for the moment they opened the lid. Inside was a neatly curled piece of yellowed paper, tied with a red ribbon. Liz slid the ribbon off and gently unfurled the paper to reveal closely packed writing in a language none of them had ever seen before.

'What do you think it is?' Lucas asked.

Liz shook her head. 'No idea. It looks ancient. What do you think, Faye?'

Lucas and Liz looked up to see Faye staring into the box. Something else was in there, underneath the scroll. It was an engraved gold locket on a delicate chain. Slowly, Faye reached out and picked it up, running the chain through her fingers as she held it up to the light.

'Faye?' Liz asked. 'What's the matter?'

'I recognize this,' Faye whispered. 'I think . . . I think it was my mother's. My dad kept it after she died. I can remember seeing him look at it sometimes, when I was very young . . .'

She dropped it into her palm and gently opened the locket. Lucas and Liz crowded closer to look inside.

'Oh my god, Faye!' said Liz. 'That's you!'

Faye nodded, tears in her eyes. 'That was my fifteenth birthday. My dad took this picture – I wondered where it had gone. He must have put it in the locket … but … but why would it be here, in your dad's desk?'

Liz shook her head, still grasping the scroll. 'I don't know, Faye. But I think we should take the locket and this paper to Joe. Right now.'

Chapter Forty-two

Choosing Sides

'Are you sure this is a good idea?' Lucas asked as Liz parked her car in the snowy woods. 'I mean, from what you were saying, they think I'm the spawn of evil . . . they're not going to be too happy about me turning up unannounced, are they?'

'Technically,' said Liz, pulling on a warm coat, 'you *are* the spawn of evil . . .'

Lucas looked at her, unsure if she was joking or not. 'Gee, thanks, Liz.'

'Liz!' Faye hissed, 'don't say that!'

'. . . but Faye and I don't hold that against you,' Liz added, quickly. 'Much. Well, not any more, anyway. I'm sure the bikers will say the same. Especially if you're willing to help us.'

'I've already said I am,' Lucas muttered, trudging through the snow.

'Well, there you go then.'

Lucas sighed as he followed the two girls through the forest. Liz was being true to her word in trusting Faye, but it was clear she wasn't sure about him. Lucas couldn't blame her, really. If the situation had been reversed, he wouldn't have been happy hanging out with someone who, only a few hours earlier, he'd been told was pure evil. Catching up, Lucas fell in step beside her, nudging her arm in what he hoped was a friendly gesture.

245

'So, you found Jimmy then, huh?,' he asked, 'He is the geeky one, right?'

'He's not really that geeky,' said Liz.

'He is a bit.'

Liz tried to suppress a grin, but failed. 'Yeah. You're right. He is a bit.'

'I've never actually spoken to him before,' Lucas went on, teasing. 'So you'll probably have to translate. I don't speak geek.'

Liz shook her head. 'Oh, *mean*. And you're trying to convince me you're not the spawn of evil?'

'How am I doing so far?'

Liz stuck her tongue out at him, a sparkle in her eye. 'The jury's out.'

The camp, once they reached it, was empty apart from Jimmy. Lucas watched him get to his feet as they arrived, grinning at Liz.

'You're up,' she exclaimed, rushing to his side. 'Are you sure you should be walking?'

'I'm fine. Anyway, I need to exercise the leg, Joe said. They're all out on patrol. Well, except Finn – he went off to Winter Mill High. Didn't you see him there?'

'We weren't there that long,' Lucas told him.

Jimmy looked at him suspiciously. 'What are you doing here?'

'It's OK, Jimmy,' Faye began. 'He's going to help us. You see—'

There was the sudden sound of branches parting behind them, and Finn came striding into the camp's clearing.

'You?' he said angrily, spotting Lucas. 'How did you find this place?'

'Finn, it's OK,' Faye said, holding up her hands as Finn advanced on Lucas. 'He's with us.'

'What do you mean, he's with you?'

'We brought him here. He's got—'

Finn turned on her. 'You brought him here? After everything we told you?'

'Finn, he's not like Mercy,' Faye tried to explain, 'He's going to help us. Look, we need to see Joe. We found—'

'*Help us?*' Finn repeated in disbelief. 'He's not here to help us. He's fooled you, Faye. He's a spy. Deception – it's what his mother's so good at.'

'And how would you know?' Lucas retorted, equally angry. 'Or do you think you can sniff it out with your super-mutt senses?'

Finn narrowed his eyes. 'What did you say?'

'You heard me. The girls have told me what you are. It figures. I always thought I could smell wet dog whenever you were around.'

Finn growled, a sound that rattled deeper in his chest than anything a human could produce. He paced closer, and Lucas saw a yellow tint in his eyes.

'And what about you?' Finn snarled, teeth bared. 'What are you, half-breed? Let's face it, with a mother like yours, no one has any idea what you really are.'

Lucas stood his ground as Finn came closer. He couldn't back down, but he was scared. Finn's anger shimmered around him like a visible glow. His hair seemed to be standing up in sharp spikes and Lucas could see that all his muscles were primed, despite the bruises that peppered his shoulders.

'Finn,' he heard Faye say. 'Calm down. Please. Lucas isn't what you think, I promise. He's with us.'

Finn bared his teeth, growling again, and Lucas saw his canines, sharp, powerful – growing. Then he saw a flicker of amusement pass through Finn's amber eyes.

'You're scared, aren't you?' The half-wolf growled, close enough for only Lucas to hear. 'Well guess what? You haven't seen anything yet.'

Suddenly, someone shoved Lucas in the shoulder, hard. He was knocked sideways and stumbled, dropping to the ground at Finn's feet. In his place stood another biker – Joe, the leader that Faye and Liz had told him about. His arms were bare despite the snow, and Lucas could see the thick hair on them standing on end.

Joe was in Finn's face, so close that they were almost nose-to-nose. 'Back off, boy.'

Lucas pushed himself to his feet, shocked to see that Joe's eyes were glowing a feral yellow, too. They were standing face-to-face, shoulders bunched, hackles raised, about to fight. Lucas backed away, one step at a time.

'He's Mercy's kin,' Lucas heard Finn say. 'He's the enemy.'

'Mercy would never have let him come here alone,' growled Joe. 'Use your brain. If he's here, he's here for a reason.'

Lucas heard Faye's voice beside him. 'There is a reason,' she said, her voice shaky. 'We found this scroll, but we can't read it. We thought you might know what it is.'

Joe held out his hand, gesturing for the paper, but didn't drop Finn's gaze. Rage radiated from the two men in waves. Faye jumped forwards, dropping the aging scroll into the biker's large hand. He held it up, shifting his gaze from Finn's to the scroll briefly as he unfurled it. As their eye contact broke, Lucas saw Finn look at Faye, and he could almost see the spark that shot between them.

'Where did you get this?' Joe asked, after a moment.

'I – I found it in my father's study,' Liz spoke up, nervously. 'He'd locked it away. With a locket that had a photograph of Faye in it.'

Joe said nothing for a moment, contemplating the scroll. Then he placed a hand on Finn's chest.

'Lucas Morrow is not our enemy, Finn.'

'How can you know that?'

'Because this is the language of Annwn. It's definitely not something Mercy would give up willingly. Especially to her enemy.'

'It could be a trick!'

'It's not a trick.'

'It's not,' said Lucas, feeling he had to speak up. 'I swear.'

Finn turned towards him, teeth still bared. 'And what makes you think I'm going to trust you?'

'Finn,' Joe said, quietly. 'You're going to have to.'

'Why? What makes him so trustworthy, all of a sudden? You might have all been taken in, but I haven't. He's a snake, hiding in the grass, that's all.'

Joe shook his head. 'He's not. Finn ... this is something I should have told you years ago. Lucas ... Lucas is your brother.'

Chapter Forty-three

Betrayal

Finn felt Joe's words hit him in the chest like a jackhammer. He blinked, staring between his father and Lucas. He shook his head, not wanting to believe what he'd just heard.

'What are you talking about?'

'I told you your mother was one of Mercy's human servants that the wolves took with us when we escaped her control.'

'Right,' said Finn. 'You said . . . you said that the two of you fell in love once you were clear of Mercy's bonds . . . That you had planned to make a life together, with me . . .'

Joe nodded. 'But life on the road was hard, especially then, and that your mother sickened and died before you were even old enough to sit up on your own.'

'So what?' Finn asked, feeling the solid ground of his identity begin to shift. 'What are you saying now, Dad?'

'That it was a lie, Finn. It was all a lie. I'm sorry. There was no servant girl. Mercy did not keep human servants, back then.'

'Then who?' Finn whispered, glancing at Lucas. 'You can't be saying . . . You can't mean . . .'

'Mercy.'

Finn shut his eyes. 'No. No . . . No, I don't believe it.' Finn turned away, every nerve suddenly raw. He knew that everyone was looking at him, and he wanted to run, to get away. How could this be true? How could his father have lied to him like this? His father, whom he had trusted so completely. To lie to him – about something so huge, so important . . .

'I'm sorry,' Joe said, quietly, taking a step forwards. 'Finn, I'm sorry. I've tried to tell you so many times . . . but it never seemed right.'

Finn opened his eyes, looking at Joe in a new light. 'I don't understand,' he said. 'I just don't understand how . . .'

'She would have enslaved you, the way she had trapped the rest of us,' Joe said, 'so I took you when we fled. You were so small, but I couldn't leave you with her, Finn. I couldn't.'

Finn opened his eyes. He could feel the wolf-rage flowing in his veins, just below the surface of his human self. He wanted to run until there was nothing of Finn left, until there was only the wolf. He wanted to hunt something . . . anything.

'How could you not tell me?' he asked Joe, 'How could you drag me around, keeping this from me for so long?'

Joe shook his head. 'I'm sorry. I truly am. When you were younger, I thought it would be better – easier – than you know-ing the truth. And then the years passed . . . the centuries . . . and there was no way to tell you.'

'There was,' Finn said, in a voice so harsh it burned his own throat. 'You just preferred the lie.'

He looked around. They were all staring at him – Faye, Liz, Jimmy . . . and Lucas. They were all so young, so clueless. How could they possibly understand? There was a battle to fight, the battle – and now . . .

Finn had to get away. He had to be anywhere, anywhere but here. Turning, he strode towards his bike. He heard his father shout after him, but he didn't listen. Throwing his leg across the seat he kicked the engine into gear and skidded out of camp.

The last thing he heard was Faye's voice, calling for him to stop. And then the wind in his ears blasted everything away.

Faye ran forwards as Finn went to his bike. 'Finn! Wait!'

He didn't stop, the bike disappearing into the trees long before the sound of his engine faded from the air. She felt a strong hand on her arm.

'Let him go,' said Joe. His face was weary. 'He'll need time.' He raised the scroll. 'You did well, finding this. It could be exactly what we need.' Joe let go of her arm and sat down, intent on the ancient paper.

Faye turned back to the others, who were standing still, in shock. Jimmy's face had lost the colour it had regained.

'Jimmy?' Faye asked, 'Are you all right?'

'Yeah,' he said, faintly, trying to smile. 'I just . . . maybe I should sit down for a while.'

Faye watched as Liz slipped her arm through Jimmy's. 'Come on,' said her friend. 'It's too cold out here, anyway. You should be inside.'

'I'm OK,' Jimmy protested. 'I'm just a bit tired, that's all.'

'I'll come with you,' Liz told him. 'I'm cold out here, Jimmy.'

A look of concern crossed Jimmy's face, and he wrapped his arm round Liz's shoulders. 'I've got a spare blanket.'

Faye watched as her two friends walked slowly to Jimmy's shelter and disappeared into the tent. She couldn't help but smile. At least something good was coming out of all this chaos. Jimmy was good for Liz, although Faye thought her best friend was probably pretty good for Jimmy, too. They were a cute couple – and she knew Jimmy couldn't believe his luck. He'd liked Liz for so long, from afar, and now they were together. He was different, Faye realized – stronger, somehow, as if this experience had forced Jimmy to stand on his own two feet and he was enjoying what that felt like.

Faye looked around for Lucas, but he'd disappeared. One

minute he was there, standing silently as everything happened in front of him, and the next he had vanished. Faye saw footprints leading out of the clearing where he had been standing and into the unbroken snow beneath the forest canopy.

She followed them, and found him, standing beneath a huge cedar tree on the crest of a ridge. Beneath his feet, the land dropped away in a sharp precipice. Lucas had wrapped his arms around himself against the cold and was staring out at the sea of snow-bound trees. Faye felt her heart go out to him. He'd learned some pretty difficult things about his family over the past couple of days, and that had to be tough.

'Lucas?' Faye stopped a few yards away, suddenly aware that he probably wanted to be on his own. He didn't move, or say anything. Faye stepped to his side and looked out at the bleak landscape. The sky was heavy with more snow.

'It's funny,' Lucas said, after a few moments of silence. 'I always wondered what it would be like to have a brother. Trust me to end up with a moron like Finn.'

Despite herself, Faye smiled. 'He's a good guy, really, Lucas. He's just . . . passionate, I guess.'

Lucas turned to look at her. 'You're always defending him, you know that?'

Faye shrugged. 'He saved my life.'

Lucas laughed drily. 'Right. That's my brother: the hero. What does that make me? The family zero?'

Faye reached out, pulling Lucas round to face her. 'I know this is difficult . . .'

Lucas shook his head, cutting her off. 'This isn't difficult. Divorce – that's difficult. This is . . . this is . . . impossible! A week ago, I was just a normal teenager who happened to be a bit richer than most. Now . . . now it's like I don't even know who I am any more. And I was never too sure to begin with.'

Lucas laughed again, a dry, short sound with no joy in it. 'You know what? When Joe said that . . . when Joe said to Finn that I was his brother, I thought he meant he was my father. Just for a second, I thought . . .' He shook his head, looking down at his feet. 'And I would have been OK with that. I would have been . . . happy with that, even. But no. I get the short straw. Mercy-the-great-evil-one is still my mother, and my dad's still some schmuck without a name.'

Faye didn't know what to say. There wasn't anything she could say. So instead, she pulled Lucas to her. She felt him hold her tightly, felt his cheek come to rest on her hair. They stood like that, quietly, for several minutes.

'You're with us now,' Faye said, eventually, into the silence. 'We're here for you.'

She felt Lucas move, pulling back slightly to cup her face in his hands. There was pain in his blue eyes, but he was smiling slightly. 'Are you, Flash? Are you here for me?'

Faye felt her stomach flip over completely as she looked into his eyes, Her arms were still around Lucas's waist, his body pressed against hers. He looked at her as if he could see nothing else. An image of Finn flashed through her mind, and Faye knew she should push Lucas away, but she couldn't. She was drawn towards him, helplessly, and it felt amazing. Lucas leaned in, slowly, his lips brushing hers.

'Faye?' Joe's voice broke the silence of the forest, loud and close. 'Faye? Lucas? Are you here somewhere?'

Lucas looked away and Faye stepped out of his arms, trembling. 'Yes, Joe – we're here!' she called back.

The biker appeared behind them. 'The patrol reports that the town is snowed in. Mercy's entered her endgame.' Joe held up the scroll. 'I think we need to talk to your aunt.'

Chapter Forty-four

Secrets and Lies

The wolf flared inside him as the cold wind cut through Finn's leathers. He rode hard, through the forest at first, and then down onto the road. At first Finn had no idea of where he was going – he thought perhaps he should just ride out of town, and never come back. But then he saw the signs, proclaiming Winter Mill snowed in, and knew that he was trapped with every other living soul inside the town limits.

Finn had never felt such fury, and certainly not directed at his father. All his life, he had looked up to his dad, Joe Crowley, leader of the Black Dogs. He'd always known his father was a good man, and he had brought his son up to follow in his footsteps. But now? Now it seemed that Finn's whole life had been built upon a lie. Mercy Morrow, the woman he had dedicated his life to tracking and stopping, was his mother.

For a while Finn rode blindly, racing through the wind and the freshly falling flakes of snow, before finding himself on the road that led to the Morrow mansion, in the depths of the woods just inside the town limits. He knew where he had to go.

Finn had never seen Mercy close-up. He'd seen pictures, of course, and he'd spied her from a distance, usually as the bikers failed to stop her latest bargain with Annwn. But he'd always been in the background, with no chance of him coming

257

face-to-face with their great adversary. Finn now understood how that had been carefully engineered by his father – of course Joe had never wanted him to meet Mercy. She would have blown his lie to pieces.

Finn had no doubt that Mercy was evil – he had seen the things she had done with his own eyes, the cruelty she had visited on mankind for centuries. But she was his mother. And now Finn knew that fact, he couldn't just ignore it. Just like he couldn't ignore the fact that he'd just found out he had a brother . . . Finn thought of Lucas, and shook his head. That was something he'd have to deal with later. He'd never even thought of the idea of having a brother before, and it would take some getting used to, for sure.

He pulled back on the throttle, slowing the bike as it reached the mansion's main gates. They were wide open, standing back on their hinges, but still Finn hesitated. He imagined what his father would say if he knew Finn were contemplating confronting Mercy alone. He knew it was stupid, he knew he should know better – but now Finn knew she was his mother, he had to talk to her, face to face. Joe would roll out a lecture about how her words could bind and her face could beguile. He'd tell Finn she was pure deceit and infinite destruction, and that to listen to her was to seal one's own cruel fate.

He'd listened to her once before in his life, in fact, and it had led to the death of the person he'd loved most in the world.

But the longer he stared at that great house, the more Finn knew he could not ignore this impulse. He wanted to see her, in the flesh. He wanted to look Mercy Morrow in the eye, and for her to say that yes, she was his mother.

Finn opted not to ride in the front gate. Instead, he hid his bike in the dense bushes at the entrance and then slipped over the wall, dropping into the soft snow the other side. Walking up the pathway would only limit his options and put him on the back foot. Finn wanted to meet his mother, but he wasn't stupid. He wasn't going to let Mercy have any advantage that she could use against him.

He headed for what would have once been the servants' quarters, set in the basement. The external door was small, and locked fast, but the panels around it were old glass, easy to shatter. His leathered fist pushed through one and the glass tinkled to the stone floor on the other side. Finn froze, listening for any sign that someone inside had heard him, but there was no movement. Reaching his hand through the broken window-pane, he found the key in the lock the other side. Finn was inside the house within three minutes, stopping to listen again. There was no sound anywhere. It was as if the house was dead.

The rubber soles of Finn's boots were quiet on the stone floor as he crept out of the kitchen and up the short flight of stairs to the ground level. There were no lights lit, and the house was cold and dark. The corridor he was in opened onto the main foyer, which was paved with pristine marble. A huge wooden staircase curved up into the gloomy upper level. Finn stood for a moment, getting his bearings. Finn wished he could use his wolf senses, but he was keeping a tight rein on them. He didn't want his first proper meeting with his mother to bring out that side of him. Over many years, Finn had learned to control when he changed into the wolf. It didn't always work – when he was very angry, for example, or under attack, Finn sometimes felt himself changing before he had a chance to clamp down on the creature within. But mostly, he tried to control that dark side of himself.

Then Finn heard a car pull in through the main gate, gravel rattling beneath the tyres. Looking around, he saw a door open-ing onto a darkened room, and slipped into it. Seconds later

Mercy Morrow opened the front door and stepped through. She paused for a moment on the threshold, listening just as Finn had done. Finn watched her from the shadows, fascinated. She was so tall, so slender – and yes, she was beautiful. He swallowed, trying to remember back through the centuries, trying to remember a time when she was really his mother. He realized, with surprise, that it was important to him to be able to see her that way. He'd never known what it was like to have a mother. And now, here she was, not twenty paces away. Finn had been brought up to fear this woman, to hate her even. But now, now that he was here . . . things didn't seem so simple, at all.

Mercy flicked the light switch. She looked around, her large eyes bright in the sudden glare.

'I know you're here,' she announced, still not moving from her spot. 'Do you think I can't sense my own son when he's so close?' Mercy took one step onto the marble, holding her head high, her neck stiff. 'I know where you have been, Lucas. How dare you think you can simply return here, to me?'

Finn felt his heart do a sick backflip. Mercy couldn't tell that it was him – Finn, not Lucas. She just knew that someone with her blood was near. He shut his eyes, briefly. Well, there was confirmation enough.

He stepped out of the darkened doorway, into the light, but didn't speak. Mercy turned sharply at the noise, her displeased frown transforming into shock, which she quickly hid beneath a mask of uninterest.

'Well,' she drawled, moving closer. 'Look who it is. My lost son, my would-be heir. So Joe finally told you, did he? He finally revealed the truth, after all these years.'

Finn said nothing, watching Mercy has she wove her way slowly closer. She smiled at his silence, a charming flash of warmth that his heart responded to. This was his mother. This was . . .

'So. What do you think of the wonderful, righteous Joe Crowley now, my sweet?'

Finn cleared his throat. 'It doesn't change anything.'

Mercy smiled again. 'Doesn't it? Then why are you here?'

She was in front of him now. She touched her fingers to his face, and they were ice cold. He felt a tremor pass through him. When he was younger, he'd longed to feel his mother's arms around him, telling him he was loved during those cold nights on the road.

'I just wanted to see . . .'

'You wanted to see what?' she whispered, again.

Finn shook his head, unable to speak. Mercy suddenly slid her hand down his arm, catching his fingers in hers. Tugging at him, she pulled him across the floor, into a dimly lit room. It held a fireplace and comfortable chairs. They didn't sit down. Instead, Mercy dragged him towards the fireplace, above which hung an ancient, large mirror.

'I missed you, my perfect little boy,' she said again, softly. 'You were so beautiful when you were born. So small, with so much dark, dark hair. I loved you so much. But he took you from me.'

Finn found himself transfixed. 'He said it was for my safety,' he managed to murmur.

'Oh, Finn – how can that be true?' Mercy asked softly. 'How can it be right to part a baby from his mother?'

He had no answer to that. He watched as Mercy lifted one slim hand towards the mirror. He followed its movement, looking at where her fingers touched the glass, and then, without realizing, he was looking at the glass itself.

An alarm bell went off in his mind. This was wrong ... something was wrong. He could feel something, pulling him closer.

'No,' he said sharply, tearing his gaze away. 'No!'

He backed away. Mercy took a step towards him, but he moved out of her reach, heading for the door.

'He was right about you,' Finn said, hoarsely. 'Everything he said was true.'

Mercy grinned, a cruel, powerful gesture that twisted her face. 'But you know that's not true, Finn. And if he lied about that, what else has he lied about?'

'Nothing,' Finn said, almost at the door.

'Oh really? What about that little girl you so loved? What was her name, now? Eve, wasn't it?'

Finn's hand was on the door handle, but he froze and looked back. 'What about her?'

'Don't you know how she died?'

He swallowed painfully. 'You killed her,' he said. 'You ordered your hounds to ... to ...' Finn faltered, shutting his eyes. Even this many years later, he couldn't think about it.

Mercy shook her head. 'I wasn't there. I didn't even know her name. Who did, Finn? Who knew about her?'

The thought popped into his mind before he could stop it. Joe! Joe knew. Joe had warned him away – just as he had tried to do with Faye. Finn shook his head. 'You're lying.'

Mercy sighed, a long-suffering susurration that seemed to fill the echoing hallway. 'Oh, Finn. Think about it. When have I ever lied to you?'

He opened the door and ran through it, slamming it shut behind him with a resounding bang.

Chapter Forty-five

Homecoming

Jimmy was fidgeting. Liz watched him, pulling the blanket he'd given her tighter around her shoulders. They'd been talking quietly for the last ten minutes, but she could tell his mind was elsewhere.

'Jimmy?' she asked finally. 'What is it? What's the matter? I mean, aside from all the weird werewolves and end-of-the-world stuff . . .

He smiled at her, and Liz couldn't help but smile back. She was doing that a lot around him lately. She couldn't believe how quickly her feelings towards him had changed. It was as if this whole crazy thing had opened her eyes. And boy, was she glad it had.

'Sorry. I didn't mean to – it's not that I'm not listening to you, Liz,' Jimmy said, sitting a little closer. 'I was just thinking about my parents.'

'They know where you are, right?'

Jimmy shook his head. 'No. Joe thought – the bikers didn't know how the bite was going to affect me. They didn't know whether I was going to survive it or . . .' He shrugged. 'If I'd gone home, Mom and Dad would have insisted I go to a hospital, and that wouldn't have helped at all. So Joe said I should wait. Until I was better.' Jimmy shrugged. 'And I trust him. I trust all of the bikers.'

Liz nodded. 'They must be worried sick, though. I mean, where do they think you are?'

'I know,' Jimmy looked down, scrubbing a fingernail against the cold ground. 'Joe's been teaching me how to ride a motorbike.'

'Wow – really?'

'Yeah . . . it's amazing. I mean, I can only do basic stuff right now, what with my leg and everything. But being on the bike – it's really incredible, Liz. I just forget everything else.'

Liz nodded, not sure what this had to do with Jimmy's poor mom and dad.

'Anyway,' Jimmy went on, nervously, 'I was thinking about taking one of the bikes and going to see them.'

'Your parents?'

Jimmy nodded. 'Yeah. I'm getting better all the time. Joe says all it's going to take is time and rest.'

'It's a good idea to see them, Jimmy,' Liz told him, touching her hand to his for reassurance. 'They'll be so much happier once they know for sure you're all right.'

He smiled, turning his hand over and curling his fingers through hers. 'Yeah, that's what I thought. So I wondered . . . I wondered . . .'

Liz put her head on one side, watching as he struggled to ask her something. 'What is it?'

'I wondered if you'd come with me. To see them. On the bike,' Jimmy said, in a rush. 'It's fine if you don't want to. I'll understand. I just don't really want to go on my own, that's all. But it's OK. I'm sure you—'

'Jimmy,' said Liz, cutting off his nervous babble. 'Of course I'll come.'

He grinned and stood up, looking the best she'd seen him look since the attack in the forest. 'Oh, that's brilliant! Thank you. Come on, I'll ask one of the pack to lend me their bike.'

'You want to go now?' Liz said, surprised. 'Are you sure you're well enough?'

Jimmy was still holding onto her hand. He pulled her up. 'I'm fine,' he told her, still smiling. 'With you around, I'm always fine.'

Liz stared up at him,

The bike ride was uneventful, but intense. Liz had never been on a motorbike before. One of the bikers gave her a leather jacket to wear against the cold – it was huge, but warm.

'Hold on to me,' Jimmy told her, as they got on. 'Whatever happens, don't let go.'

She reached around him, feeling Jimmy's hand clasp the two of hers over his stomach, holding them together. Liz was tall enough that her chin rested on his shoulder, his hair tickling her nose as they moved off. Jimmy didn't gun the bike – he seemed to be taking it easy for her benefit, perhaps worried about her safety. He kept turning his head to look at her, checking to see if she was OK. Every time he did his cheek would brush her forehead, and a little pulse of delight would flood through her belly. It felt as if every nerve in her body was sparking at his touch. She shut her eyes, enjoying the feeling of safety that being so close to Jimmy gave her. She felt one of his hands trace over her joined ones again, and opened her eyes.

'You OK?' Jimmy yelled, over the wind.

'Perfect,' she yelled back.

There was a light burning outside the house as they pulled up, a little lantern that lit the snowy pathway. Jimmy pulled the bike over and jumped off before helping Liz down. He slid his arm around her waist and lifted her as if she weighed nothing. Liz was surprised – she had no idea that Jimmy was so strong. He put her down, but didn't let her go. Liz placed her hands against his chest as Jimmy held her, firmly. His eyes were troubled, but he smiled anyway.

'Thanks for being here.'

'Any time. Do you want me to wait with the bike?'

Jimmy pulled her closer, resting his chin on her head. 'No. Come with me to the door. Please?'

She nodded and he let her go, taking her hand instead as they walked up the path. Jimmy hesitated for a second before ringing the bell.

'I lost my keys and phone in the chase,' he explained. 'Anyway, I can't just walk straight in. I don't want to give them both heart attacks.'

'It'll be fine,' she whispered. 'They're just going to be happy to see you, that's all.'

Jimmy sighed. 'Yeah. Then they'll probably ground me for, like, ten years.'

He rang the bell. There were a couple of moments of silence, and then the sound of shuffling inside as someone came to the door. It opened into gloom – there were no lights on inside the house.

'Mom?' Jimmy asked, into the silence.

The figure inside the door moved forwards, into the meagre light cast but the lamp at the end of the pathway. Liz recognized her as Mrs Paulson, but only just. There was a strange, faraway look in her eyes, and her forehead was creased in a frown. Liz shivered. Jimmy's mom looked just like everyone in town.

'Jimmy,' she whispered, 'We have to go . . .

She looked up at Jimmy, and saw his stricken face. 'Mom?' he said again, 'It's me, Jimmy.'

Liz reached out, putting one hand on Jimmy's arm while keeping a wary eye on his mom. 'Jimmy,' she repeated, more urgently. 'I'm sorry, but—'

'Mom, it's me.' Jimmy pulled away from Liz. 'Jimmy, your son. Mom?'

Mrs Paulson retreated into the shadows, still staring blankly ahead. 'Please go away now,' she said, flatly. 'We don't want to buy anything. Go away.'

'Mom!' Jimmy shouted, as she shut the door. 'Mom, wait—'

Liz, shaken, grabbed his arm. 'Jimmy, stop.'

'But—'

'Jimmy,' she said again, softly. 'Mercy has got to them. I'm sorry. We've got to go.'

She led him back down the path to the bike, but Jimmy couldn't ride. They stood, silently, side by side. Liz didn't know what to do, or how to help him, but her eyes filled with tears at the look of pain on Jimmy's face. He looked as if he was trying to say something, but finally, he reached out to pull Liz to him, clutching her tightly as he cried.

Faye pushed open the door to the bookstore. Aunt Pam appeared from the back room almost immediately.

'Faye!' she exclaimed, rushing over. 'Where have you been? I'd have called the police if I thought it would do any good. This town . . . ' she shivered. 'I'm truly scared, Faye.'

Faye pulled her aunt into a fierce hug. 'I'm sorry.'

'I've been worried sick. The town is snowed in, and I seem to be the only person who isn't wandering around like a lost soul. It's terrifying.'

'I know what's happening, Aunt Pam,' Faye told her. 'Look – this is going to be a lot to take in, but we need your help.'

'Who does?' asked Pam, confused. 'Faye, what's going on?'

'I can explain everything – but first, I need you to meet some people. OK?'

Aunt Pam had gone very still. She was looking over Faye's

head, out of the shop's front window. Faye turned to see Joe and Lucas watching them.

'That's the leader of the Black Dogs, isn't it?' Pam asked. 'And that's the Morrow woman's son. Oh, Faye, what have you got yourself into?'

Before Faye could answer, Joe had pushed his way into the shop, ducking to avoid the wolf amulet that still spun gently on its little thread. He offered Pam a friendly smile, pointing at it.

'Nice totem you have there, ma'am.'

Pam smiled back, polite but guarded. 'Thank you. In fact, it was a gift from one of your men.'

Joe smiled knowingly. 'I thought it might have been. Finn, was it?' Joe asked. He stepped further into the store as Lucas quietly closed the door behind them.

'That's right. He's very talented.'

Joe nodded. 'That he is. He's also my son. Did you know that?'

Faye watched as the suspicious look on Aunt Pam's face softened. 'I did not. But I have always felt that goodness in the child reflects goodness in the parent. And if that is the case with you, then you are welcome here.'

The biker nodded, still looking at the wolf amulet. 'Thank you. Do you know why Finn gave it to you?'

Pam looked at him seriously. 'No, I don't. But I chose to hang it because it felt right to at the time.'

Joe smiled again, holding out his hand to shake Pam's, gently. 'My son says you are a smart woman. It looks to me like he was right.'

'Well, Finn's a good young man.'

Joe nodded. 'Ms McCarron, Finn is almost two hundred years old.'

Aunt Pam stared at Joe for a moment, and then nodded calmly. 'I see.'

268

Faye was shocked to see that her aunt seemed to be taking all this in her stride. She'd always known Aunt Pam was strong, but right now, Faye saw that perhaps there was even more to her than she had realized.

'My name is Joe Crowley,' he went on, 'and I'm here to stop what's going on in this town.' Joe nodded at Lucas. 'Lucas told me about an incident here, in this shop, with his mother, Mercy. Apparently your pet dog objected to her?'

'So Mercy Morrow has something to do with this, does she?' Aunt Pam nodded gravely. 'I think you'd better tell me everything, Joe Crowley.'

Chapter Forty-six

La Belle Dame

Aunt Pam pulled down the blinds at the shop windows and Faye brought out chairs. They sat in a circle as Joe told his story, Faye filling in the parts that she had been personally involved in, with Lucas explaining the little that he knew himself. Pam listened quietly, nodding occasionally but asking no questions. Several times, Faye found her mind wandering to Finn, wondering where he was and what he was doing. Joe had said it was best to let him find his own way back, and that his son needed to work out his anger, alone. But Faye was still worried. If there was evil abroad, she wanted him to be safe.

'Well,' Pam said, when they had finally finished. 'What a thing to come to our sleepy little town.'

'I wish it hadn't,' Joe told her, his voice sincere. 'But it has, and now we need your help. I'm told you're a history and culture expert.'

Pam smiled. 'I know some useful bits and pieces – used to teach folklore at Miskatonic. And what I don't know, I can usually find,' she said, indicating the books stacked high around them. 'What do you need?'

'I need to translate this,' Joe told her, pulling out the scroll and passing it over. 'You probably won't recognize the language.'

Pam unfurled the scroll and examined the text for a moment

before looking up. 'It looks like a form of ancient Cyrillic script,' she said. 'Though the language seems to be a variation of something non-Slavic that I've never seen before. Moldovan, perhaps? Or the Bashkir tongue? It bears enough resemblance to both of those be translatable, though, I think.'

Faye watched Joe, who was evidently impressed, and felt another swell of pride for her aunt. 'I can read some of it, but not all,' he said. 'That region has so many dialects.'

Pam nodded, still looking at the scroll. 'Well then, together we should be able to make sense of most of it.' She stood up, crossing to the bookshelf that held the old volumes of illustrated poetry. 'First, though, I want to show you this.'

They got up and crowded around Aunt Pam as she pulled out a large, leather-bound volume and cleared a space on her desk. Thumbing through the delicate pages, she opened it and laid it flat for all of them to see.

'*La Belle Dame sans Merci,*' Faye read.

'The Beautiful Lady Without Pity,' said Aunt Pam, translating from the French. 'It's a ballad by the English poet John Keats, about a good and pure knight who finds himself enchanted and bound by a beautiful woman he stops to help. In a glamoured dream, he sees the stranded bodies of other men who have been similarly taken in by her cruel beauty.' Pam looked at Joe. 'Sound familiar?'

Joe bent closer. 'How old is this?'

'Keats wrote two versions, the first in 1819,' Aunt Pam told them. 'But the title of his ballad is far older than that – he took it from a piece by Alain Chartier, who wrote his poem sometime between 1392 and 1430.'

Faye stared at the words on the page, transfixed. 'Can it really be Mercy Morrow?' She asked, looking at Lucas. 'Has she really been doing this for so long?'

Lucas shrugged and shook his head. 'Don't ask me,' he said, clearly upset. 'I don't think I have any idea who that woman is any more, but I'll never call her my mother again.'

Joe straightened up. 'This is her,' he said, quietly. 'I'm sorry, Lucas. But this is truly your mother.'

Outside, the silence of the street was shattered by the growl of a motorbike engine. It pulled to a stop beside the shop's door, and a second later someone banged on the glass. Faye answered it to find Finn standing on the step. He was breathing hard, his eyes wild.

Mitch Wilson strode out of the mansion and into the deep snow. It had fallen so strongly in the past few hours that it seemed as if the drifts would soon touch the sky, enclosing the earth in never-ending ice.

The large set of keys Mercy had entrusted to his care jangled against his belt. He walked towards the decrepit outbuildings that stood apart from the house. Like the rest of the estate, they had been abandoned for years until Mercy arrived. But unlike the mansion, they had not survived as well. The roofs bore holes where slates had tumbled to the ground, and the wooden doors were warped, their bolts rusted.

Reaching the door of the farthest stall, Mitch fitted one of the keys into the large silver lock. It was new, added only when Mercy had arrived, and it undid smoothly. Mitch wrenched the old door open and stepped inside.

The smell of hay and dirt was strong. A sort of moaning chatter echoed up around him, from beyond the inner pen that had been built to secure cattle and horses. Mitch ignored it, even when it grew louder, begging.

Instead, he turned to a rusted iron rack. On it was hanging a suit of ancient, ornate armour. It was made of a metal he couldn't name, richly engraved and riveted together with tiny, intricate pins. It had

belonged to Ballard, but it fit Mitch as if it were made for him alone. Slipping on the helmet, he buckled it beneath his chin before reaching for the breastplate.

Behind him, there was a soft whinny, and Mitch smiled. 'Hello, girl,' he whispered to the great horse hanging her head over one of the partitions. 'Ready to ride?'

The mare raised her head and dropped it as if she knew what Mitch was saying. She was white, no – paler than white, a milky, translucent shade of opal that made her look even more ghostly.

Mitch stroked her nose. 'Let me just get the dogs,' he whispered, opening the paper bag he was carrying and pulling out a large slab of raw steak.

The chattering whine immediately rose to a clamour as the smell of meat wafted through the stable. Mitch moved to the furthest pen and looked over the wooden rail. Inside were a host of men – wild and dirty, dressed in rags. Their faces were hungry, their bodies wasted; around their necks were chains of shining silver. They were all on their haunches, looking for Mitch and what he held in his hands. He slapped the meat against the fence that held them in, and the men went crazy, scrambling towards the steak, snapping at each other as they crashed together.

'Come on then, boys,' said Mitch, with a smile. 'Time to hunt.'

Chapter Forty-seven

Eve

'Finn?' Faye said, relieved to see him, standing on her doorstep. 'Is everything OK?'

He shook his head. 'No. No, it's not. I need you to come with me.'

Faye felt her eyes widen. 'What, now? Where to?'

'I don't know. I haven't worked that out yet, but—'

'Finn?' Joe stepped to Faye's side. 'Why don't you come in?'

Faye saw Finn's face darken as he looked at his father. 'What are you doing here?'

'Faye's aunt is helping me translate the scroll,' Joe said, frowning at Finn's expression. 'Why don't you come and help us? You know as much of the old language as I do.'

'No,' Finn said, shortly, looking back to Faye. 'Please, Faye. Come with me. You can't trust anyone here. No one.'

Faye stared at him. 'Finn, don't. You're scaring me.'

'What's happened?' Joe asked, taking a step towards his son. Finn backed away, grasping Faye's hand.

'I don't know, Dad.' Finn said, his voice cracking slightly. 'Why don't you tell me?'

'What do you mean?'

'Eve,' Finn said hoarsely. 'I'm talking about Eve.'

Faye looked at Joe, confused. She thought she saw a flicker of something like guilt pass through the big man's eyes.

275

'You went to see Mercy, didn't you?' Joe asked. 'Finn, you know you can't believe anything she says.'

'Whereas you never lie, do you, Dad?' Finn spat. 'Faye. Just talk to me. Please – out here. Alone.'

Faye was still scared, but nodded. She looked up at Joe. 'I'll be back in a minute.'

After a moment Joe nodded reluctantly. Finn ignored him, pulling Faye with him as he walked out into the dark, abandoned street. He carried on walking until he found a darkened alley, out of view of the street, and pulled her into it.

'Finn,' Faye said. 'What's going on? Please tell me. Who's Eve?'

Finn stared at her. Faye felt that familiar pull again, the one that she'd had inside her every time she saw him, ever since that day in the mall. She looked away, staring at a neon sign further down the road. Its bulbs were dying, flickering sickly and casting an unnatural night.

'Faye,' he began, 'I know this is strange . . .'

'Just tell me,' Faye said, again. 'Just tell me who Eve was. Who was she to you?'

Finn took a deep breath. 'Eve was your great-great-great-aunt. She wasn't from here – she lived in eastern Europe, where I guess your family emigrated from a long time ago. And she looked – she looked just like you.'

Faye nodded, numb, her mind spinning. 'Wait,' she said, 'Wait . . . Lucas showed me a picture, of a woman that looked like me, but wasn't me. Oh, God. Was that her? Was that Eve? '

Finn nodded. 'Mercy was terrorizing her village. We heard about her arrival and came to help, and I—' Finn paused, shutting his eyes, the look on his face distant, as if he were watching the past replay behind his eyelids. 'It was like a thunderbolt as soon as I saw her. I was young then, truly young, and they all said it would fade with time, but it didn't. It never has.' He looked at her. 'Until now. Until you, Faye.'

'What happened to her?' Faye asked, quietly.

Finn opened his eyes, staring at the drawn blinds of the bookstore. 'She died,' he said, shortly, his voice full of pain. 'And I thought I knew how, until today, and now . . .' He shook his head, tailing off.

Faye stared at him, feeling the anger build in her chest, beside the pulse of energy that always seemed to be there when she was with him.

'So what?' she asked. 'You've just been looking for a replacement ever since? You just figured I could slot right in and be your Eve again? Because I looked like her? Because I share her blood?'

Finn's head snapped towards her in shock. 'No!' he said. 'Of course not! Faye – how could you even think that?'

'How could I not?' Faye asked, distraught. 'I look like her, Finn! I look just like her, and that's the only reason you're even talking to me now!'

'No!' Finn said again. 'Faye – don't you feel it? It's like . . . it's like a thing in your chest, right? A thing that ties you to me as if we were joined together with a rope, or something. Except that it's stronger than a rope. I know it is, because it's been there for years. It's always been there. And I know you feel it, because I do too.' Finn placed a hand over his heart. 'It's right here. Isn't it? I swear, Faye, the moment I saw you – that moment in the mall, it felt like everything was falling into place, and I could feel you, right there, I could hear you breathing as if there were no one else there but us.'

'But how do I know?' Faye asked, wanting to cry. 'How do I know whether that's for me, or Eve? She's always there too, isn't she?'

Finn rubbed his hands through his hair, screwing his eyes shut. 'No. No. It started being Eve. In some ways, you are so alike. But in others, you're not. You're so strong, Faye. You face things head on. You don't flinch. You look after yourself. Eve was different. She was delicate – she needed me to protect her. And I didn't. I couldn't. She slipped out of my grasp like water, and I didn't even see her go.'

Finn stepped forwards, grasping Faye's arms and pulling her towards him until their foreheads touched. 'You're my second chance, Faye,' he whispered. 'I loved Eve for one hundred and fifty years. *One hundred and fifty years!* But I love you ten times as much, and it's going to last ten times as long. The thought of losing you . . . I have to keep you safe. I have to. If I lose you – if I fail again . . . I don't think I'd even want to live. Please come away with me. Just you and me, Faye. Please.'

With a gasp, Faye wrenched herself out of his grasp and backed away, tears flooding down her face. 'I can't!' she said, agonized, 'I can't do this – I can't deal with this. I don't understand any of it . . .'

'You don't have to,' Finn pleaded. 'Just accept it.'

'How can you say that?' Faye shook her head. 'I don't even know you!'

'You do,' he whispered. Finn stepped forwards, cupping her face in his hands, so close that she could feel his heart, beating hard against her chest. 'You do, Faye. We've known each other for ever, it's just taken this long to find each other.' Finn took a deep, shaking breath. 'Tell me you don't feel what I feel, and I'll leave you alone.'

Faye stared at him, trying to force the lie through her lips, trying to tell him she didn't feel anything, but she knew he could see the truth in her eyes. She reached up, pulling Finn's hands from her face. Then she turned on her heel and fled back to the shop.

Finn walked to the end of the alley stood in the empty street, watching Faye disappear into the bookstore.

'You can come out now,' he said into the empty air, as the door shut behind her.

There was a moment more silence, before cautious footsteps echoed out of the shadows. Lucas walked towards Finn slowly, stopping where Finn could see him.

'How did you know I was there?'

Finn glared at the boy. 'The wolf is pretty close to the surface right now,' he said. 'So I'd really recommend not pissing me off.'

Lucas nodded. 'Right,' he looked down, digging his hands in his pockets. 'So. . . I heard all that.'

'So?'

'Pretty heavy stuff. I guess I didn't realize . . . what you and Faye were all about.'

'Yeah, well,' said Finn. 'It's not really any of your business, is it?'

'Why are you being such an idiot?' Lucas asked, his sudden anger surprising Finn. 'You can't protect her by running away. She's safer here – with all of us.'

'Is that so?'

'Yes! It is! And if you didn't have your head so far up your own—' Lucas cut himself off with a sigh. 'Look, you're not the only one who cares about her. But . . .' Lucas looked away with an embarrassed shrug. 'I've never had a brother, I guess. And now that I have one, I don't want to fight with him, you know? So why don't we start again? I seem to be doing a lot of that, lately. It seems to be working out so far.'

279

Finn looked at Lucas properly for the first time. They were alike, he could tell, despite the centuries and the father that separated them.

'Come on,' Lucas urged. 'I'm not going to chase after my brother's girl. But I will help you keep her safe. OK?'

Finn nodded, slowly.

'All right, then,' said Lucas, with a tentative smile. 'Let's forget this getting-out-of-town stuff and get back inside. They're working out a battle plan in there.'

Chapter Forty-eight

The Choice

Faye tried to concentrate on what Aunt Pam and Joe were saying, but her mind kept wandering to her confrontation with Finn. He seemed so convinced of what he was saying, so passionate. And that connection between them was there, in her chest, thrumming even now.

'If you look here,' Aunt Pam was saying, 'I think this refers to the prince, not to the Immortal. I know the preposition is confusing, but . . .'

The door opened and Lucas came in, followed by Finn. Faye felt her heart tumble over itself and looked away, pretending to be focused on the notes Aunt Pam was pointing at.

'Welcome back, boys,' she heard Joe say, drily. 'Finn? Are you here to stay?'

There was a pause before Finn's quiet voice cut through the silence of the shop. 'For now. But we need to talk, Dad.'

'We will, I promise,' Joe assured him. 'But right now we have to apply ourselves to this.'

'What have you found out?' Finn asked, apparently deciding that right now, all he could do was join them. 'Anything useful?'

'Well,' said Faye, feeling Finn's eyes rest on her as she spoke up. 'Apparently this isn't a spell. It's an account.'

Finn took a step towards her. 'What do you mean, an account?' he asked. His voice was soft and full of concern. Faye

281

tried to ignore what it was doing to her insides, and leaned over the scroll again, instead.

'Aunt Pam says it describes a ritual,' Faye told him.

'A ritual for what?'

'That's what we're trying to work out,' said Joe. 'Finn, why don't you take a look? We could do with another pair of eyes on this, I think.'

Faye stepped out of the way as Finn moved nearer, but not quickly enough to stop his hand brushing gently against hers. She felt his fingers curl around hers briefly before Finn let go and concentrated on the scroll. Faye swallowed, hard.

Finn watched Faye, trying to catch her eye, but she deliberately avoided his gaze. He wondered if he'd done the right thing in telling her what he had – maybe he'd pushed her too hard. But if his dad was right, they were running out of time, and Finn was terrified to think that something might happen to her. After what had happened to Eve, all those years ago . . . He had to find a way to protect her from whatever was coming. Whatever it took.

Finn stepped into the space Faye left at the desk, beside her aunt. The scroll was held open by a couple of books, and he frowned as he leaned closer.

'What have you worked out so far?' he asked.

'Well,' began Pam, after a deep breath. 'As far as we can make out, the text talks about a feudal prince who ruled a now-forgotten land in eastern Europe, centuries ago – during the Dark Ages, when Immortals were pure creatures and still walked the Earth. His land had been overrun by Mercy's kin, his subjects held in her thrall.'

Lucas shuddered. 'This is so weird. That's my mom you're talking about.'

'The prince was desperate to find a way of helping his people,' Joe went on, taking up the story. 'But Mercy's powers were growing strong in his land, swarming over it like darkness itself. The prince had fallen in love with one of the few Immortals that had not fled the region. The couple were happy – devoted, and so in love that any who saw them together were blessed.'

Finn nodded, pointing at the scroll. 'It says here they were planning marriage. A huge celebration of their love, to bring cheer to the whole land.'

'Right,' Aunt Pam agreed. 'And that's about as far as we've got.'

Finn studied the scroll, frowning. He couldn't make out all of it, but there were a few words he recognized. 'It's talking about a bargain with Annwn,' he muttered, reading on.

'One of Mercy's?' Joe asked.

'No, I don't think so.' He frowned. 'It was a bargain that the Immortal suggested. To the prince.'

'That doesn't make sense,' said Faye.

Finn looked up at his father. 'Listen to this,' he said, translating the scroll aloud. 'Though the Immortal was consumed by her love for her One, her soul was in torment. She could not look upon the suffering of his people and enjoy her own happiness.'

'So what does that mean?' Lucas asked. 'Did she not marry the prince after all?'

Finn stared at the ancient writing, feeling something dark and cruel settle on his shoulders. He could feel Faye, standing just a few feet away, but suddenly he couldn't look at her.

'She did,' he told them, quietly. 'That's where the bargain comes into it. The Immortal knew what Annwn craved. What

283

would provide them with so much emotion that they would no longer need Mercy's offerings.'

'True love,' said Joe, quietly, and Finn knew at once that his father understood.

Finn nodded. 'She told the prince that they could offer up their love, in exchange for the lives and souls of their people. They could set them free, if they sacrificed their love to Annwn.'

There were a few moments of silence as everyone in the room tried to take this in.

'I don't understand,' said Faye, sounding confused. Finn forced himself to look at her face, and his heart ached at the distress he saw hidden there. 'What does it mean, that they sacrificed their love? You can't just give love away. You can't just decide to stop loving someone. Can you?'

'No,' said Joe. 'Which is why it was such a great sacrifice. Am I right, Finn?'

Finn nodded, scanning the scroll again. 'The Immortal knew how to create a ritual that would cast their love into Annwn,' he explained. 'It would drain every ounce of that emotion from them both, dragging it through a mirror that had been enchanted as a route to Annwn. That part of themselves would be gone for ever, taken into the underworld to feed those spirits for a very long time. The prince hated having to do it. But he knew it was the only way to free his people. The Immortal wrote the ritual into the marriage ceremony. The kiss that declared them as man and wife became the focus of her magic – a Mortal Kiss that sealed the ritual. And their fate.'

A sad silence settled on the room again, thinking of these two who had loved so much, but were destined never to be together. To Finn, it seemed the cruellest fate of all.

'What was left?' Faye asked, her voice shaky and quiet. 'When the ritual was complete?'

'Nothing of their love,' he told her, quietly. 'They were shells, empty of what had made them so happy. They didn't know each other. They became strangers from that day on, destined never to know each other again, or what they had given away.'

'That's horrible,' Faye whispered, tears standing in her eyes.

'Yes,' Finn agreed. 'It is. It really, really is. But it worked. Mercy and her kin abandoned the land. The people were safe.'

'Well,' said Joe. 'I can see why Mercy was so keen to keep this scroll locked away.'

'What do you mean?' Lucas asked. 'To be honest, I know this is a terrible story, but I don't really understand why you all think it's so important.'

Finn turned away from Faye, looking at his younger brother and wondering how they could be so alike, but so different at the same time. 'Because the scroll also includes the words and symbols needed to complete the ritual,' he explained. 'And because that means it can be performed again.'

'But how?' Lucas asked, 'I mean, it's not going to work with just anyone, is it?'

'No,' Finn said, though the words stuck in his throat. 'It's not going to work with just anyone.'

'What are you talking about?' Faye asked, faintly, but when he turned to look at her, Finn saw from the look in her eyes that really, she already knew. 'Me?' she asked, shakily, into the silence. 'You think this is about me?'

'It explains so much, Faye. About why Mercy chose Winter Mill. You're a danger to her. And you're also a card to play against us, if need be. Mercy likes the high stakes.' He looked at aunt Pam. 'I'm guessing that your family originally came from somewhere in eastern Europe, right?'

'That's right,' Pam nodded, standing up to pull an old leather-bound book from the shelves.

285

Faye spoke up. 'Yes,' she whispered. 'Dad used to tell me about our family tree. But that was centuries ago. And it still doesn't make sense. How would Mercy know about me? How would she know about my family's past, and that I was here?'

Finn was about to answer when Faye put a horrified hand to her mouth. 'Oh no. Oh no . . . Liz found dad's letter opener in the woods. And Sergeant Wilson had my locket . . . And dad's been out of contact for weeks! What if . . . what if . . .'

She looked so desolate that Finn reached out to her, gripping her arm. 'We don't know that anything's happened to him, Faye. She could have met him somewhere, seen the locket, and enchanted him for information, that's all.'

'I think it's pretty clear,' Joe's strong voice said. 'Faye, your family is descended from the line of that prince.' He looked at Finn. 'So was Eve. It's why the two of you look so alike, Faye, and it's why . . .'

Faye shook her head, and before she shut her eyes, Finn saw them fill with tears. 'I don't want to hear this. I can't hear this. You're just making this up – it's just a coincidence, that's all!'

'I'm sorry, Faye, but it isn't.' Aunt Pam looked up from the book she'd been searching through. 'This is our family tree. Eve's listed here. Joe and Finn are right.'

'So it's me?' Faye sobbed. 'This is about me, and I'm the one that has to stop Mercy?'

'Yes,' Joe told her quietly. 'You and . . .'

'Don't,' Faye cut him off, brokenly. 'Don't say it.'

'Are you actually serious?' Lucas asked, in disbelief. 'Have I been following this right? You're telling Faye she has to perform this ritual?'

Joe nodded, gravely. 'Yes.'

'Who with?' Lucas asked.

'That's down to Faye,' said Joe. 'The blood of the Immortals is in both Lucas and Finn.'

Lucas glanced at Finn, and then said, 'Well, I'll volunteer. Faye? I'll do it.'

'Lucas, it doesn't work like that,' Joe said. 'Faye has to choose. And it has to be the person she loves – truly, truly loves. The ritual won't work, otherwise. The emotions released won't be powerful enough.' He looked at Faye. 'Faye? Do you understand?'

Faye shook her head. 'I can't do this!'

'You have to,' Joe said. 'I'm sorry, if there was any other way, we'd take it, but we're running out of time and this is how it must be. You have to choose.'

'But I don't know!' Faye cried, looking between Finn and Lucas. 'I don't even know myself!'

'You do,' Joe told her. 'It's there, Faye. Just look inside yourself, and be honest. Choose.'

Chapter Forty-nine

Consequences

Faye pulled away from Finn and turned her back, covering her face with her hands. She just couldn't deal with any of this, it was too much. As Joe said, deep down, she knew the name of the person she truly loved. But she couldn't bring herself to say it, to condemn their love to an underworld that would so cruelly tear it apart.

She felt gentle hands on her shoulders, pushing her forwards. It was Finn, guiding her towards the store's little back room. He shut the door behind them, but she kept her hands over her face. Finn pulled them away, holding her wrists gently.

'Hey,' he said, with a faint smile.

'Hey,' she whispered. She looked up at his face, trying to make sure the sight of it was so deep in her memory that nothing, not even magic, could erase it from her mind.

'Is it me?' Finn asked, quietly.

Tears filled Faye's eyes again. 'Oh, Finn . . .'

'If it's not,' he said, suddenly unsure, 'that's fine too. You have to be honest. What I said out there – I probably said too much. Maybe all of that – maybe that's just me. So if it's actually Lucas . . .'

Faye shook her head, once, the tears spilling down her cheeks. 'It's you, Finn. Of course it's you.'

A flicker of delight sparked deep in his eyes, followed

289

quickly by a burst of pain. Finn pulled her against his chest, wrapping his arms around her and holding her tightly, as if just being close to her could stop what was coming. Faye rested her head against his chest and cried for everything they would both be forced to lose.

'Ssh,' Finn soothed, stroking her back. 'It's OK.'

'It's not!' She told him. 'It's not OK! Everything you said – all of it was true, all of it. And we've just found each other, Finn. We've only just found each other, out of all the people in the world, through all the years that you've been alive. And now we have to let go? It's not . . . it's just not fair.'

'No,' Finn agreed. 'It's not.' He pulled back enough to cup her face in his hands, smiling gently. 'But just listen to me, Faye. All I ever wanted to do was keep you safe. I just never realized that it was me putting you in danger – my Immortal self, combined with your heritage. This is the way I can keep you safe. For good, Faye. We wipe that slate clean, once and for all.' He traced a finger over her heart. 'We sever that tie, and you'll be free. You'll be safe. For ever.'

Faye shook her head, her eyes filling with tears again. 'But afterwards . . . We won't know each other, ever again. I'm not sure I can bear that.'

Finn smiled, leaning forwards to kiss her forehead. 'But we have known each other,' he said softly. 'There are so many people in this world, Faye, who never know what it's like to really love. We have that, even if it's only right now.'

Faye shut her eyes again. 'We could just run away. There must be a way out of town, somehow.'

'Come on, Faye McCarron,' Finn said. 'I know you better than that.'

She sighed, wiping away her tears. 'Yeah. I guess you do.'

The door suddenly banged open, making them both jump. It

was Liz and Jimmy, dressed in leathers and dusted with fresh snow.

'Whoa,' Liz said, stopping dead when she saw Faye and Finn standing so close together. 'Sorry – are we interrupting? Where is everyone? The store's empty. If they're all upstairs eating Aunt Pam's cookies, they'd better have saved some for me.'

Despite herself, Faye smiled to see her friend, rushing over to engulf Liz in a hug. 'I'm so glad you're here. Where have you been?'

Liz hugged back before glancing up at a grave-faced Jimmy. 'To Jimmy's parents. It's not good news.'

'Oh, no – not them, too? Jimmy, I'm sorry.'

Jimmy nodded. 'We didn't know where else to go. The biker patrol told us you were all here – looking at the scroll?'

Faye nodded. 'Let me get the others. There's a lot to tell you.'

The others had indeed gone up into Aunt Pam's apartment. The four teens followed them, and sitting around the kitchen table they filled Liz and Jimmy in and drank strong coffee to keep themselves going.

Liz could hardly believe her ears as she listened to Faye's explanation of the text and what it meant. She shook her head. 'I never realized,' she said softly. 'Why didn't you tell me you felt so strongly about Finn? I never would have been so against him, if you had!'

Liz watched Faye smile slightly. 'I don't think I even realized it myself, Liz. It was just there, as soon as we met. Like a part of me. Such a big part that it felt as if it had always been there.'

Liz smiled back, but then frowned. 'So, hold on,' she said. 'You're telling me that Finn's your long-lost Immortal love, and now you're just going to sacrifice that?'

Faye held Finn's hand tighter as they sat side by side. 'We

291

don't have a choice, Liz. We just need to work out when to hold the ritual.'

'It needs to recreate the marriage ceremony that would have joined the ancient Immortal and her prince,' explained Aunt Pam. 'I don't know how we're going to arrange and stage that, and get enough of the enchanted townspeople to witness it, at such short notice when Winter Mill is snowed in.'

Liz frowned. 'Would a party do?'

Joe shrugged, 'Yes, anything like that, as long as there's a mirror present we can use to perform the ritual. The symbols in the text on the scroll have to be written on it to open the path to Annwn.'

'There's a really big mirror in the school gym,' Liz pointed out.

'There is,' agreed Lucas, 'but how does that help us? How would we set up a party and get everyone there?'

Liz smiled. 'Have you guys totally forgotten what the date is?'

Jimmy laughed, softly. 'Liz, you're a genius!'

'What?' asked Finn and Faye, together.

'Oh my god,' said Aunt Pam, looking at the calendar on the wall. 'It's Halloween.'

'Yup,' said Liz. 'And whatever else our zombie friends have been doing, they've been setting up for the biggest Winter Mill High Halloween Prom ever, remember? We came here that way – there were hundreds of students, all dressed up, heading for the school.'

Aunt Pam looked at Joe. 'Do you think that could work?'

'Yes,' he said, 'if we could find a way of engineering a focused moment for the ritual to begin.'

'Wait a minute,' Faye spoke up. 'Don't they usually crown a king and queen of the Prom?'

'Yes, they do,' Liz exclaimed. 'We could rig it for you two to win. The crowning ceremony would be the perfect focus for the ritual, wouldn't it?' Liz watched as Faye nodded. Then she saw the colour drain from her friend's face. 'Faye? What's wrong?'

Faye shook her head. 'I've just . . . Are we really going to do this? Right now? So soon?'

Finn put his arm round Faye's shoulder, leaning in to kiss her hair. 'The sooner the better,' he said, quietly. 'Mercy's closing in on her goal, and we can't let her win.'

Liz reached out, taking Faye's free hand and squeezing it gently. 'Forget what's at the end of it,' she said. 'Just think – this is your first date, with your true love. It doesn't get much more romantic than that, right?'

Faye smiled, even managing to laugh a little. 'Well, when you put it like that . . .'

Liz stood, pulling Faye up with her. 'Exactly. Which also means that you need a really, really killer outfit.'

Chapter Fifty

Preparations

Faye stared blankly at her wardrobe. She couldn't help but think that trying to choose something to wear with everything that was going on was just plain wrong, somehow. Her mind kept going over and over her conversation with Finn – he had looked so happy when she'd told him he was the one. But that happiness wouldn't last – couldn't last. All because of her: her family, a past she'd had no idea about. Faye blinked, feeling tears prick at her eyelids. And her dad – what had happened to him? Everything was a mess, and yet she was expected to carry on as if the world wasn't falling down around her ears.

'I'll just wear the prom dress I bought for last year,' Faye said, eventually.

'No,' Liz said firmly, 'Faye, you've got to wear something worthy of being crowned Queen of the Prom – even if we're going to rig the ballot, it's got to be believable.'

Faye rubbed a hand across her eyes. 'I just can't think straight. Trying to choose an outfit right now ... it seems stupid.'

'That's why I'm here,' Liz told her, patting her shoulder.

'But the last time we were at school, everyone was acting like a zombie,' Faye pointed out. 'Are you sure they're even going to be holding the Prom at all?'

'That's definitely what was going on when Jimmy and I

295

came past,' Liz insisted. 'They've been planning it for weeks, so maybe it's a kind of autopilot thing? It's not as if anyone has anything else to do, what with the town snowed in.'

Faye shuddered. 'We still don't know what Mercy's plan is,' she said. 'They could all be part of it.'

'I guess that's why we have to act now,' said Liz. 'You know, before she can do anything?'

Faye nodded miserably. 'I guess you're right.'

Liz watched her for a minute, as if trying to decide what to do. 'I wish I could help, Faye. But I don't know what to do, other than make sure you look amazing.'

Faye managed a watery smile. 'It's OK,' she told her friend. 'I just have to do this. You're helping with that.'

Liz nodded, looking unhappy as she said, 'From the look of everyone heading to the Prom, it's a full-on ball theme. You need something really spectacular. It looked like one of those festivals in Venice, or something.'

Faye shook her head. 'It's no good,' she muttered. 'I don't have anything like that.'

'Maybe I can help?' The girls turned to see Aunt Pam standing in the doorway, holding a large cardboard box. She walked in, setting the box on the bed.

'What's that?' Faye asked, intrigued.

'Something I've had under my bed for a very, very long time,' said her aunt softly. 'Take a look. I think it'll fit you. I was only a few years older than you when I bought it.'

Faye and Liz went to the box, lifting off the lid together. The dress inside was soft, and had been carefully wrapped in tissue paper. The girls took it out, uncurling the paper.

'Wow!' said Liz as they removed the last of the paper. 'Wow . . .'

Faye pulled out the gown and both girls gasped. It was silk, a shimmering, peacock-blue with a full skirt and an elegantly boned corset top that laced up at the back. As Faye held it up to the light, something that had been rolled inside the dress fell to the floor. Faye bent down and picked it up. It was a lace veil. She was stunned.

'Is this – Aunt Pam, is this a *wedding* gown?'

'Yes, it is,' her aunt admitted. 'Not that I ever wore it.'

Faye and Liz stared at her. 'I – I had no idea,' Faye stammered.

Aunt Pam smiled sadly. 'Well, let's just say you're not the only one to know what lost love feels like,' she said quietly. 'But that's another story. Come on, hurry – I'll find something of your father's for Finn to wear. He can't turn up in his dirty old leathers.'

Finn was waiting at the bottom of the stairs when Faye appeared. He'd thought he was prepared for anything, but he hadn't expected her to look so beautiful. He stared at her dumbly as she smiled shyly, moving carefully down the stairs to avoid stepping on the skirt of her dress. Finn recovered himself before she reached the bottom, holding out his hand to help her from the final step.

'Faye,' he whispered, taking in her hair, pinned in loose curls. 'I – uh . . . I don't know what to say. You look amazing.'

She smiled again, blushing. 'You too. Nice . . . shirt.'

Finn looked down at his outfit, self-consciously. He was wearing a pair of black pants and a white dress shirt. 'I'm sorry,' he said. 'Your dad's jackets were too small for my shoulders. And,' he indicated his open collar, 'I can only fit in the shirt if I don't do it up around the neck.'

Faye laughed. 'Don't be silly. You look gorgeous.'

Finn wanted to stand there, looking at her for ever, but there

297

was so much at stake. 'I'm sorry, ' he said quietly. 'But we have to go, right away.'

Faye nodded, looking around at their little group. 'What is everyone else going to do?'

'Lucas and Jimmy will come with me back to the camp,' said Joe. 'We've got to pack everything up, then we'll all head down into town. I'm taking the real scroll with me for safe keeping, but I've copied the signs and incantations you need here.' He handed Faye a piece of paper. 'Just make sure you mark the mirror exactly as I've written, OK?'

'I've got the fake ballots,' Liz said, holding up the papers before stuffing them into her purse. She was wearing Faye's old prom outfit, a short yellow satin dress with delicate spaghetti straps that showed off her shoulders. She walked to Jimmy, and reached out to take both his hands. Jimmy leaned forwards until their foreheads were touching. They stood like that briefly before Liz took a deep breath and stepped back. 'Now come on,' she said, firmly. 'Let's go.'

Everyone headed for the door, but Finn held Faye back, just for a moment. They looked at each other, and he saw tears glimmering in her beautiful eyes. Finn tried to find something fitting to say, but there was only one thing in his head.

'I love you,' he whispered. 'I don't know how I could ever stop.'

Faye smiled, the tears threatening to fall. 'Then don't,' she whispered back. 'Just . . . don't.'

Chapter Fifty-one

The Prom

Despite everything, Faye had to admit that the school looked amazing. All the lights were on, and black gauze had been pinned over the windows so that the building glowed in the dark. Candles flickered inside hand-carved pumpkins, leading the way to the school gym, where the dance and crowning of the king and queen were due to take place.

'You know,' muttered Liz, 'for zombies they've done a pretty good job.'

The lights in the gym had been dimmed to a low glimmer, but the glitterball that hung from the ceiling was on, casting a dense pattern of circling pinpoint stars throughout the room. Black paper bats flickered overhead in the dim light, suspended on invisible thread. The dance floor was already full, the dancers a twirling, spinning riot of colour as they moved to the music.

'Look,' said Liz, louder this time, nodding towards one corner of the gym. 'There are the ballot boxes.'

Faye nodded, 'And that's Ms Finch guarding them,' she said, seeing her teacher hovering beside the decorated cardboard boxes.

'Don't worry,' said Liz. 'I'll find a way past her.'

'Are you sure?' Faye asked, worried. 'We know now that she's been Mercy's for weeks, Liz. What if—'

299

Liz shrugged, cutting her off. 'We don't have a choice, do we? Wish me luck.'

A second later, she set off through the masses of students, weaving around the dancers.

Finn slid his arm round Faye's shoulder. Faye leaned into his touch. 'She can do it, Faye,' he said.

Faye sighed. 'I know.' She looked at the large mirror that stretched along the far wall, touching the lipstick she held in one hand. 'I have to get to the mirror as soon as possible.'

Finn nodded, and they began to cross the crowded dance floor, holding hands.

Liz looked enviously at her classmates as she passed them, dancing as if they had nothing to lose. There was Candi, looking awesome as usual in an amethyst-coloured full-length dress. Rachel was with her in a floaty outfit that almost seemed as if it was spun from silver. This prom was the best Winter Mill High had ever staged, and here she was, worrying about the end of the world. Oh, what she wouldn't give to have everything back to normal! She bit her lip, realizing that 'normal' is what they would have by the end of the night – and Faye would lose Finn for ever. Her heart ached for her best friend, but she also wanted it to be over with as soon as possible. At least if neither Faye nor Finn remembered each other, they wouldn't be in pain. Her mind wandered to Jimmy, and she wished he was there with her. His lop-sided smile always seemed to make her feel better, these days.

She sidled up to Barbie Finch with an innocent smile. The teacher smiled back, her eyes vacant as she scanned the dance floor.

'Hello, Liz, dear,' she said absently.

'Ms Finch,' beamed Liz, turning her back so that it was

against one of the ballot boxes. 'Isn't it a great party?'

'Oh yes,' the woman said, her voice a hollow echo. 'Just wonderful. Wonderful.'

'That's good. Except—' Liz cut herself off, shaking her head. 'Well, I wondered if those bikers were supposed to be here?'

At the mention of the bikers, Ms Finch snapped her gaze to Liz's her eyes narrowing. 'Bikers?'

Liz felt herself shiver at the cold look in the teacher's eyes. No, she definitely wasn't herself at all. 'Y–yes,' she said. 'They're outside the gate—'

Barbie Finch stared at Liz for a moment. 'I must investigate,' she said, before sweeping past Liz.

Liz nodded, watching as the teacher headed for the back doors. She waited until Barbie had left the gym, and then turned around, swiftly splitting her fake ballot papers into two piles and stuffing them into the two boxes. She turned round, checking that no one had seen, but the students were all dancing as if hypnotized by the music – or something worse.

Faye edged towards the mirror, letting go of Finn's hand and twisting off the cap of her lipstick as she did so. No one took any notice as she checked the piece of paper Joe had pressed into her hand. There were two symbols she had to scrawl onto the lower corners of the mirror, and a third that needed to be placed equidistant between the two.

She'd just finished the first symbol when someone bumped into her, making her jump.

'Sorry,' said Finn softly, into her ear. He was scanning the room, keeping watch.

She took a deep breath and smiled shakily, moving on to the second corner with Finn beside her, blocking anyone from seeing what she was doing.

The bikers were finishing loading everything onto their bikes. Lucas, having helped with the quick pack-up, had taken a seat beside the dwindling fire as Jimmy went to get them both coffee. They were cold and tired, but both knew there was a lot more that had to be done tonight.

As he waited for Jimmy to return, Lucas took out the scroll and looked at it. He ran his fingers over the creased, ancient paper. He couldn't believe that Finn and Faye's fate had been sealed by what was written here, or that the ritual described in the scroll was all aimed at stopping his mother. Lucas shook his head. He hadn't really worked out what was going to happen to him now that he was, basically, homeless. It seemed selfish to worry about such things when his newly found brother and the girl he loved were about to sacrifice everything to save the town.

Lucas was still looking at the scroll as Jimmy returned with the coffee and sat down beside him. He took the tin mug held out to him, glad to have something warm to wrap his fingers around. The snow was falling again, and the temperature had dropped even further.

Jimmy, trying to get comfortable, shifted suddenly, knocking Lucas's elbow. Hot coffee splashed out of the mug, drenching Lucas's legs and hands.

'Oh, no – the scroll!' Lucas stood, frantically shaking the now-wet parchment, trying to remove the droplets of coffee.

'I'm so sorry!' said Jimmy, jumping up, distraught. 'I can't believe I did that – is it ruined?'

Lucas squinted at the scroll with a frown. He stopped shaking the paper, letting the coffee run along the yellowed text. 'No,' he said, quietly. 'No, it isn't.'

Jimmy let out a sigh of relief. 'Thank goodness for that. If we hold it near the fire, maybe we can dry it out.'

Lucas wasn't listening. He was watching the droplets of coffee on the paper. Putting down his mug, he ran one finger along the wet words, feeling his heart begin to hammer wildly.

'Lucas?' Jimmy asked, 'What's the matter?'

'I'm no expert,' Lucas said, hoarsely, still staring at the scroll in his hand. 'But shouldn't old ink run when it gets wet?'

Jimmy leaned forwards, and Lucas heard his sharp intake of breath at he looked at the paper in his hand. 'Oh no . . .'

Lucas jumped up and ran straight for where Joe was packing his bike, Jimmy beside him all the way.

'This is a fake,' Lucas shouted, 'This text is a fake!'

Joe looked over his shoulder, 'What?'

'Look at it,' Lucas hissed, shaking the scroll. 'If this had been written in ink from centuries ago, it would have run. But it hasn't. Joe – it must be modern ink on old paper!'

Jimmy looked between the two of them. 'What does it mean? For us? For Finn and Faye?'

Shocked, Joe rubbed a hand over his eyes. 'That Finn was right. The ritual – the whole thing – it must be a trap.'

'But—'

Lucas's question was cut off by the long, haunting call of a hunting horn floating out of the forest.

Chapter Fifty-two

Trapped

The sound of the horn went on and on. It echoed around the camp, eerie and chilling. Jimmy froze, remembering the last time he'd heard it so close. He remembered the fear of being in the woods alone, the sight of the wolf's horrible yellow eyes at it came at him from the darkness. He shuddered. The bikers, though, sprang into action, standing up and watching the edges of the camp carefully.

And there they were – dark slinking shapes, sticking to the gloom of the undergrowth. They slid along the edges of the light cast by the fire, a flash of yellow eye here, a glimpse of harsh white teeth there. Jimmy turned, slowly, and saw that they were surrounded. He felt Joe place a hand on his shoulder, and jumped.

'Be calm,' Joe cautioned. 'They won't attack – yet. Mercy wants something.'

The hunting horn sounded again, and out of the forest slid a pale horse. It was clad in ancient battle armour, engraved black metal encased its nose and flanks. On its back sat a rider, also armoured. The horse stepped forwards proudly, heading straight for Joe Crowley. The bikers, suspicious, moved to circle their leader and his visitor, obviously ready to defend him if they needed to.

The rider of the pale horse pushed back the visor of his

helmet, and Jimmy was shocked to see the face of Sergeant Wilson beneath. He took something from one of the horse's ornate saddlebags and thrust it towards Joe without speaking.

It was a silver mirror. Joe held it up, and Jimmy was close enough to see the icy patterns coalescing on its surface. And then, suddenly, Mercy Morrow's beautiful face shimmered into view. She smiled.

'Joe Crowley,' she whispered. 'It's been a long, long time.'

'And yet,' Joe answered, 'it's still not long enough.'

Mercy pouted as if this were a game she was losing. 'Oh, come on, Joe. You'd miss me if I wasn't here. In fact, I know you miss me even now.'

'You're wrong. You always were, Mercy, about so many, many things.'

A flicker of anger passed through Mercy's eyes, and the ice on the mirror grew thicker. 'Well, let's see if I'm right about this. You know now that you and our precious son have been caught in a trap of my making. I knew, as soon as I saw that girl's face, that Finn would be just as enchanted as he was with the last one. You should have been smarter, Joe. You should have found a way to keep them apart. The end is nigh, Joe Crowley, and you've brought it on yourself. But I offer you a choice. Come back to me. Come back to me, be my servant again, and I'll let you and the son you took from me live.'

Joe was silent, and for one terrifying moment Jimmy thought he was considering Mercy's offer. But he shook his head. 'Never, Mercy. I would rather suffer in Annwn for all eternity than be your slave again.'

For a split second, Jimmy saw something like grief in Mercy's cold eyes. Then it was replaced by a fury that burned so hot the ice on the mirror's surface began to steam.

306

'Then, Joe Crowley, you have sealed your fate. Yours, and all those with you.'

The light in the mirror died and Mercy's face vanished. The air was suddenly full of snarls, echoing from the forest as Mercy's hounds sensed a battle.

Joe barked an order and as one, the bikers began to transform. Jimmy watched as they fell to their knees, faces twisted in agony. Their skin began change, fur sprouting. Their faces became masks, bursting opening to reveal the wolves beneath. Joe did not change, and Jimmy saw him take up a position behind the wolves, as if to command their movements. Within seconds, only Joe, Lucas and Jimmy remained human, surrounded by the ravenous sounds of two wolf packs.

The hunting horn sounded once more.

Finn felt something ripple through him – a shiver across his skin as he sensed his pack change. Forcing himself to concentrate, he watched as Faye tried to speak to her friend, Candi. It was no good – Finn had seen the look in the girl's eyes before. She was too far within Mercy's influence to really know who Faye was any more.

He took Faye's hand. She was trembling. 'Hey,' he whispered, ducking his head to brush his lips against her ear. 'Let's dance.'

Faye shook her head. 'It's not the right time.'

'We won't ever have another,' Finn reminded her, with a sad smile. 'And anyway, we have to keep up appearances, right?'

He pulled her to the dance floor, glad that the music had slowed. They stood, close together, and Faye looked up at him with such a look of desolation that Finn couldn't help but pull her tight against him, tucking her head under his chin. They swayed, gently, to the music, as Finn tried to imprint the memory of her into his mind.

'Tell me something about you that I don't know,' Faye whispered, pulling back slightly to look at his face. 'Not werewolf stuff . . . something about you.'

Finn looked down at her. It had been a long time since he'd tried think of himself as separate from the wolf. He shrugged. 'I like writing letters,' he said, eventually.

Faye looked surprised. 'Letters?'

'Yeah . . . you know – before things like email happened. Letters, sent by mail. I like writing them.'

Faye smiled. 'I would have loved you to write me a letter.'

He pulled her closer again. 'I will. I promise. Somehow, I'll write you a letter.'

'Ladies and gentlemen!' Barbie Finch's voice boomed across the room, making them both jump. She was standing on the school stage, holding a microphone. Reluctantly, Finn let Faye go as she moved out of his arms to see more clearly. 'As you know, tonight we have been voting on a king and queen of the Winter Mill High Halloween Prom. And I'm delighted to say that the votes have now been counted!'

He reached for Faye's hand.

Liz listened to Barbie's announcement with a frown. Surely they couldn't have counted the votes so quickly? She'd been watching for Ms Finch's return after the wild goose chase Liz had sent her on, and the teacher had arrived back in the gym barely five minutes ago. It was only then that she'd removed the boxes for counting.

'I have to say,' Barbie continued from the stage. 'I am very, very pleased with the result, as I am sure you all will be.'

Liz looked around the hall. The dancing had stopped, as had

308

the music. But not all the students were looking at the teacher on stage. In fact, most of them were looking at Faye and Finn, who were standing in the middle of the dancefloor, holding hands . . .

'The honour of king and queen of this Halloween Prom will this year go to one of our most diligent, popular students,' went on Ms Finch.

Liz wondered if she was imagining things, but no – Faye and Finn seemed oblivious to it, but everyone was looking straight at them. Almost as if they already knew who was going to be crowned . . .

'And also, to one of our newest students,' Barbie went on. 'Which I think is a truly wonderful way to welcome him to our school. So, it is with great pleasure that I announce the winners to be . . .'

Liz shivered as a cold wind passed over her skin. In fact, the temperature in the gym had dropped so suddenly that she could see the gathered students' breath pooling in the air.

'. . . Faye McCarron and Finn Crowley!'

The applause was deafening. It echoed around the freezing room as people pushed forwards to congratulate the lucky pair. Liz tried to catch Faye's eye, to warn her that something wasn't right, but it was impossible. Finn and Faye were surrounded.

Alone on the outskirts, Liz backed towards one of the smaller doors out of the gym. She had to find out what was going on, right now. The vote had happened too quickly – it was almost as if Faye and Finn had already been chosen as king and queen. And if that was the case . . .

Liz slipped out of the door as Barbie Finch announced that the coronation would take place in ten minutes. It was even colder outside the gym. Liz turned left, towards the school's main entrance, but felt the temperature rising as she got closer.

Turning, she retraced her steps, feeling the ice in the air increase as she stepped further and further along the echoing corridor. Back here, behind the school hall, were the offices that students never went in – Liz was sure that whatever was going on, it would be happening back there, where none of her friends would dream of going.

The lights were out, and it was dark, illuminated only by the lamps at the other end of the hallway. Liz kept walking, wrapping her arms around herself as she shivered in the cold. There was a door at the end of the corridor – it was shut, but there was no lock. Reaching out, Liz grasped the metal handle and turned it, hissing in pain as the extreme cold bit into her skin. The door swung open, and Liz let go, looking down at her hand to see that some of her skin had been ripped away, stuck to the frozen handle. She clenched her fist against the pain, looking into the darkness beyond the door. It was another passage, with a second door at the end of it. This door was shut too, but around the edges, light filtered through. It was colder still here, so cold that icicles had begun to form on the ceiling.

Shuddering with cold, Liz went on, looking about for something to protect her hand as she opened this door. There was nothing, so instead she hitched up her skirt and grasped the handle with it, pushing open the door and stepping into the room beyond.

It was flooded with a cold light that burned a fierce blue. In the centre of the room, on a tall wooden chair, sat Mercy Morrow. Her eyes were cast in shadow, her hair a pale halo around her head. At her feet lay a huge grey wolf, its tongue lolling from between wide jaws full of sharp teeth.

Liz screamed. She turned to run, but the door slammed shut, trapping her inside.

'Now, now,' said Mercy in a soft, dangerous voice, leaning down to scratch the wolf behind the ears. 'There's really no point running. I'll only have to send Peter here after you if you do.'

Chapter Fifty-three

No Mercy

There was a moment of silence as the sound of the horn echoed away. Then all hell broke loose. Lucas watched as one of Mercy's hounds took the first leap. It plunged forwards, foam flecking its open mouth. Joe shouted an order and the biker-wolves attacked. Within seconds, both wolf packs were tearing at each other. Seated high on his horse, Mitch Wilson watched from the edge of the clearing, horn ready at his lips to spur his pack on.

Jimmy stood, terrified, not knowing what to do.

'We need weapons!' Lucas shouted, over the roar of snarling dogs, searching for something suitable.

'How do we know which are which?' Jimmy shouted back. 'The wolves all look the same!'

Lucas watched as Joe stood his ground amid the mêlée. To his left, two wolves battled each other to the ground. One sank its teeth into the other's hind-quarters. With a howl, the injured wolf wrenched itself away, splattering blood across its enemy's snout. It turned, ignoring its torn flank, and plunged forwards again, grazing its canines along the other's spine. The other wolf screamed in pain, an animal sound that wrenched at Lucas's eardrums.

'Lucas! Look out!' He heard Jimmy's yell and turned to see a wolf coming right at him, fangs bared. Its yellow eyes were full

313

of hate. Lucas froze for a moment, but then he heard Jimmy shout again. 'Here! Catch!'

From the corner of his eye Lucas saw something come soaring through the air towards him. It was a tent pole, with the ground spike still attached. Lunging sideways, Lucas caught it and turned in one movement, planting the blunt end in the ground behind him and angling the other towards the leaping wolf. It caught the creature full in the chest. The wolf howled in pain, struggling to pull itself from the spike. Lucas, shocked, let go of the pole and backed away.

All around them, the sounds of snarling and snapping filled the air. Mercy's pack was desperate, crazed by the smell of blood and the promise of food. Joe, still human, ran to the pale horse, lashing out at Sergeant Wilson with a burning branch he'd taken from the dying fire. The horse reared, terrified of the flames. Mitch Wilson clung on, swinging at Joe with one fist as he battled to stay on his ride. The horse dropped to all fours and then twisted sideways, dislodging Liz's dad and sending him to the ground with a clang of metal. Joe lunged towards him, turning back to look at Lucas and Jimmy.

'This is a distraction,' he shouted, over the noise. 'Get to the bikes. We have to get to Finn and Faye – we have to stop the ritual!'

Liz froze with her back to the door, shaking badly. Mercy rose, smoothing out the sumptuous layers of her white satin gown. The wolf moved with her, yellow eyes fixed on Liz.

'What a pity you weren't there when they began to translate that scroll, hmm?' Mercy purred, weaving her way towards Liz. 'You're obviously the smart one, aren't you? Just like your father. You wouldn't have taken it at face value, would you?'

'What have you done?' Liz asked, fearfully.

314

'Oh, nothing much, my dear,' Mercy said, touching an icy finger to Liz's cheek. 'But of course you must realize that this little ritual Joe had you plan out is simply a trap? Do you really think I would let such a valuable text out of my sight?' The woman shook her head, her bright eyes piercing in the weird blue light. 'Really, Joe should have known me better.'

'So it won't work?' Liz asked. 'The ritual won't do anything?'

Mercy laughed, a jangling sound that grated in Liz's ears. 'Oh, it'll do something all right. Just not quite what you all wanted. My dear boy, Finn, so willing to sacrifice himself . . . Well, he'll get his wish. But it won't save her. It'll save my kin, instead.'

'Your kin?'

'The ones Joe banished to the depths of Annwn, leaving me so, so alone. I worked out a way to bring them back, you see. A big enough sacrifice that the spirits of Annwn will return them all to me, every single one.'

Liz blinked. 'Finn and Faye? That's what will happen when they perform the ritual?'

'It really took me such a lot of trouble to put those two together,' Mercy sighed, reaching out lazily to stroke the huge wolf at her feet. 'I practically had to chase her into his arms. But it was really just luck that I met her father, carrying that quaint little locket.'

Liz stared at the wolf, feeling her blood run cold. What did Mercy mean? Oh God, had she killed Mr McCarron? Had she fed him to the wolf?

'As soon as I saw her picture,' Mercy purred, 'I knew that it was fate. Of course Faye was destined to love my errant son. And that love was just what I needed to bargain with Annwn once again.'

Liz felt tears in her eyes. 'So you're going to sell them both to the underworld?'

'Oh, Liz, my dear, do please learn to think bigger,' Mercy drawled. 'Their love is important, yes, but I'm not just thinking about them. All those beautiful, juicy teenagers, dancing away in that gym . . . don't you think Annwn would love all of them to play with?' Mercy smiled, showing her teeth. 'That's the kind of exchange the underworld demands. That's what it will take for me to receive my kin again. And lo! The time is upon us. The trap is set and baited. The game is almost won. At last!'

Faye grasped Finn's hand again, overwhelmed by the crowd of well-wishers. It seemed that everyone at the Prom wanted to shake their hands and congratulate them. Everyone was smiling and laughing, hugging and chatting. Then the music started up again, and another dance began. It was faster, this time, a hypnotic beat that whirled with the mood.

'Are you OK?' Finn asked her. She nodded. 'It must have worked – Liz did it,' he added.

'Can you see her?' Faye asked, looking around.

'Not at the moment. She must be here somewhere.'

Faye looked up at his strong face as Finn scanned the crowd. She squeezed his hand tighter, and he looked down at her. 'I'm not ready,' she said, desperately. 'I can't do it.'

Finn raised his free hand and stroked her cheek. 'I know how you feel, but you can do it. *We* can do it. I promise.'

'But I don't want to.'

He smiled, a world of sadness in his eyes. 'Neither do I.'

She nodded, leaning against his chest.

Jimmy and Lucas reached the bikes first, with Joe close behind them. Jimmy saw Lucas hesitate.

316

'The key will be under the back wheel,' he shouted. 'Come on, hurry.'

'I don't know how,' Lucas shouted back. 'I've never ridden a bike before.'

'Trust me,' Jimmy told him, kicking the stand of his chosen ride shut. 'If you can handle that Ferrari, you can handle this. Just get on it, and follow me!'

Joe leaped onto his own bike, taking the lead away from the camp and through the woods. Jimmy nodded for Lucas to go between them, looking over his shoulder as they rolled out.

None of the wolves was following, too intent on their savage combat. But Mitch Wilson watched from the back of his pale steed.

They raced through the woods, ducking branches laden with heavy snow. Twice Jimmy saw Lucas falter, his bike threatening to skid out of control on the icy hillside, but he managed to right himself. They rushed out of the woods and onto the road into town, sliding on the gritted tarmac as the snow-clogged tyres tried to deal with the change. Joe didn't slow down, racing onwards, the lights of Winter Mill in the distance.

Then a new kind of light lit up the road in front of them, blue and red. They were climbing the snowy road towards the bikes, travelling fast.

'Squad cars!' Jimmy yelled, but the wind tore his words away. A few second later the sirens could be heard, chasing over the cold air on the hill.

Up ahead, Joe turned briefly, looking back at Lucas and Jimmy, lifting a hand to spur them both on as the cars drew closer. Joe was betting on them being able to filter past all four before the squad cars could turn and follow.

Jimmy hunkered down on the bike. His heart was banging

317

against his ribcage, his ears full of the sound of sirens and wind. Ahead of him, Lucas wobbled, and Jimmy prayed he could hold on.

Chapter Fifty-four

Crowned

'And so, I give you ... your Halloween Prom King and Queen!'

The rest of Barbie Finch's words were drowned out as the assembled students erupted into wild applause. Finn and Faye stood at the bottom of the stage steps, looking at each other. Faye tried to say something, but the words stuck in her throat, and anyway, Finn wouldn't have heard her over the noise of the crowd. Finn smiled at her gently, taking her hand and leading her up the steps to where Ms Finch waited.

A sudden, eerie hush fell on the crowd as the couple walked across the stage. Barbie smiled at them, a radiant, empty gesture that did not light up her eyes. She turned, beckoning to two students who stood, waiting in the wings. In their hands they carried velvet pillows that each held a crown.

Faye heart began to hammer, her eyes a blur of tears.

'There's no need to cry, dear,' murmured Ms Finch, into the silence. 'This is *glorious*.'

Faye shut her eyes, forcing the tears to fall. A cold wind shuddered through the hall, rustling in the silence. She shivered, but when she opened her eyes again, all she could see was Finn, standing close to her, looking down.

'Now,' he whispered.

And quietly, too quietly for anyone but Finn to hear, she

began to recite the text that Joe had written down; in a language she did not even know.

The cop cars came at them out of the gloom, sirens wailing like banshees in a storm. Jimmy saw Joe throw his bike sideways, between two squad cars, weaving to avoid the wing mirrors as they passed, almost touching him. Lucas pulled to the right, out to the edge of the road, bumping along the icy edge of the tarmac. His back wheel kicked out and he almost lost it on the still-frozen ground, but somehow Lucas held on.

'Where did these guys come from?' Jimmy heard Lucas shout at him, over the wind.

'Sergeant Wilson must have called for reinforcements before the town was stranded,' Jimmy yelled back.

'Great!' bellowed Lucas. 'That's just . . . great!'

Jimmy wrenched his ride left, holding his breath as one of the cars streamed past him, so close that he felt the turbulent air trail it left in its wake. Seeing him move, the car behind changed direction, trying to cut him off, forcing Jimmy to run right, into the middle of the road. The bike shuddered and he felt the front wheel catch a stubborn patch of ice, threatening to slide, but he pulled it back, holding on. He felt his injured leg protest a little, but he ignored it. Roaring onwards, they left the cop cars behind in a flurry of snow and screaming rubber.

Barbie Finch's gaze was fixed on Faye, and she was saying something, some sort of congratulations before Finn and Faye were crowned. Faye wasn't listening. Finn's hands felt warm where they covered hers, his lips moving silently in time with her own as she recited the incantation under her breath.

A strange sensation washed over her, as if she were somewhere on the ceiling, looking down at what was going on. Faye felt calm, the fear draining away as she stared into Finn's eyes. She glanced towards the mirror, seeing that it had grown dark, as if there was a maelstrom brewing, just below the glassy surface.

'Again,' she heard Finn whisper, as the two crown bearers stepped forwards.

'This love, for ever . . .' she echoed back under her breath, beginning the incantation again. 'One love, for ever . . .'

A cold wind blew through the hall, snatching at Faye's breath. She shivered, stepping closer to Finn, feeling herself caught by his gaze, unable to look away.

She felt the crown settle on her head.

'Again,' Finn whispered.

The squad cars were fast, but no match for the bikes in bad weather. The snow was falling so thickly that by the time the three men reached town, it was almost a blizzard. Lucas wiped at his eyes, clearing them of the slush, but he could hardly feel his fingers, they were so cold.

Ahead of him, Joe waved them forwards, faster and faster through the empty streets, heading for the school. Lucas glanced behind him, half-expecting to see the police come storming down the hill, but the road up into the forest was dark and silent.

The three bikes sped into Winter Mill High's parking lot, sliding to a stop in front of the main doors. Joe jumped off immediately and ran up the steps. He tried to push open the doors, but they were locked. Lucas leaped off his bike, joining Joe in his attempt to open the doors, but it was hopeless – they were locked fast.

'We can try another way in,' Lucas said, out of breath, but Joe shook his head.

'If this one's locked, they'll all be locked. Mercy won't take any chances.'

Lucas bent double, still trying to catch his breath. The mention of his mom cut like a knife beneath his ribcage. All of this was his mom's fault . . .

There was the sudden roar of an engine behind them. They turned to see Jimmy on his bike, revving and wheel spinning as he held it in place.

'Move!' He shouted.

'No, Jimmy!' Joe yelled back. 'You'll kill yourself!'

Jimmy didn't listen, letting the engine go instead. The bike leaped forwards and Joe and Lucas jumped out of the way as it screeched towards the entrance. Jimmy and the bike hit the double doors head-on, ripping them open as the bike tore through the wood. Lucas saw the bike swerve and Jimmy flew over the handlebars, crashing against the wall before sliding to the floor in a motionless heap.

Lucas and Joe ran to Jimmy. He was conscious, but bloodied and bruised.

'Leave me,' he told them. 'You've got to get to Faye and Finn.'

Lucas knelt beside him. 'But you're hurt—'

'I'm fine,' Jimmy said, pushing Lucas away. 'Really. Go!'

Joe pulled Lucas to his feet. 'We'll be back,' he promised Jimmy, before turning to Lucas. 'Which way?' he asked, urgently. 'Show me!'

Lucas took the lead, running down the corridor and turning left, towards the school gym. There was no sign of anyone, no sound at all. But then, as they approached the gym's doors, a strange kind of murmur started up. It turned into a chant as Lucas reached for the door handle. He grunted as he touched it, pulling his hand back.

'It's freezing!'

Joe pushed him aside, grabbing at the handle with his calloused hands and throwing the door open. The three rushed inside, stopping dead when they saw the scene inside.

The room was crowded with students, all looking towards the stage. Over their heads, Lucas could see Finn and Faye, standing close together, crowns on their heads. They were staring at each other as if nothing else existed. Faye's lips were moving, but whatever she was saying was drowned out by the chant of the crowd.

'*Kiss* . . .' they were all saying, '*Kiss* . . . *Kiss* . . .'

'No!' shouted Joe, 'Stop! Finn, stop!'

Lucas shouted too, but there was no sign that Finn and Faye had heard them. Joe leaped forwards, forcing his way through the crowd, trying to reach the stage.

Lucas looked at the large mirror on the wall. Beneath its surface boiled angry black waves of what looked like smoke. They burst up from within, cracking against the wall of glass holding them in.

'Look at the mirror!' he shouted. 'It's going to break, it's going to—'

He tried to raise his voice against the chant, which was growing louder and louder. Lost in the crowd, Joe couldn't reach the stage. He was becoming entangled in the wall of bodies all staring adoringly up at Finn and Faye.

Lucas forced his way to the edge of the room, trying to make his way along the wall.

Chapter Fifty-five

Last Stand

'Oh, now don't cry, there's a dear,' Mercy drawled with a sigh, circling around the chair she had forced Liz to sit on. 'I do find girls who weep so tiresome.'

Liz put a hand up to her face, surprised to feel tears on her cheeks. She was so numb she hadn't thought she could feel anything at all. She was shaking, from deep cold and an even deeper fear. The wolf had moved closer to her, and Liz looked up to find it gazing at her. For the first time, Liz found herself staring right into its yellow eyes, and was surprised to see something other than evil there. It looked not angry, but . . . sad. Yes, that was it. The wolf's eyes were sad. Liz frowned, and the wolf dipped its head and moved it, just slightly, from side to side, as if it were trying to tell her something.

Mercy returned to her seat, reaching down to pet the wolf as she passed. She picked up a delicate lace shawl and threw it over her pale, bare shoulders.

'I know what will cheer you up,' she said, brightly. 'Let's go and watch all the fun, shall we? They've gone awfully quiet out there – the game must almost be played out.'

Mercy took a step towards her again, but then froze for a second, listening. A new sound had joined the humming chant floating in from the school gym – a chorus of shouts.

As Mercy hesitated, Liz took a chance. Leaping up, she raced for the door, but the wolf was quicker than its mistress. It lunged towards her as her hand grasped the handle, its teeth snapping so close to Liz's ankle that she felt saliva spatter across her leg.

Heart hammering, Liz reached for something – anything that she could use to ward off the wolf. Her hand came in contact with the back of another chair, stacked beside the door. Grabbing it, Liz swung it towards the wolf, smashing it around the head with enough force that it yelped in pain, skittering sideways and slamming into a bookcase.

Liz heard Mercy roar with rage, and glanced back to see the woman coming for her, her face a mask of anger. She screamed too, flinging open the door as the wolf began to stir. Slamming it shut behind her, Liz ran down the corridor.

Behind her there was the sound of wood shattering as the door exploded. Liz held her arms up to shelter her head as a shower of lethal wooden splinters peppered the air. Glancing back, she saw Mercy advancing, the wolf at her feet. Around them both was a dense aura of flickering electricity, sparking blue as Mercy's magic drew itself to the aid of her anger.

Liz slammed the second door behind her and skidded along the corridor, her borrowed heels almost impossible to run in. She reached the door of the gym and threw herself headlong through it, dragging it shut behind her.

'Finn!' she screamed. 'Faye! Wait – don't – it's a trap!'

'Liz!' Lucas's voice sounded beside her. She turned to see him pushing through the crowd towards her.

'It's a trap, Lucas – the ritual's a trap!'

'We know – Joe's trying to get to them, but I don't think he's going to make it!'

The ground began to shake. Liz looked back towards the door she'd just crashed through.

'What is it?' Lucas asked, grabbing hold of her to stop them both falling over.

'Mercy! She's coming – and she's angry!' Liz looked up at Finn and Faye as they began to lean towards each other. 'What are we going to do?'

'The mirror,' Lucas shouted, over the growing roar around them. 'If we can smash the mirror, nothing can be sucked through it – right?'

'But we'll never get there!' Liz looked across the room at the mirror, now a dark, swirling morass of evil.

'I need something I can break it with,' Lucas shouted over the noise, 'Give me something I can throw!'

'I don't have anything! Can't you use a chair?'

Liz watched as Lucas ran forwards, trying to find a way through the dense crowd of students, but it was hopeless. There was no way they were going to get closer to the mirror.

Liz felt something behind her, and heard Lucas shout. She turned to see the wolf – it had run ahead of Mercy, and was now beside her, looking up at her with those sad, yellow eyes.

'Liz,' Lucas yelled. 'Run! Run!'

He lurched forwards, trying to pull her away, but the wolf jumped at her. Liz flinched, expecting to feel its fangs biting at her. But instead of teeth, she felt its soft fur, brushing against her leg. The wolf was butting at her purse with its head.

A light went off in Liz's mind, and she scrabbled in her bag, pulling out the letter opener that had belonged to Faye's father. 'What about this?'

Lucas grabbed it from her hand, turning towards the mirror. He frowned in concentration, leaning back, his hand stretched far over his head. Then he threw himself forwards and let go with every ounce of energy in his body.

The knife flew across the room, spinning over the heads of

the gathered students. It soared in an arc through the air before striking the glass and clattering to the ground.

The mirror began to crack. It splintered silently, a slow ripple of fractures tracing up and out. They covered the mirror's surface, disrupting the smooth glass like a miniature earthquake.

In the gym, time slowed. Liz felt as if her body had turned to jelly. She could hardly move. She wanted to ask Lucas what was happening, whether it was working, but she had no voice. She couldn't hear anything, as though there was cotton wool stuffed in her ears. Liz turned her head to see Mercy, frozen, still in the act of coming through the imploding door. The wolf at her feet was stuck in mid-leap, paws outstretched, fur wavering.

Then, time started again. There was the resounding crack of glass breaking, the harsh tinkle of shards crashing to the ground as the mirror's surface disintegrated. Sound rushed in, and Liz was suddenly drowning in it as every student in the hall snapped out of whatever trance they'd been in.

'Oh my god!' Liz heard Candi scream, as she spun around in a circle. 'What's happening? Is this the Prom? I don't—'

'Look at the mirror,' Hart Jesson shouted, drowning out Candi's confusion. Everywhere, students were in a state of panic. It was as if they'd all woken from a collective dream, and had no idea what was real and what wasn't.

Then Rachel Hogan saw the wolf, and screamed. She pointed a shaking finger at the animal, still standing beside Liz. The screams spread, the fear catching, until the gym was full of piercing shrieks. On stage, Finn and Faye, woken by the noise, sprang apart. They looked out, over the chaos in the gym. Liz saw Faye grab Finn's arm and point at the mirror.

The glass was continuing to fall from the frame, a thousand tiny, shining reflections tumbling as the cracks continued to grow. But instead of leaving the blank wall behind the mirror, there was a dense, black pit of dark smoke and flame. It rose in oily puffs, bubbling up through the cracks as the glass disintegrated.

The terrified students, afraid, stampeded. Liz and Lucas were shoved aside as they rushed for the exits, still screaming. Through the mêlée, Joe reached the stage and in a second was with Finn and Faye.

'Fools!' Liz heard Mercy scream, over the noise. 'What have you done? What have you *done*?'

The wolf dodged the running students, paws skidding on the polished wooden floor. Mercy's aura sparked in the gloom as the terrified students streamed around her.

It took only moments for the gym to empty. The screams echoed away with the sound of running feet. Mercy strode into the room towards Liz and Lucas, the wolf with her, always.

'What have you done?' she asked again, grabbing at Lucas.

'We've stopped you!' he shouted, defiantly. 'We knew your ritual was a fake.'

Mercy pushed him backwards, a suddenly look of fear crossing her face. 'I am still your mother, Lucas,' she hissed. 'You must help me. We must—'

Liz saw Lucas shake his head. 'I'll never call you my mother again,' he said, his voice trembling with anger. 'And I will never help you! How could you do the things that you've done? How could not tell me what you really are?'

Mercy shook her head. 'When you were old enough, I would have,' she told him. 'Lucas, I still can! You must help me, before it's too late. Before we both die—'

'Never,' Lucas hissed. 'I don't care what happens to me. I will never help you. *Never*.'

Mercy spun on her heel to look up at Joe, still standing on

329

the stage with Finn and Faye. Raising one arm, she pointed at the fractured mirror and its roiling sea of black mist.

'Don't you understand?' she shrieked. The sound of Mercy's terror chilled Liz to the core. 'You interrupted the ritual! The mirror was enchanted, and now the path to Annwn is left open!'

Joe shouted at her, stalking towards her angrily. 'I've had enough of your lies.'

Mercy began to laugh hysterically, a high-pitched, fearful sound that filled the empty gym. Then from somewhere, a low rumble began to tremble beneath their feet.

'You always were a fool, Joe Crowley, and now you've killed us all. You've given them a way in. And not one of us can escape!'

Chapter Fifty-six

The Final Bargain

The rumbling went on, growing louder and louder. Above them, the glitterball still spun slowly, casting weird, looping patterns of light against the gym's darkened walls and ceiling.

'What's happening?' Liz shouted, raising her voice over the noise.

'I don't know!' Lucas shouted back.

Joe jumped from the stage; Finn and Faye close behind him. Liz looked around. 'Hey,' she shouted, shaking Lucas's arm. 'Where's Jimmy?'

She saw the hesitation on Lucas's face, and a new kind of fear seeped into her veins. 'Where is he, Lucas? Tell me!'

'I'm here,' came a voice calling from behind her. 'I'm here, Liz . . .'

She spun round to see Jimmy, limping slowly across the trembling floor. He was bent almost double, obviously in pain. Liz ran to him. 'What happened to you?'

He tried to shrug, but grimaced in pain instead. 'Bit of a battle getting in. What happened to the mirror?'

Liz looked up at it to see the roiling darkness that had been contained behind the glass moving like a living thing. It surged and rolled inside the frame, testing its boundaries, trying to find a way out.

'The creatures of Annwn are rising,' Mercy cried, reaching

331

down to grip her great wolf's collar. The creature, afraid, tried to twist from her grasp.

'How do we stop it?' Faye shouted, over the din. 'Mercy, tell us how to stop it!'

'We can't!' Mercy screamed. 'They will come for all of us! They're coming now – look!'

Amid the smoke were faces, fleeting among waves of black flame. They rose to the surface, twisted, demented, skeletal, baring evil teeth and staring with blank eyes before sinking once more out of sight.

'They're looking for a way in,' Mercy cried. 'And they'll find it. They can feel us, feel our fear . . .'

Joe grabbed her by the forearms, shaking her violently. 'There must be something we can do!'

Mercy shook her head hopelessly. 'There's nothing – nothing! There's no way to seal the mirror again now. Before, I could control it. It was . . . It was mine . . .'

'It was never yours, Mercy,' Joe shouted back. 'Don't you see that? Don't you understand?'

'It could have been!' Mercy raged. 'This is your fault, Joe Crowley! We should have been completing this together, side by side – you should never have left me!'

Joe shook his head. 'I never had your cruelty, Mercy,' he said. 'And I'd rather die than see it drag another single soul into Annwn.'

There was a loud crack, and Liz turned. The frame of the mirror was smoking as it burned. The black maelstrom began to seep out like bubbles rising to the surface of a boiling pot. It surged out of the mirror and up the wall to the ceiling. It crept onwards, a malevolent dark fire, eating everything in its path.

* * *

Faye tugged at Finn's hand. 'The ritual,' she shouted, over the ever-growing noise. 'Your dad said that when he escaped Mercy before, he twisted it. Can't we do that again?'

Finn shook his head. 'It won't work – Annwn has already been awakened to what's here. They're expecting the bargain they agreed to.'

'Then what?' Faye asked, looking at Joe. 'Come on – there must be some way we can stop this!'

'They'll want something of equal value,' Joe told her. 'We have to give them that, nothing less.'

Finn looked at his father. 'Dad?'

Faye saw the look that passed between father and son – sadness, and understanding.

'I'll do it,' said Joe. 'I'll sacrifice myself to Annwn.'

Faye felt Finn's hand tighten over hers. 'You can't,' he shouted. 'Dad, it's not—'

'It's the only way,' Joe shouted back. 'An Immortal life, given willingly. I have to, Finn. Or everything we've worked for is lost, and so is this town. Quickly – you have to help me. We must do this now, before it's too late.'

'But there's no mirror,' Finn pointed out. 'It's smashed, gone. There's nothing to perform the ritual with.'

Faye raised her head to stare at the ceiling, watching the writhing blackness spread, imagining it devouring the world completely. They were lost, surely. With no mirror to complete the ritual, everyone in Winter Mill would be engulfed by Annwn, lost to the horrors of the underworld for ever.

Something shone on the surface of the darkness, a pinprick of light. It was there for a second before dancing away across the room. Faye blinked, seeing more and more, a halo of stars, picked out in light.

'The glitterball!' She shouted. It still hung above them, turning, casting tiny fractured lights to the four corners of the room.

Liz looked up, confused. 'What?'

'The glitterball! We can use the glitterball!'

'What are you talking about?' Lucas asked.

Jimmy pointed up, frantic. 'Faye's right! Look at it! Mirrors! It's made of mirrors!'

They all looked up at the turning orb. 'Oh my god,' said Liz. 'You're right! Can we use it?'

'We have to mark it with the symbols,' said Finn. 'Can we lower it?'

'I know where the controls are!' Liz said, pulling out of Jimmy's arms. She ran to a lever on one of the walls.

'Liz!' Faye shouted after her. 'Look out!'

She heard Liz scream as one of the twisted black figures made a grab for her out of the smoke. It lunged at her friend, ghostly fingers scraping sharply along Liz's spine. She ducked, grabbing the lever on the wall and wrenching it, hard.

The glitterball began to descend, even as the blackness threatened to hide it completely.

'Quickly,' Joe shouted, 'we're running out of time! I need something to write with!'

Faye thrust her lipstick towards him, the one she'd fatefully used to enchant the now-destroyed gym mirror.

Finn watched as his father prepared to write the symbols. Above them, the darkness swirled like a living thing. The dark figures were stronger now, creeping out of the mirror on all fours, crawling jerkily along the walls, watching the play unfold below them.

'This won't be enough,' Mercy screamed. 'Don't you understand? What Annwn wants – what it demands – one Immortal life won't be enough to sate that!'

Joe turned to look at her. 'Then what about two, Mercy?'

334

She stepped backwards. 'No. No, I won't.'

'But would it work?' Finn shouted at his mother. 'Would two work?' Mercy didn't answer, and Finn turned to Joe. 'What about two?' he asked. 'Two Immortal lives, given willingly, out of love. That has to be enough, doesn't it?'

He felt Faye tugging at his hand, but forced himself not to look at her. Finn's gaze was locked with his father's, and he saw the answer there.

Finn nodded. 'I'll give myself, Dad. I'll come with you.'

'Finn, no!' Faye cried, clutching his arm and trying to get him to turn towards her. 'You can't! Please, please don't!'

Joe nodded back at him, a sad look on his face. Then he turned towards the glitterball and reached out to paint the first of the symbols on its mirrored surface. His voice rose as he began to chant, ancient words that immediately added to the electricity in the room.

Finn faced Faye, seeing the tears in her eyes. All he wanted to do was wrap her up in his arms and hold her there, for ever, but there was no time for them. If he didn't do this now, they'd all be lost. He pulled her close, feeling her head come to rest against his chest.

'I have to,' he told her, as gently as he could over the roaring maelstrom around them and the sound of his father's incantations.

Faye looked up at him, the despair in her eyes suddenly replaced with steely determination. 'Then I'm coming with you.'

'What? No, Faye, you can't—'

'I can, and I will. Annwn wants as much emotion as it can get, right? Well, I'd say right now I've got quite a lot for it.'

'You don't understand,' Finn said, pleading. 'It'll be worse than you can imagine. I can't let you go through that. I won't.'

335

'So you expect me to live, here, without you, knowing that you're there, in pain?' Faye asked. 'You think that won't be torture for me?' She shook her head, standing on tiptoe to place her hands either side of his face. 'Finn, I love you. Where you go, I go. I won't leave you.'

Finn stared into her eyes, so fiery, so determined, so beautiful. He wanted to kiss her, and realized that this may be his final chance. His father's chant was rising, reaching its conclusion. Finn leaned in, but before their lips could meet, he was wrenched away. It was Joe, pulling Finn towards the glitterball.

'There's no time!' Joe shouted. 'Touch the glass, now!'

Finn did as he was told, reaching out to press his palm to the mosaic of glass. Faye moved with him, and before Finn could stop her, she'd placed her hand beside his. Joe stood beside them, his huge hand joining theirs on the glitterball. He shouted one final incantation, his voice echoing away into the storm around them.

There was a long, low shriek from somewhere. It sounded more animal than human. Inside the mirrored surface of the glitterball, a column of black smoke grew, and grew, until it was too big to be contained. It shot out of the shining globe, pluming above them. Inside it were more creatures, writhing, their skeletal faces looking down at the humans below them.

Faye screamed as the column descended, ready to swallow them up, and Finn held her close. He shut his eyes, expecting to feel the grip of Annwn taking hold at any minute. But then there was a pause.

Finn opened his eyes, and saw that Faye was staring up, into the billowing column of oily black. One single figure had emerged from the tangled mass of lost souls. It was a woman, gaunt and skeletal, but still recognisably sad. She stared down at them.

'I know her,' Faye shouted. 'I've seen her before. In the mirror, at the mall . . .'

The figure swooped towards them and Finn felt Faye flinch. But the creature did not attack. It hovered in front of them for a moment. And then she spoke.

'Not you,' it whispered, in a voice like a thousand dull knives sliding against each other. 'Neither of you. My masters will not take these souls. They are not enough.'

Panic sped through Finn's veins. If this didn't work, they had no other option. 'No,' he shouted, as the figure began to sink into the smoke once more. 'Wait! Please, wait—'

The lost soul turned away. Finn thought it was going to disappear, but instead, it shot towards Mercy Morrow. The enchantress shrank back, but the figure wove through the air, riding the tide of smoke until they were nose to nose.

'This one,' it hissed, its ghostly voice echoing clearly through the hall. 'This one has fear enough to feed us. This one.'

'No!' Mercy screamed. 'No, you can't!' she scrambled backwards. 'Without me, who will bargain with you?'

The figure smiled, and in its spectral face, Finn could see a line of sharp, terrifying fangs. 'My masters will find a way,' it whispered. 'They always do.'

Mercy turned, trying to flee, but suddenly the great grey wolf was there, blocking her way, snarling and snapping.

'What are you doing?' Mercy screamed at the creature. 'You're mine! Mine!'

The wolf drove her back towards the ball of mirrors, yellow eyes consumed with rage. It didn't stop until she was pressed against the shining orb.

Finn felt something cold spark under his hand, and suddenly he and Faye were flung backwards. Finn threw his arm out, trying to protect Faye's head as they both crashed to the floor. Finn looked around for Joe, but his father was still standing, hand fused with the glitterball. Around him and Mercy, the air shimmered black.

'Dad?' Finn shouted. 'What—'

At that moment, more electricity burst out of the mirrored orb, silhouetting both Immortals against the darkness. A loud crack sounded above them as the glitterball came free of its moorings, crashing to the floor. Its mirrors shivered, a thousand reflections of Joe and Mercy shuddering on its surface. Around them, the writhing smoke descended, snaking towards the ball in one smooth stream. It engulfed the two Immortals, swallowing them whole.

The rumbling grew louder still. The floor of the gym shook, the wooden planks shearing underfoot as they were torn to pieces. Finn saw Lucas, Liz and Jimmy fall to the floor. The blackness poured into the huge glitterball, filling the tiny mirrors one by one. It blew past them all, faster and faster, like a storm rushing through a valley. The last ghostly black flame fled into it, and for a brief second, the reflections of Joe and Mercy's faces were repeated over and over as they sank into the darkness within.

The glitterball exploded. It splintered into tiny shards too small to count, sending showers of glass into the air to tinkle to the ground like tiny bells.

And then the rumbling stopped.

They all lay still for a while, catching their breath. Lucas was the first to get up, looking at the place that his mother had been standing before the hordes of Annwn had claimed her. There was no sign that she'd been there at all. He felt a gentle hand on his arm, and turned to see Faye looking at him sympathetically.

'I'm sorry, Lucas,' she said.

He shrugged, trying to smile, trying not to think of the only parent he'd ever known, lost somewhere in the underworld, suffering at the mercy of those monsters. 'I guess that was karma in action, huh?'

He looked around the gym. The room was a wreck, the floor torn up, the ceiling tainted with what looked like oil. On the wall, all that was left of the mirror was its smoking frame. The darkness had gone, leaving only singed brick where once had been the path into Annwn.

'Well,' he said, wryly, 'Looking on the bright side, I guess this means—'

He stopped mid-sentence, spying something in the corner of the room. It was a man, lying on his side, clad in rags and apparently unconscious.

'Hey,' Lucas said. 'Who's that?'

Finn took Faye's hand, looking to where Lucas pointed. 'Anyone see where the wolf went?'

Lucas shook his head. 'No . . . it just kind of vanished.'

Finn nodded. 'With Mercy's magic broken, the wolves that were under her control will be wolves no longer . . .'

'Faye,' Liz said, suddenly, in a voice that made Lucas look at her immediately. 'Doesn't that look like . . . Isn't that—?'

Lucas heard Faye's sharp intake of breath as she looked at the crumpled man. 'Oh god! Oh god . . . It's my dad! That's my dad!' Faye ran to the slumped figure. She crouched beside him, shaking him. 'Dad! Can you hear me?'

Liz knelt down next to Faye. 'Mercy called him Peter . . . but I thought she was just being clever,' she said. 'You know, Peter and the wolf . . . I never thought . . . Oh my god, and the wolf tried to help me! With breaking the mirror – and when Mercy tried to get away! I should have known! Mr McCarron!'

'Dad,' Faye said again. 'Daddy, please wake up!'

Peter McCarron opened his eyes, slowly, blinking as he looked up at his daughter. Lucas could see how alike their eyes were. 'Faye?' Her father asked, hoarsely. 'Faye, is that really you?'

'Wait . . .' said Liz, looking up at Finn as realization dawned. 'Wait a minute – does this mean my dad's going to be OK too? If the magic's gone – will he be back to normal? Oh, Finn, please say he will!'

Lucas saw Finn nod, wearily. 'He should be fine,' his brother said. 'All the men under Mercy's thrall should be back to normal.'

Lucas raised an eyebrow. 'Does that go for the bikers, too?'

Finn frowned. 'I don't think so. We left her influence centuries ago.'

Liz jumped up, grabbing Jimmy's hand. 'Jimmy, we have to find my mom and dad! And yours! Please? Right now?'

Jimmy smiled. 'Let's go.'

Lucas watched the pair head for the exit with before looking at Finn. 'I'm sorry. You know – about your father. He was a good guy.'

Finn nodded, grimly. 'Yeah.'

Lucas shrugged unhappily, staring at his feet. 'I guess you and I are kind of in the same boat now, right? With the no parents thing, I mean.'

He felt Finn's eyes on him and looked up to meet his brother's gaze. 'That's a pretty big house you've got up there in the woods,' Finn said, quietly.

Lucas nodded. 'It is.'

'Too big for one person, I mean.'

Lucas stared at Finn, and then smiled. 'Yeah. I could probably take in a few lodgers. The sort that have spent a lot of time on the road, maybe?'

340

Finn smiled back. 'You know, Joe told me once that Mercy used to keep diaries.'

'Diaries?' Lucas repeated, confused.

Finn nodded. 'An account of where she'd been, the people she'd met . . .' he looked Lucas in the eye. 'Her conquests. Might be worth looking up the one that involved your dad. Don't you think?'

'Did you find my locket?' Peter McCarron asked, as Faye helped him to stand. 'You know, the one that was your mom's?'

Faye slipped her arm through her dad's as they walked slowly outside. 'Yeah, Dad. We found it. Don't worry, it's safe.'

'Oh,' he said, relieved. 'I thought it might be gone for ever. Mercy ordered one of her wolves to take it from me. I tried to hold on to it. I tried to fight them off, too, you know. That was such a chase, through the woods. Lost my little silver letter opener in the process. I really thought I'd nicked one of wolves in the struggle, but maybe not.'

'Don't worry about anything right now,' Faye told him as reached the school steps. 'Everything's fine.'

Overhead, the heavy snow clouds were slowly slipping away. A late fall sun filtered down over Winter Mill. Faye shut her eyes, lifting her face to the warmth. She felt her father squeeze her arm, and smiled.

'Looks like the thaw has begun,' said Peter McCarron, weakly, as Faye looked at him. His face was shadowed with hunger, but the smile Faye remembered so well was there. 'Mercy's influence is fading already.'

'Yes,' sighed Faye. 'Well, it's about time.'

Her father nodded. 'I think I'd better go and see Pam,' he said, heading down the school steps. 'She's going to want to know where I've been . . .'

341

'I'll be right there,' Faye said, hanging back. She watched as her father nodded with a wave. In another moment he'd blended into the groups of students still milling around, confused.

'You don't want to go with him?'

It was Finn's voice that spoke behind her, softly. Faye turned. He was watching her with that quiet, intense way he had, as if trying to tell what was in her heart.

'I will. In a minute.'

Finn nodded, moving nearer. 'It's funny . . .' he said slowly. 'I don't know about you, but I kind of feel as if . . . I don't know . . . as if there's something missing.'

'Missing?'

He took another step closer, right into her space. 'Yeah,' he said, quietly. 'Like . . . there's some unfinished business, somehow.'

Faye looked up into his dark eyes. 'Unfinished business?'

Finn shrugged. 'But maybe that's just me.'

Faye smiled, reaching up to wrap her arms around his neck. 'No,' she whispered. 'It's not just you.'

Finn's lips met hers in a gentle kiss that turned Faye's legs to jelly. She wanted it to go on and on, this kiss that she'd been wanting for so long. But Finn pulled back, his hands on her hips. She opened her eyes to see him looking down at her.

'What?'

He grinned, looking up at the sky. 'Just waiting to see if the world is going to end.'

Faye laughed. 'It hasn't.'

'No,' he said softly. 'It hasn't . . .'

Finn scooped her up. He held her close as he kissed her again, and this one lasted for a long, long time.

Epilogue

Wind whistled through the mansion. Somewhere, a door banged on its hinges. No one had set foot here for days, too busy clearing up the mess at the school and the slush of old snow from the streets.

In the old living room, ice crusted the mirror despite the warm sun outside. Cold gusts of air eddied against the reflective glass. Frost danced on the surface, creating its own rhythm.

The sound of running feet echoed from somewhere. Not human – this creature was on all fours. It was fast, stealthy. Inside the mirror, something trembled. In its depths, darkness grew. It flowered, suddenly, blooming against the inside of the glass as frost danced at its edges.

Eyes peered out of the deep gloom. It was a wolf, running, running. The creature leaped towards the glass, exploding out of the centre of the mirror, shattering the ice that blocked its path. It entered the world in a flurry of cold, pausing to look around.

Its eyes were the bluest blue. It shook the frost from its fur once, and then trotted out of the open door, disappearing into the dense forest outside.

HAVE YOU EVER FALLEN IN LOVE?

978 0 552 50173 0

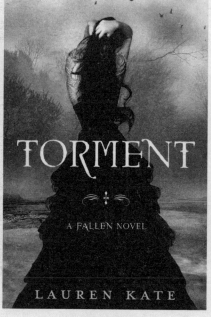

978 0 385 61809 0

Discover the series that the
whole world is talking about.

'**Dark and romantic, an absolute
blinder of a book**' *The Sun*

By Lauren Kate

A glamorous slice of vampire life
– with a sinister edge …

Jason has just moved to Malibu – home to rich kids
and fabulous parties. He's flattered to be included – and very
flattered by the interest of the stunning Sienna. But Sienna
and her friends hide a dark secret … and Jason is
risking his life by falling for her.

Two Vampire Beach novels in one.

'Outrageously addictive, super cool …'
The Bookseller

978 1 862 30896 1